Dear Rock Angel

by

Annaliese Morgan

Black Daisy Press

Dear Rock Angel

First published in the UK by Black Daisy Press, London
© Annaliese Morgan 2024

Formatted by The Book Khaleesi
www.thebookkhaleesi.com

Other Books by

Fiction

Stay Wild
The Book of Lights
The Witches Post (Blog)

Non-Fiction

The Moon Telegrams Volume One
The Moon Telegrams Volume Two
Breaking Chains – autobiographical inspiring vignettes
Desperate Housepets – Become a chic pet owner without
being a bitch
How to get through NVQ 2 veterinary Nurses
How to get through NVQ 3 veterinary Nurses
A-Z for veterinary nurses
Anaesthesia and analgesia chapter in BSAVA Manual for
Veterinary Nurses

The Dagger

A tool of carnage, wounding and violence to an untrained mind. To those who can see beyond, it's a tool of great power. It slices through the unnecessary and excess, slashes roots and skins attached to darkness and the rotten; it cuts entanglements leading to creative minds and self-healing. Much like the colour red, a dagger is doubled-edged: life-taking or life-giving, a warning or passion, love or anarchy, and the choice is in the hand that holds its hilt.

Dear Rock Angel.

A few London moons ago I was dropped some advice, by the self-help vagina power gurus I'd found myself watching online to – gulp – begin journaling. From what I've seen, this is meant to be done whilst all pretty in pink, in a journal with a cover that 'speaks to you.' What the fuck? Whilst beautifully written with dates and goals stamped with unicorn stickers, wearing comfy socks and burning a scented candle to infuse one's aura. I can't. I refuse to be a pink fluffy journal smelling of begonias.

It's an idea that repels me but continues to prod me on the shoulder. I repented slightly last week and bought a yellow legal notepad to give this so-called life-changing technique a shot. Yet I feel stupid writing and bearing my inner self to an emotionless page, not to mention the time I'm wasting by doing this. How does chronically my life and thoughts help in the emergency creation of my phoenix moment? Seriously – who am I writing this ridiculous verbiage to? So, I didn't. I drew the design of my next tattoo on the first page and wrote three words on the next find my nirvana and there it ended. I'd left the notepad on my desk in the cave room ever since hoping three words were all the participation required to cast a magic spell across my life.

My cave room is the spare bedroom across the hall from my bedroom, I converted it to mimic a mystical library and now it houses all my books, oddities and curiosities. Instead of quietly disappearing though, the notepad huffs at me in frustration. I've considered recently maybe the huffs I sense are not merely frustration and annoyance at being ignored but a friendly nudge telling me it holds answers if only I'd dare to walk through the illusion.

Prod

Prod

Prod

Huff

Prod

Huff

Damn it

I decided at the weekend, I would instead write a private blog on an anonymous platform using my sticker-covered laptop to a rock angel. I think Aerosmith was playing on my tape deck at the time and it's possibly where the idea of writing to a rock angel came from. It could also have been due to too much vodka, but here we are, regardless of how I conjured this up.

My spirit can no longer function in the relentless torment of life's invisible cage. The monotony of society and its people who endlessly follow the last person or latest trend, more concerned with someone else taking their moment than questioning the whereabouts of their own identity. Society thinks it is the wild horses of this world like me, who need to be tamed, so we can understand and fix ourselves to fit neatly into the pattern. I retort – why are they –afraid to be untamed?

My father had been my lantern, my Holy Ghost, and the one to encourage me to hunt and grow the dream seeds planted within us all, until he left seven years ago with his paella-making girlfriend he'd been living a double life with for two years. I haven't spoken to him since. I may have cut my ties with him but my grand lofty visions, rockstar soul and vintage heart he taught me to find I did not. I cultivated and strengthened them instead, and now they're mine. They're me. And I'm keeping them.

This brings me to the problematic endeavour of being me. Deemed too off the mainstream beat, too much, or not enough I have learnt to hold on tight to myself because when the sun sinks and the moon rises, myself is all I have. I ignored the early strums of a strange noise deep within believing I should be able to chisel my way into the life around me and eventually make it all work out. What other option is there? Except, it hasn't worked out. I'm like a power station at over capacity, with a purpose as powerful as electricity but nowhere to channel it. My life and old-fashioned heart, which no modern man knows how to approach, let alone take care of, have reduced me to think the unfortunate. Originality, romance and depth have been lost for good in decades past.

Where am I supposed to go then?

Sat in my kitchen typing this my reality is sadly clear… I am going to self-detonate by the power of my own soul if I am not serious enough to take a chance on myself.

Therefore, I have two choices to make this life malarky work; one, suppress the pure essence of me to match them – or two – machete my way through to create a new world. My world. In other words, it's time to ride or fucking die, and I'm not about to do the latter.

I have now moved from the kitchen island to outside on the balcony as I watch another hustling South Kensington summer evening evolve into the night. I light another cigarette and consider whether to continue writing these entries and what value they might hold. Penning these blogs reminds me of my 16-year-old self when I used to write a diary. Bearing all my secrets of unrequited love and fantasies of being a famous singer whilst being cloaked in embarrassment should anyone find the diary. Whilst no one did find it, nor did I get the guy or become a famous singer. I can't even hold a note. Same for love. There's no room within me anymore for men and romance who are all but carrots dangling themselves everywhere. It hurts because it's always mañana when I can get over the disappointment. Macheting may not be subtle or precise, but I am no longer a 16-year-old girl. I'm a 23-year-old woman who needs to create a path when there isn't one. To where I'm unsure. I do know though, only I can leap for the future and leap I must. For this reason, I conclude, I'll try anything to land the jump, and if that means having to write to a crazy arse rock angel – I'll do it.

Stamped with the heel of my studded suede fold-down ankle boots – not unicorn stickers.

No. 1

Thursday 1st July

I'd had a strong word with myself the night before and again in the morning before handing my notice in at the magazine. One week ago, I'd instructed myself to not be blunt or scathingly honest with my thoughts about the publication or most of the staff. Keep doors open and bridges intact I continued instilling into my brain. Be smiley to my editor boss and spin her a polite sentence such as, 'Monica Blue is moving on to pastures new. Thank you for the incredible position and experience of being a writer for you. It has given me plenty of–' Blah, blah... it sounded easy in my head. Straightforward. Unoffensive. Professional.

So much for not burning bridges. You can still see that fucker burning from Paris.

The magazine is a national success built from the ground

up by the editor herself who began it from her studio apartment in Shepherds Bush over twenty years ago. Now it runs out of offices in Soho with a readership of millions. This part is inspiring, it's why I took the job a year ago, and I still admire her achievements. However, the magazines' content and style are against every value I hold. A view I extended to the rest of the staff who work for it. The editor and her minions remind me of the self-help vagina power gurus. All blue jeans and tiny dresses bound for cocktails in Ibiza with an inflatable flamingo. I mean - dear Lord - how mundane. And don't get me started on smoky eyes and duck lips. How can these people have vagina power when they are all regurgitations of the same thing? Where is the meat of their own fucking bone marrow? I don't see it anywhere.

This is exactly what I'd said to my editor when I informed her I was leaving. I had handwritten my notice on thick cream paper and requested to speak to her in her office as soon as I arrived. My intention of an amicable parting soon became a distant memory, promptly joined by not working my notice period. I had, of course, intended to see out the notice period but changed my mind once all the words were falling out of my mouth and thought what the hell. I've made my decision. No point lingering about, and I'm certain she wanted to drag me out of her office by my bandanna, not work my notice, and be a disruption to others. Our conversation had silenced when she made a heavy hmm sound. I watched with a quizzical gaze as she rubbed her chin and smoothed her hand along her jawline to her ear before pulling her hand back down the same route. A cringing face, as she continued to tug on her ear lobe, had me asking her why she was doing face yoga at such a pivotal moment. I thought smoke might steam out from her ears instead she grimaced at how my decision was rash and foolish. I didn't care.

"I'm sorry you think this way," she said. We stepped out of her office onto the main floor, "but thanks for letting me know, there are plenty champing for a writer's position who won't feel it's a hardship to work here."

I stared over at the intern filling cup after cup up at the water dispenser because you can earwig conversations in the office from that spot. I wanted to spray her smug slug impersonating eyebrows off her face with the glugging water container, but I refrained. I shouldn't get so irritated about other people's slugs and ducks ... eyebrows and lips.

"Exactly," I said looking her right in the eye. "Exactly."

I cleared out my drawer of the usual pens, cinnamon bun crumbs, lone earrings and rogue cigarettes. I also found a Van Halen tape I thought I'd lost and last took all my notebooks I'd stuffed at the back. Each one was jammed with story ideas, contacts and information I had garnered over the previous months. I had planned to add more connections and data to these notebooks during my notice. A smart tactical move but then my mouth spoke, and I was asked to leave the office keys on my desk on my way out.

The normal jovial atmosphere of the office had paused itself as speechless staff peeked over the top of their computers and I walked a lone finale across the marble floor to the lift. Did they feel envious of me I thought for boldly leaving or righteous in their self-fulfilling prophecies that I am, indeed, a freak? The click of my ring-laden hand flicking the lid of my silver Zippo lighter up and down was the only sound as I entered the lift and examined my reflection in the internal mirrors.

"One hundred you've done the right thing," I said into the mirror, pressing the button for the ground floor for the last time.

Outside, the streets of London remained the same. Hundreds rushed somewhere or nowhere, oblivious to anything lateral of their stony gazes. There was no fanfare of my morning's achievement, no one cared but me and it was enough. I triumphantly planted earphones firmly in my ears, escorted my backbone to the tube station and disappeared down the steps into the underground.

I emerged in Notting Hill and sat with coffee and a cinnamon bun outside the Book and Beans shop people watching. Tourists posing with a thumb's up next to flash parked cars or against the coloured painted houses versus the elegance of true Notting Hill women walking their dogs or handbags. At my table for one, relief from unchaining myself from a misfit experience had me in a good place. Everything and anything seemed possible. I felt possible and prayed this new era was the real deal and not a mere flash of it before reality's other shoe drops. Eventually, I realised I didn't want to people-watch all day and headed down Portobello Road to Martha's vintage clothes shop.

"Hey, Martha," I called out, walking in the door and dodging a copper bird cage swinging from the ceiling puffing out bad-smelling incense. "Martha!" I yelled to a silent shop.

"In the back, Monica."

I found her reading tarot cards at her table in dim light, a plastic blue lighter and a used bong perched on the shelf behind her. The stale smell of weed clinging to the back-rooms air and furniture has become a familiar ambience, in the same way incense loiters in my bedroom. Martha, however, refuses to open the little window on the far wall or spend money on one of those air ventilator who-jars.

"Was just thinking about you," she said, not lifting her eyes from the cards. "The cards tell me an unexpected change is coming and new love is storming in. It's right here." She tapped a few of the cards with her coffin-shaped nails foretelling her vision before raising her chin to look at me. "The Celtic cross doesn't lie but something don't feel right… I think the message is for you, not me," she said, tapping them again. She blew out a big sigh and dropped her shoulders, scooping the cards back together into a neat deck. "The good messages are always for someone else," she wittered.

"No shit. I'll try to remember but… about the job. I'm available from tomorrow, as I don't need to work my notice. Cool, huh! Loving the new line of studded flares, spotted my size too."

Martha's was one of my favourite shops. I'd shopped there for years. Rammed with too many rails of kooky clothes, accessories, dangling objects from the ceiling and old posters on the wall, mainly from the '70s-2000s, Martha's is an endless playground.

"Oh, about that," she said. "Bit unfortunate as I've always liked you, but I've had to give the job to someone else, thinking you couldn't start for a few weeks."

"I'm sorry. What?"

"Yeah, this guy can sew and design, too. Makes sense to have someone who can, and who plans on being here long-term … good for the bottom line. I'm sure you could see my predicament."

"Less smoking the old pipe is also good for the bottom line. What the fuck, Martha? This job was to be my wage, a tiny one, but with better hours. *Thus,* allowing me to set up my own magazine. I've left my old one for it. You knew this!"

How could she be so blasé about putting me in the shitter?

Martha examined the air and launched into a rambling monologue about how her offer wasn't in writing, and she carpe diem-ed an opportunity with the other guy.

"It slipped my mind to call you. I wasn't sure you were all that serious about it," she said, attempting a friendly smile but changing her mind when her violet eyes (contacts) met my fierce glare.

"Damn right you should have called me. It's me with the predicament, not you."

"See… the cards are never wrong. Unexpected change," she nodded.

I couldn't bear to talk to her any longer and thundered out the back room across the shop floor, grabbing a pair of the new black studded flares and a jacket with a dragon on the back from the rails. Martha yelled after me and stood at the shop entrance to put the clothes back immediately.

"Payment for time wasting. Carp diem-ing the opportunity. You'd know all about that," I shouted back, not looking at her.

I held the hangers high up in the air and swaggered down a crowded Portobello Road until my arms ached and I collapsed onto a bench down a side street.

Shit.

No. 2

Friday 2nd July

I need to snap out of it. I've barely left the house to avoid running into anyone I know and having to explain why I'm not at work. It happened a week ago, yet I cannot remove myself from the loop of those scenes playing over and over in my head. I am stuck under the rubble of the mind yet part of me feels better staying in the unfairness, making voodoo dolls of Martha, than it does to claw my way out.

I received a letter this morning in the post. From the magazine, formally announcing I no longer work for them. Due to conduct, it was mutually agreed I left with immediate effect. I wouldn't have handed my notice in if Martha had thought to call me first and let me know she'd given my job away. I'm mad at myself for trusting her and for not checking before flying into the editor's office like a rocket, fuelled by my fantastical idea of a new print magazine.

My magazine and publishing empire is a dream seed of over half my life. A secret thought my mind naturally wandered to from the days of early adolescence and I haven't let go of it since. I've told no one about it, not even Bootsy. Only Viv, and briefly Martha, when we discussed one Saturday afternoon how she needed a new assistant as her old one was leaving. Swapping jobs from the magazine to Martha's couldn't have been a more perfect solution to begin escaping where I don't belong. Across the years I've often thought about what Dad would advise me to do with this larger-than-life plan of mine. He knows how to create an iconic legacy and as much as I might want to, I can't dis this fact or take it from him, but nor is he here to rely on for support or permit me to go for it. If I put a positive spin on it, his betrayal and absence is an annoying blessing in disguise. It forced me to make decisions myself, to stop seeking permission from others and trust in the work I do, rather than wait on a platform for a train that never arrives. I diligently crafted this venture regardless of how sound a project others would analyse it to be because I know deep in my bones, dream seeds are true. They are the holy essence of our purpose on earth, pray tell, why has the divine spectacularly destroyed its own vision the first day out of the gate? I have no job or savings. Only an idea with a bunch of computer files and ring binders containing half-completed work and it appears, unfortunately, it shall be no different for the foreseeable future.

Having known Martha for years, I trusted her offer. She's an interesting woman with the gift of the future's eye and rides a cruiser motorcycle. Martha can be found periodically with the biker crowd at Smokes Club, she doesn't have set nights she goes but recently I've noticed her there more. I wonder frequently if she has a thing for one of the biker guys, which would be cute if not weird as I have never seen Martha with another. I could be way wrong though, her mystical elusiveness leaves Martha hard to read.

By the age of seventeen, I was a regular at her shop and hanging out at Smokes once, twice, thrice a week. Not with Martha, I don't socialise with her. We get along great at the shop but at Smokes we stay in our own lanes, only acknowledging each other in passing. It reminds me of high school and the invisible yet palpable divide between sixth formers and the rest of the students.

The bikers, and Martha when she is there, hang outside the club by the wooden tables gathering in an intimidating group like pigeons do in Trafalgar Square. If the weather is rubbish, they congregate on the elevated floor area in the far corner on the way to the loos. It's where bands play when gigs are on. I don't believe the biker's choice of placement is random because whether you are inside, outside, arriving or leaving, you are unlikely to miss their presence. Viv, Ronnie and I stay in our space by the pool table nearer the entrance, I'm not *friend friends* with the bikers but there is no hate between us either. I keep it that way while considering more than once if the bikers are, despite appearances, more neighbourly and loyal than Viv and Ronnie. Then I dismiss the thought, Viv and Ronnie are my close friends I shouldn't think these things.

I'm due to meet Viv and Ronnie at Smokes tonight and uncharacteristically I don't think I'll go, I'm down and out in hermit mode and do not want to run into Martha. Then again, why should I stay home and miss out on beers and a few rounds of pool with friends because of her? A pint of beer may be thought of as unfeminine and I don't love the bloating belching brown beverage, it's just cheaper than *my* drink, vodka. It's also safe to say the lady etiquette ship sailed without me a long ago. I can only afford to drink vodka at home or in the bar over the road from my house where Bootsy, my best friend who managers the bar, and I have a small deal in place.

I'm not going out.

I don't need to bloat.

I don't want to go.

No. I will stay home, meditate, drink lemon water, be as pure as undriven snow and transform into the next Anna Wintour. I bet she would know what to do about money and career – and – what the hell to tell my mother…

Three hours later, I dragged myself out from the safety of a nap and met up with Viv and dodgy Ronnie at Smokes Club. Viv doesn't know I call him dodgy it would offend her blinkers. Though Smokes is becoming worn and old on me these days and it needs a new carpet one's shoes don't stick to, it beats staying in listening to This Woman's Work by Bush and hurtling myself off a bridge into the Thames.

No. 3

Later that night...

Returned home in the middle of the night completely wasted dressed in black lace and velvet. In thigh-high boots, I sat unproductive on the lounger outside on my chunky white balcony. Meaning, proper full-length thigh-high boots. Not those half-ass ones claiming to be thigh-high when they're just standard over-the-knee boots. These boots are not the same, it's an important distinction to make.

I'd become unnerved by how practical it is to change life on a dime. Reinventing myself is real now and no longer a dream residing in the comforting space of an idea. Its urgency pecks at me constantly, especially as all I have left is a rock angel to help turn my 18-wheeler of a life around. A mess I need cleared up and sorted out before Mother returns from the South of France at the end of August. I didn't know how many weeks away the end of August was; I couldn't work it out. I tried to calculate it on my phone's calendar, but the screen glare pierced my eyes and a gazillion dates blurred as I stabbed at the wrong ones in the wrong year.

I rang Viv, but any question beyond her location proved to be complicated. She and Ronnie ended up hanging out with the band who played a gig at Smokes Club tonight. I thought Viv and Ronnie were only doing snow with a few others when I left, not hanging out with the band.

"It's the beginning of July, Mon," Ronnie slurs down Viv's phone, off his face.

"Ica. It's Mon – ICA. You loser of a cokehead."

"Don't call him that," Viv added. "I know you're annoyed about the job, but don't take it out on us."

"I'm not. I truly think the man is a sinking cokehead, and he'll take you down with him."

"Says you, who practically has vodka for a bloodstream."

"I'm not enjoying this conversation, Viv. Goodbye," I said, ending the call.

Jeeze, I only rang about dates and timelines.

I question if I missed a perfect opportunity by not staying on at Smokes with them. Not for snow, drugs are a dirty game but for the whiskey and sin of interesting musicians with interesting talk. People with a passion for their craft. Instead, I came home to write useless words to a rock angel on my balcony, in a house bigger than my hair. Even Bootsy over the road had closed the bar for the night. He would have known how many weeks it was until the end of August.

I sat in a sour vapour of second-guessing my decisions until my love of lone time on this street in starlit hours pulled me. At 2 a.m., no tourists are scurrying for the museums, souvenirs and overpriced water, and it gives one a moment to be free of living in a South Ken fish tank, as tourists take their busyness and itineraries back to hotels.

My freedom was only for a moment though, as a battle then commenced with my thigh-high boots to get them off. I fought to pull my leg out of one of them rolling dramatically off the lounger onto the hard concrete floor of the balcony during the mission. I stood up, wobbling on the other killer heel and whanged the now free, infuriating boot through the balcony doors into the sitting room. Uninclined to attempt the other, I hobbled to the balcony's ledge. Its bright white stone was cool against my fingers as I grabbed another moment to escape... only to see a guy wearing white trousers, a white T-shirt and a thin grey cardigan. He was hovering by Bootsy's bar and the hotel next door to it across the road opposite my house. He stretched out his arms, arching his back; outside lights from the (now) closed bar highlighted rolled-up sleeves and tanned forearms. He drifted up and down the front of the hotel and Bootsy's bar and lit up a cigarette. It struck a chord, as it was unusual to see people out here at this time. Most of the large white buildings on my side of the road were once all houses; now they're offices and empty spaces, so it's quiet up this end of town late at night. *Must be a late-arriving guest at the hotel.*

When he finally glanced up from scuffing his dark sliders into the pavement, it startled him to see me watching him from my balcony. I would have been startled too, in fairness, but something was different about him. He appeared uncomfortable I'd noticed him. Checking the street left and right as a fugitive would, paranoid a bystander had seen him. Unable to remove my attention, I said nothing but joined him for a long-distance smoke, via a lopsided lean over the balcony. What for I don't know, I'm not into stranger connection... come on; it's London. He had an enchanting spirit all around him and its potency infiltrated me as only energy exchanges can, and we locked eyes. I think this is how it happened... hard to tell at two o'clock in the morning when massively pissed – me not him – he looked tired and massively sober. I couldn't move my gaze from him; perhaps he's been infusing his aura with begonia candles.

Maybe I do need a begonia-smelling candle after all if that's the magic it will make me effervesce with too.

Or maybe not.

I'll stick to 90s rock girl.

But his initial strange alarm at seeing me in all my wild glory dissipated as our smoke clouds merged mid-air above the road. He gave me a salute as he stubbed his cigarette out before he slinked up the steps into the hotel and disappeared through a revolving door.

Still entranced, I watched the door until it slowed to a stop. He didn't circle around and back out onto the street, as I'd hoped.

"Good night smoking friend," I sighed, as a group of five young sparkly dressed women tottered up the road from the centre of South Kensington, jarring me out of what was a rare, beautiful moment with a blond-haired carrot.

"There are no clubs up here. You guys lost?" I shouted over.

Living here my entire life you get a feel for people, and I could tell they weren't from around here. They blanked me dawdling around the outside of the hotel's entrance instead. Not going in, not doing anything except craning their necks up at the floors above and leering to the side of the potted tall plants to snoop through the glass revolving door.

"I can give you directions if you need help?" I added.

They glanced over at me casting a look as though I was one of the city's morons and ignored my offer of assistance.

"Fine. Fuck off then," I muttered, firing my cigarette end over the balcony with a flick and staggering into the sitting room.

I realised as I crawled into bed for the second time today with one boot still on, the rookie mistakes in recent times I had been making. Trying to make room for *myself* in a world that isn't mine, instead of extending my universe outwards. Thinking I needed to find myself more than I already had, and for a moment there, these errors made me invisible to the world at large I did want. I picked apart the exhausting ache to live a life of *my* creation not one via a hope in a maybe of a glamorous magazine and others I considered radical. Perhaps I hadn't missed an opportunity to hang out with the band at Smokes tonight or messed up leaving the magazine, but on reflection, had been missing the obvious answer for some time. The opportunity I am looking for is – me.

No. 4

Saturday 3rd July

I awoke with a stormy head and heavy body, but all told, I didn't feel as dire as I had expected to When the morning after a hard night on the drink is brighter than anticipated, it's an achievement. It's a special pass that life hands out occasionally to miss a lesson one didn't want to be at in the first place. It never gets old, and I confirmed a small victory in winning at life to myself. Gone are the teenage days when I could drink all night, wake at three in the morning somewhere along the track by the river Thames squished between a group of friends. Then wander home and be all perky and very fine hours later. I used to howl with laughter at the adults who warned of hangovers.

This morning though, my waking moment held something worse than a monstrous hangover. Looming thoughts of my mother. My mother is a pleasant woman but a trip. I can't put my finger on why. It's more of an unsettled stomach I've grown to live with than anything I can articulate. I think she wanted a more conventional daughter, a cooperative corporate, not a woman who reminded her of her own inability to go after the bit in her teeth she dropped at the altar.

I should ring her tomorrow to plant the impending seed of change. To shoehorn her into reality – I am not the next mogul of the glossy's she spews proudly about to people. She thinks her words fool me because if you asked her what I last wrote about… she won't have a fucking clue. Much like my life choices and fashion style, my recent actions will appal her. I couldn't care less; I'm only narked I'm still answerable to her. Society, including my mother, is an invisible cage, and all is well if I conform to its restraints of normalcy. When I don't, it rattles the cage. It becomes nervy and unsure how to handle a truth-seeker about to emerge and when I make people uncomfortable, they pull the trigger. They fire words to threaten my deepest fears. They try to ban or fight me, test my skills and patience or disregard me entirely all in a bid to keep me whipped.

Satisfied I had at least entertained the sensible approach of dealing with this situation and my mother, I finally declared to myself I had no intention of informing Mum about my departure from the magazine and plans, not until I sussed out my next moves. Moves I didn't have the motivation or passion to turn and toil over today.

I needed to calm my swirling stomach and loitering headache and knew the solution… my long hooded cardi, hot sugary tea, iced water and two episodes of the TV series I had become hooked on. I propelled myself out of bed into the cardi and made a delicate descent downstairs. I loved this house with all my heart but it's changing, and I don't know why. Its many rooms and long winding staircase once bursting with joy and warmth now could be a fruitless maze. It's sad if I think about it too long. I often thought Mum would sell it; the house is unnecessarily big and has only been us two since Dad left. It became Mum's as part of the divorce settlement, along with her stake in the ownership of the house in the South of France but surely, she could either do more productive endeavours with the house. Or from the money of the sale of it? I'd always envisaged transforming part of the house into a magazine office and creative studio. Why not? It's a positive use of the enormous space half of which remains unused most of the time. Dad has the other half of the French house; I don't know if he uses the place anymore. I no longer go with Mum either on holidays to France as I prefer the Gothic and ancient finds of other European countries and the idea of a Spanish love affair in salty air.

I managed one episode before I fell into a mouth-open slumber on the sofa. I resurfaced an hour later with a desert mouth and the overbearing dazzle of the TV streamer's latest film recommendation – a new twenty-something rom-com smash.

"It's not a 95 percent match; it's a 25 percent match," I groaned, flicking the TV off.

Rising carefully from the sofa, I reassessed the hangover situation upon standing. *Pretty good, pretty bloody good* I thought and drained the last dregs of water from the glass on the floor, when I remembered about *him*.

I paced to the closed balcony window doors and from under my hood, surveyed the comings and goings over at the hotel, and next door at Bootsy's bar. Bootsy, an unlikely best friend, is eight years older than me and adores the bar he manages over the road. He tried to buy it once. The hotel said no. Idiots. It's only a success because he turned it around from near ruin two years ago. It's not the type of joint I'd usually hang out at, I only going to chat and visit Bootsy or to annoy him. The bar is Bootsy's baby though and he's wanted his own since I've known him.

You in today? I need coffee, I texted Bootsy, craning my neck to view the hotel entrance.

No, Marco is taking me out for dinner. In tomorrow after four. You're out of vodka too, he texted back.

I'll bring a bottle in tomorrow, I replied, still craning. '*I jacked the magazine in last week.*

Shit. Is that why you've been avoiding coming in, aha? What's the plan? he asked.

Raincheck.

… An answer only you could give.

I can't be arsed to think of a witty comeback. Go away.

Talk to you tomorrow. X.

I clicked the phone off. Slid it into my cardi pocket and collected my lone boot from across the sitting room, picking the lamp up it had knocked over, before turning afoot to steal another glance over the road.

I swear I saw *him*. He carried his blond messed up curtains confidently as he walked out of the hotel. Dressed in pale blue straight jeans, a white T-shirt and a cream V-neck cable knit edged with dark green, the old money style was oddly alluring to me. A suited man and suited woman pillared either side of him. The magic I felt last night was still there. A low-lying mist which seeped across the distance, through the windows of my house and commanded my jaded heart. Strange… I prefer brunettes. The three of them made a swift beeline into the back of a parked shiny black car waiting outside the entrance. I also swear he sneaked a peek at my balcony and clocked me standing there, hugging my boot looking like a cloaked mystery before he sank into the plush car. I pulled my hood completely down to cover my face and leapt to the side of the balcony doors. Frozen. Like a feline in the headlights of a speeding vehicle.

No. 5

Saturday Evening, 3rd July

I had grown bored moping around the house all day. I didn't smell much better either; the stench of stale alcohol had followed me around like condemnation. Somewhere between another cigarette and blasting Disturbed, Land of Confusion in my bedroom, I decontaminated myself in the shower and watched the water disappear down the plughole and out of sight. I spent twenty minutes unknotting my back-combed hair and coated my fresh skin in some coconut shit left over from Christmas and wrapped myself in a dressing gown.

I needed to think, find a solution, an idea. Something.

I pushed on the heavy wooden door into my cave room, a room of books, music (cassette tapes mainly), information and treasures. Everything from the ancient

Egyptians to symbols to travel to cave paintings, mythical legends, and fantasy stories are housed in this room. Plus, my treasured collection of cassette tapes arranged in alphabetical order, most are my dad's, but I add to them when I can. I'd kept all the tapes when Dad left because why the fuck should I let him have them? Not that he's asked for his extensive collection. He'd be able to source them all again easily enough, anyway. My cave room is the coolest Gothic mystical library there ever will be.

I'd claimed the fourth floor of the house with its four rooms as *my floor* when I was sixteen. I've spent hours, days, and months crafting these spaces to mould them into unique pieces of me ever since. Aside from the cave, my bathroom and bedroom there is my dressing room. Another space I've developed with collections of vintage, edgy and elegant rock fashion, accessories, makeup and footwear. None of these would feature in mainstream fashion publications, but I find each piece inspiring and interesting. I've lost hours of my life to my style, apparel, the cave room and rock music. None of these let me down or make me wrong.

I am writing this uninteresting information about my floor because I realised something. During my evening house wander, smelling like a foreign holiday, it dawned on me these rooms are more than they appear. They are a representation of what I'm able to create and do when left to my own devices, without interference or opinions from other people – because I trusted myself. They are straight-up Monica, and I am arriving at the conclusion straight-up soul answers most questions.

I didn't understand, back then, the depth of what I was doing. I thought I was merely decorating and collecting. Investigating this further one could say my past self, unknowingly, had been smart enough to stay connected to the soul within. My actions then, prepared me for the era in which I now find myself. I must stay alert to following *my happy* because this is how the mother ship guides us.

From my cave room I selected a book, my yellow legal notepad and an old shoe box covered in a collage of stuck-on magazine pictures and newspaper headlines. I keep the shoe box in a cupboard next to the bookcases on the far wall only bringing it out occasionally. From the dressing room, I retrieved my portable tape and radio deck and proceeded to set myself up on the lounger outside on the balcony.

It was still light enough to see and it's nicer outside. Less claustrophobic than being encased by walls. The hard-core tourists and workers remained despite the evening hour, darting or sauntering, either way making a high level of background noise distracting my thinking. I leaned down and pressed play on the tape deck grimacing when I noticed I'd forgotten to bring a tape out. Too focused to go back in and up to the cave to pick a tape out, I turned the radio on instead.

The voice of the radio's DJ drowned out the outside hullabaloo, but he grated on and on and I wished he would stop talking and play something.

"Lenny James and his co-stars, pictured together earlier today, have confirmed the sequel of the latest smash rom-com and he's…"

Ugh. I turned the radio off. *Who cares.*

Examining the contents sprawled out around me, I picked up the book and fanned through it, making odd notes in the margins until sometime later I heard distant yelling. I ignored it, but the shouting continued, and eventually, I heard my name being called out. Curious, I leant over the balcony edge, still holding my book to keep the page, to find Bootsy standing below on the pavement, holding his arms up.

"Finally," he said, dismayed. As though I was supposed to know he was coming around.

"I've been busy. What are you doing here? You're meant to be out with Marco?"

The thick book was becoming heavy in my hand as Bootsy detailed a moan about Marco cancelling to go to his parents and how Marco goes running over every time they so much as sneeze. Bootsy came round instead here to see if I wanted a drink over at the bar.

"Thought you might need an ear about whatever it is you've done with your job. You don't look dressed for over the road though," he said.

Just then my aching fingers called time. The book slipped out of my hand and tumbled down, smacking Bootsy on the head and knocking him sideways for a second.

"God, sorry, are you all right?"

He rubbed his head and picked the book up, turning it over to read the cover.

"Bonked by… Barcelona in Full," he said, reading out loud.

"You've been bonked by worse, Boots. Wait there. I'll come down and let you in."

I rapidly collected the cards and letters I had pulled out from the old shoe box, placed them back in, and kicked the box under the lounger. Headed down and opened the front door with a cheery smile. He thrust the book into my hand.

"Your weapon, madame," he said, then he acknowledged someone over the road near the hotel with a raised arm and sauntered on in.

"Cheers. Go up. I'll make coffee."

By the time I peeked around the doorframe to see whomever it was he was he'd seen, they'd gone.

No. 6

Sunday 4th July

I'd planned to be at Viv's around 8 p.m. and left earlier than normal to visit Bootsy over in the bar. I handed him the bottle of vodka I'd bought at the cheap shop and watched him glug fresh orange juice into a tall glass containing a good measure of vodka. Tapping my card on the machine to pay for the orange juice charge… our arrangement I'd managed to talk him into, I hooked the heel of my ankle boot around the foot ledge of a barstool behind me. Admiring the long, black tassels hanging from my shorts making them appear to be trousers, I picked up a three-day-old London Newspaper laid on the bar. I read a headline about politicians up to spicy things they shouldn't be. Then another covering young celebrities about town and the outfits they wore to a recent film premier – and how we – can recreate the style. Is this the most interesting news our most wonderful city has to offer on the front page?

A thought entered my mind from somewhere else that it's not the celebrities and the politicians bugging me, so much as it is the journalists and editors who think this vanilla reporting is interesting It's not interesting, it's horse manure. Churned out time and time again, and I worry there are few members of the public left with the bravado of their own imaginations. No wonder the London paper turned me down to have my own column ages ago. I wouldn't have lasted two minutes there. I put the newspaper back down as Bootsy faffed about cutting fruit up at the other end of the bar.

Bootsy's disappointment at Marco is becoming more of a regular conversation between us. After three years, Marco continues to be averse to the engagement and marriage Bootsy longs for. I'm beginning to wonder about these two and their cute over the top romance. A lot of people – including myself – have envied and yearned for a love like theirs. Now I'm not so sure. Then again, I don't know much about rings and marriage either.

"If it was the other way around," I'd said to him last night at mine. He spluttered in objection at the smoke I blew above his head on the loungers outside, "you'd tell me I'd deserve someone who is certain. A guy who was proud to stand by my side at the altar, if that's what I wanted. Which I don't but you do."

Bootsy didn't answer, only stared up at the starry sky from the lounger.

"Spill on your latest shenanigans then," he finally said, changing the topic. "Sounds like we need to find you a new job."

It wasn't my fault Martha had shafted me, but this didn't stop Bootsy from repeatedly reminding me I needed paying work. I do realise the pressing need for a job, especially if I don't want my mother in my face, but pointing out the obvious every two minutes wasn't helpful. This is exactly the type of thing to ruffle my mother too. It will embarrass her status, which generally leads to threats of refusing to continue supporting me with a roof over my head and food in the fridge. Whilst 9-5 employment and starting again is logical and my only option, none of it feels right. None of it. It makes my stomach plummet to the floor.

A voice to the left of me leaning on the end of the bar interrupted my fussing mind.

"Hey, someone like you shouldn't be drinking alone," a striped shirt-wearing man said.

"I'm not," I replied, picking up the newspaper to read the front page, again.

"Well, you look alone to me. Come on, let me buy you a drink." All grin and full of veneers.

"No thanks," I said, sighing without moving my eyes from the newspaper.

"Any drink you want. Unlike whoever stood you up, I'm great company. It's just a drink," the buffoon who thinks he's entitled continued.

I unhooked my boot from the stool, squared myself up, and dropped the newspaper on the stool in front of him.

"I think you'll find you're better at reading *that* than you are me," I replied and walked to the end of the bar where Bootsy was arranging his sliced fruit for the night's drinkers.

"Have you told your mum you've left yet?" Bootsy asked, wedging the bottle of vodka I'd brought in into a cupboard under the till.

"Sort of," Bootsy pulled a face at me as he closed the cupboard door. "Okay, no. I told her how something bigger within me has been stuck and is bursting to get out."

"And?" he said, turning his hand over and over. "What did she say?"

"She told me to eat fresh figs. They work wonders for flushing your system out… I didn't pursue the conversation after that." Both of us exchanged incredulous smiles, yet neither of us was surprised.

"Any clearer on what you're going to do?"

"Maybe. Don't know. Who knows. I'm in a raincheck."

Bootsy raised his eyebrows at me.

"I don't want to talk about it. End of," I replied.

Crawling back to the magazine is not an option and nor will I entertain it. Ditto for working a job requiring a hairnet, rubber gloves or a uniform with an embroidered logo. True, any of these would bring in a few needed pink ladies and there are plenty of this type of employment in London compared to writing positions. The obstacle in my way, though, isn't securing a job. The obstacle is my magazine. The thought of starting my own publishing company and magazine brings life to my soul and makes me feel possible yet impossible at the same time. I dare to question Bootsy about how he can continue to settle for what he doesn't sincerely want or deserve from Marco, but am I doing the same thing by delaying my publication dreams to a more sensible time? Is it wrong to want what you want? Is it wrong to go straight to the end?

"I'd offer you a job here," Bootsy said, "but there isn't any at the moment."

"I don't think working in hospitality would be my forte."

"That, dearest Monica, is a truth no one could deny."

I pulled one of his black braces toward me and let it snap back into his chest.

"Vicious. Yes, sir?" he said, moving to a grey-haired man standing next to me who had walked in with his lady.

I gazed around the familiar wood-panelled bar room; the old-fashioned candle wall lights keep this old haven dimly lit and alive. Unlike the proverbial knight in shining armour, dangling a precarious sword stood in the corner. It's a dated, if not cliché accessory, but the hotel refuses to let Bootsy remove it. Bootsy put the knight in the underground cellars once; the hotel returned it the next day. Over time Bootsy has - almost - come to accept the statue he hates… We've called it John, and he joins us for late-night lock-ins.

Music strummed softly in the amber-lit background. A few more people arrived and stood at the bar, the buffoon man had left, and others sat at the cosy tables chatting as the place slowly awakened. It's still early for those here to parlay London's nightlife, but in another hour, it will be heaving. I scarcely noticed the solo character in an open-neck chocolate shirt slumped in one of the high-back wooden chairs by the fireplace. A chunky watch and beaded bracelets were more obvious than his identity. His face half-hidden by a tilted Stetson covering it. A white espresso cup sat on the table in front of him.

"Tired tourist?" I asked, with a sly flick of my head toward the camouflaged character as Bootsy returned from serving the grey-haired man.

"Just a hotel guest," Bootsy replied and placed a glass of rattling iced water nonchalantly on the shiny bar, his stubbled face grinning stupidly behind it. "Drink that before you go," he instructed, pointing at the water that I stared at in horror.

"I'm only going to Viv's house, not on a night out."

He pointed to the glass of water and moved on to the next hotel drinker drifting in. I swigged the water and slid off the barstool. Checking I'd put my bank card back in my bag I jiggled the glass of half-drunk water at Bootsy and made my way toward the door.

"I'm trialling a new juice I created – hangover blaster," he called over to me whilst shaking a mixture to death in a silver contraption. "I'll leave one on your doorstep – don't kick it over."

"Put it in the middle so I see it," I said.

I watched Bootsy slide two elegant drinks and the printed bill to another suited man and his lady. A well-dressed lady giving me the subtle up and down eye body scan some women irritatingly do to other women. I was about to repay her gesture with a Scorpio death stare when the hat moved by the fireplace. His eyes became visible from under the brim and searched around, landing finally up front and centre on me. Emitting that unmistakable enchantment I had met before and I had to snap my head away because it was *him;* I didn't know what else to do.

"Someone ought to tell him one's hat should be removed when inside," I hollered out to Bootsy, flinging the glass door open.

"I'll be sure to give him the message," he replied. "Don't trap your tassels," he smirked.

"I might want to trap my tassels," I returned, essentially throwing myself out of the door because something about that man stops me in my tracks and freezes time.

I might want to trap my tassels. What the fuck was that, Monica?

No. 7

Monday 5th July

Early Hours

For as long as we've been friends, Viv and I have planned on creating and running our own businesses. Viv has been saving and plotting a jewellery business whilst I plotted my publishing and literary dreams. Unlike Viv, I did not save a single penny. A choice I regret; savings would have saved the day. The nights we have lost listening to Vixen and Heart. Describing and discussing our designs, products and fan base. The imaginary living we've both encountered daily reaches far beyond what I can document here, other than to say we live another life in our heads. We've known each other since before the days of dodgy Ronnie, crossing paths in a Gothic jewellery store. Although Viv's a more dyed black hair and tie-dye purple T-shirt type of person, the same as Ronnie is. I like to make a statement and put on a show with my rock fashion. Despite our visual differences, we clicked over a silver cross pendant displayed in the window. I still have the pendant in my collection today. Turns out, she wasn't shopping for jewellery as I was, but for design ideas, and we've stayed close ever since.

I wanted her to be the first person I told. The first to know my intention of not bothering with a bread-and-butter job but going for the dream because if not now, when? Women have waited and farted about for long enough. I'll figure out the finances and all the stuff I don't know along the way.

"I know enough to get my vehicle moving, and you do too, Viv," I said, "AND you've saved money for it; you absolutely can do this!" I said to her.

Viv only scoffed and sat down next to me on the sofa in a grubby jumper, flicking the tops off two beer bottles and handed me one. The chance for Viv to make her dream real was staring her right in the eye. I fear she's either unable or unwilling to realise this herself.

"It's not the right time for me but you'll be great," she said with a tightly closed smile. "I'm helping Ronnie find a new drumming gig at the moment. Perhaps after that."

I knew he'd be involved somehow. Can't he find his own drumming gig? He's 26, a grown man, and Viv's a capable 24-year-old woman who's lost sight of this detail.

Suspecting I had become salt to her wound as the atmosphere in the tiny one-bed flat turned stiff and awkward. I abandoned my initial agenda for the magazine and moved our talk onto her office work gossip and helped her clean the fridge instead.

"No one is standing at the end with a gold medal for you. For tolerating shit you don't want to or shouldn't be," I said, sliding on my dragon fairy denim jacket ready to leave.

Outside, the Polish shop underneath Viv's flat was all shut up for the night and Hammersmith had become colder both in temperature and in heart than when I arrived. A few hours ago, I was alive with life. Viv's pretend happiness about my venture invaded me more than she knew, and more than I expected. I don't understand what's going on with her or why it dims my flame. I would have been cheering for Viv from the rooftops in the reverse circumstances.

I grabbed a late tube on the underground to go home and took a detour on the way to wander. Deflated I circulated the tree-lit streets of South Kensington, listening to Ballard of Youth by Ritchie Sambora on my phone. It felt better here, alone with myself, music and fairy-lit trees than at Viv's flat and gradually a soothing comfort recalibrated me. Almost as if the romance of the fairy lights lit up a personal renaissance as well as the trees and buildings they encased. As Sambora's guitar played and time ticked, my annoyance with Viv grew. Until I had to ask myself midstride why it bothered me, why I needed her blessing. Am I not a real friend to take this opportunity to start my magazine? Does being a solid friend mean I wait for her, and let Viv have her business first? These questions bubbled up from deep canyons within and I didn't like it. I couldn't let Viv's reaction dissuade or diminish me. As uncomfortable as it is for me to write this blog about my life and feelings, I'm still doing it. Each day I let the pages flow, not my fear. I needed to do the same with the magazine and Viv. I turned around and frog-marched myself back home vowing not to feed the wrong wolf.

I jogged up the few steps to my front door, a glass bottle filled with a rank-looking green liquid perched on the top step with a smiley face stick-it-note stuck to the glossy black door –

The hat would like to meet you. B 😊

"What are we, ten years old, passing notes under a table?" I said, peeling the note off the door.

I picked up the bottle of green gunk and clicked the door shut, leaning against it for a beat. I strode down the black and white tiled hallway, gripping the glass bottle I'd stuck the note on, and rounded the corner. Was it a serious note or a classier version of the usual shitfuckery? … men all gung ho then instantly have no time for me once they meet the deal behind the mysterious eyes and sexy boots.

I wasn't sure how to answer this man's invitation. As much as he intrigued me, and the thought of having something different and unique happen in my life for a while refreshed me, it all felt too cloak and dagger. Then again, Bootsy wouldn't have left me the note if this man was a rat. I wondered if he knew him. By the time I reached the kitchen, I decided on the possibility it might be an original, possibly cute gesture.

I plonked Bootsy's green wonder drink on the kitchen island while circling it and reading the note again. It's been an age since I went on a date. I enjoy being alone, it's easier. It's not disappointing and most importantly, I can fully focus on my career and success. These two are my priority, not a hat with a crush. Career and success have my heart and it's where my arrow of focus and love will be aimed, not at dangling carrots to trip me up.

Thinking more about the situation it brought me to consider, have I assumed the wrong idea about this chap's intentions? He might not mean a date. The 'meeting' could be for a friendly chat, work-related, could be anything… yet he's like a déjà vu; maybe I've seen him previously in the hotel, or in the bar. Many regulars stay there when in town. Perhaps I met him once at the magazine office, or…

"Wait a minute. Wait a goddamn minute." I pressed the TV remote and clicked on the TV hung on the wall across the island. Inhaling at length, my eyes expanded to the size of Mars, as I recognised the enchanting image eyeballing me from the recommended trailers and rapidly, I googled Lenny James.

"Oh, fuck."

I kept ringing Bootsy's phone until he answered. He was all mad and huffy I'd woken him up, not that this concerned me.

"Do you know what time it is?" he shot.

"No. Do you know who he is?"

"A good bartender never tells. Goodnight."

"Who does he think he is… requesting to see me? I am not an appointment to be made. I'm not interested but tell him thanks."

"Monica. You're going. We'll discuss it later," and he hung up.

I could have been mistaken for clasping my pearls the way I studied my phone screen after he hung up. If it was anyone else, I would have called them right back. I don't know what Bootsy thinks there is to discuss, but it'll be a short conversation.

…no thanks I'm not going. I'm busy creating my empire and have more pressing and interesting things to do than go on a date with a film star because he has shiny thing syndrome.

No. 8

Tuesday, 6th July

Feeling someplace north of a strategy for my magazine and empire, I spent an unproductive morning flitting around a black hole. Scrutinising a long list of to-do points, I investigated templates, then layouts, and moved on to fonts, headlines, print runs and content. It never ends. Then there are branding colours and style to decide. I had no idea about any of it, other than how to cycle around and around in indecision, until, when I could take no more, I held my hands up in defeat. Acknowledging all these pieces of my puzzle were not going to be finalised and fit together today, I quickly ushered away the thought they ever will.

I wrapped my laptop up in a velvet scarf and packed it into its special carry case. A small old brown square suitcase to which I'd added black leather strands. Silver bison heads, meant for pendants, swung from their handles and a sticker reading Aeropuerto had been stuck on the front years ago. It fits everything in – cigarettes, notepads, phone, book, pens, purse, plus space for a cinnamon bun. One could say… the contents of my life from my time at the magazine. I'm lucky they are all compact enough for my case and able to become part of my portable world. If they could speak, I think they would say they prefer the vintage case to a modern desk in an office.

My case and I bounced around coffee shops and a couple of libraries writing ideas down for the magazine and only one measly mini-story for it. I've always thought there is something mystical and inviting about writing in libraries, whether they are old and elaborate buildings or not. Except today. Today, not even the inspiring environments of libraries or the aroma of real Italian coffee and chatter at cafes could pull me out of amateur into professional. Why is this all harder to do when it's just me in charge? I could knock out various tasks and pieces of writing confidently when working at the magazine. Now living my dream by working on my own publication, I'm second-guessing if my name is even Monica Blue. Creative ideas and stories, I believe, live in an invisible stream in the ethers. Only arriving in the mind when searched for. Then they become like rivers endlessly delivering tempting ideas and stories, but at some point, choices must be made. Not all ideas make it. Not all ideas an individual may receive are meant for them, but when you know the idea is a hunch, and it's yours, the nettle must be grasped. If ignored for too long, those hunches move onto someone else. Onto another who *will* take them on with serious doses of action. Are ideas and hunches, (whether they are stories, experiences, inventions, businesses or adventures) actually alive in the supernatural needing homes? Aren't we all looking for home?

I borrowed a few business books from the library and embarked on the commute back to South Kensington. En route, I accidentally found a coffee shop on a corner of Gloucester Road. It's one I hadn't noticed before. Drawn to its old-school style, I immediately swept in across the wooden floorboards in my black maxi dress and black sunglasses and sat down. I ordered fizzy iced water only, no food despite a ravenous stomach. I'd already spent enough on unnecessary expenditures like coffee and public transport when I could have stayed at home avoiding such things. I pulled out a bun from my case and sunk my mouth around it, swilling it down with the fizzy water as I scowled at other customers' snooty glares for eating non-purchased food.

I mesmerised myself with the décor, rubbernecking the black and white photographs on the walls and reading all the messages carved into the wooden furnishings. It intrigued me enough to ask the staff about the messages and I discovered this place had been open for twenty years. How I hadn't known about this coffee shop before astonished me whilst delighting my hunger for finding parts of undiscovered London. These types of places and random finds make me feel included. Take the messages on the wall, for example. I haven't seen this done anywhere else, and I found myself wistfully smiling reading all of them. Customers ask the owners to inscribe love messages with a burning pen tool thing, something the owners are allowed to use. The personalised short messages are etched into the wooden countertop. As their popularity grew, the messages extended onto the wooden tables and now spread onto the wood panels on the lower half of the walls. There must be thousands of comments and hearts encasing initials and names with hopes of forever love...

Kiara M + Michael L
LD 4 GB
S + R 4ever

And written calculations of couples' names with their percentage of love for each other, according to the love calculator. A playful but supposedly accurate tool to indicate the strength and compatibility of a relationship, achieved by crossing out the letters for numbers and then reducing those to a percentage.

How fun.

I'd forgotten the magnetism and excitement of reading a person's name next to mine. How I secretly miss the juvenile giddiness and hope of more life in something as simple as a love interest's name. I'd certainly discounted the possibility of the dream of *te amo*, being just for me.

I wondered about all these people... did love conquer all? Does it last forever? Do twin flames unite?

It all reminded me of old high school desks and roller discos I see on the internet; a visage uplifting to the heart... wouldn't get away with that kind of coolness in school today.

No. 9

Wednesday 7th July

My first week as a magazine boss is not going well. Bewildered, I laughed out loud to myself this morning. I didn't know what else to do, three plans had collapsed in a matter of days.

First plan
Hand notice in at the magazine and work the notice period – tapping the marketing department for low-cost ideas and more contacts in the process. Save my final wage and move on to working at Martha's. Whilst working at Martha's, create and write a magazine and build a reader/fan base. Leave once it's making money. #fail

Second Plan
Begin working at Martha's immediately. Utilise staff discount

for clothes. Create and write a magazine, build a Reader / fan base and sales pronto as no last wage from the magazine and have little savings. Leave Martha's once it's making money. #fail

I've read the world wide web dry of blog posts and articles about creating a new magazine, researched and calculated figures. It's eye-watering. Not only financially but the impracticability of this being a one-woman show. My show. Most successful people, I have learnt, don't do it alone. They have another working with them or mentoring them. Someone else, usually with the opposite skills to their own, to enable all the ores of the boat to be rowed at the same time. If not a business or creative help, then a love partner or supportive parent... a champion of some description lurking in the background. I have no one and only half the skills I need to make it.

Do I need to rethink my game? Is it a magazine I want to do after all? I'm questioning all of it because the once-inspiring idea has unexpectedly transformed into a beast who has me in a headlock.

Whichever way I try to slice the tiny current I have to spend; I can't do it. Marketing is an astronomically high cost or too hard when you're nobody or both. However, with elbow grease and a lot of nerve, some of it's doable. The publication won't be featured on the screens at Piccadilly Circus or on posters on the underground anytime soon, but with a lack of a following, money, technical and photographic skills and rising costs, it's making any form of marketing overwhelmingly impossible. Therefore –

Third Plan
Don't find a new terrible boring job paying pittance which

makes the brain die. Instead, use the time to build a huge following and reader base online, create the magazine and sales by bootstrapping and winging it. Also, don't waste money on lattes, cinnamon buns and takeaway food deliveries… or living life in any way. #fail

I should adhere to the last point regardless as I don't want a figure like a budgie.

Despondently I flipped the laptop shut and the stupid stick-it-note from the other night was staring at me with its smiley face. I'd stuck it on my bedroom wall behind my desk the other night. Peeling it off, I threw it in the bin and then promptly retrieved it, smoothing out the small square piece of paper and placing it in the desk drawer. I changed from pyjamas, given it was noon, into a sleeveless black mid-length dress with seamed tights. Added a few silver pendants; crosses, bats and a lightning symbol. Stacked on silver cuffs and bracelets, rings (3 fingers on both hands), earrings… honestly, the jewellery deciding and putting on takes longer than the clothes. I tied a fringed scarf around my head hippie style because I couldn't be bothered to wash, scrunch dry and back-comb my hair. Applied lashings of eyeliner into a long cat eye and went out on the balcony with my pack of cigarettes to converse about life with Egyptian Goddesses. I saw Bootsy arrive for work but ducked down, I didn't want him to see me and start hassling me about the note.

I refuse to believe my pounding desire is a dud. It can't be. How can a thing feel so alive but be dead? I often tune into the quiet of myself and ask for wisdom from the ancient Egyptians, but I couldn't hear it. That, too, was lost to silence. Equally, I struggled to drum up a logical answer too, other than a miracle investor or business partner, but would I want that? It would be like splitting a baby in two or your favourite rock album. I needed to divert my attention to something else and away from the mounting frustration and pressure hurting my shoulders.

There was no sign of *him* over the road. Hadn't spotted him all day. Now I understood those five women the other night, hovering outside the hotel. Fans. And according to his social media, there are 5.5 million more of them too. At least he has some. Unlike me and sloth angel here.

Which reminded me...

I stubbed out my cigarette and went to the bureau in the sitting room, pulled out cream paper and a pen and wrote *him* a letter back.

I was not about to reply via a friend in a bar or on a bloody stick-it-note.

Dear Hat,

I received word of your invitation to meet. I thank you for this, but I must note a gentleman should ask for a date or meeting, in person or with his voice.

I am exceptionally busy at present and will be for the foreseeable future. I am quite certain my declining your unrefined request will be of no consequence.

Good luck with the tele stuff.

Sincerely,
Monica Blue

No. 10

Thursday 10th July

I stirred sugar into a hot coffee across the road at the bar. It was mid-afternoon and with the bar being empty, Bootsy flitted about checking stock and penning orders while pitching all the reasons I should meet Lenny. He told me Lenny is in town and living at the hotel until the autumn when he will return to New York. Bootsy getting to know those staying at the hotel isn't anything new. Hotel guests often use his bar. Technically, it's the hotels, but this is a sore point with Bootsy. However, apparently, he and Lenny met one afternoon, hit it off and a new bromance was born.

"He's here for promo stuff, work and then some time off," Bootsy said.

"Oh, how darling."

I edged the white ceramic sugar pot back and forth on the bar with my index finger.

"I understand you have a new friend," I added, "but I don't care how great you think he is, or how your romance radar fucking things are bleeping. I'm not meeting him. It's a waste of time."

"Loosen your chains," Bootsy said, removing the sugar pot from out of my reach. "He's not a vampire plotting his next bite."

"He's the latest craze riding his wave, same thing."

"Now who's all judgemental? Pot. Kettle," he smirked.

"And he lives in New York. How can you think this train wreck in waiting is a good idea?"

Bootsy huffed as I did earlier at figures and the laptop, as I reminded him his new fabulous friend doesn't speak to me, and nor did he take the time to ask me directly.

"You're not the most… approachable a lot of the time," Bootsy said diplomatically.

"That's not my problem, is it? He should grow a pair."

Bootsy groaned in irritation whilst running a hand down over his face.

"He's in a different position to those idiots you meet from hanging around Dave's kebab shop. Give him a chance."

"Dave. Who's Dave? I don't eat kebabs."

Bootsy placed his arms out wide on the bar taking in a long breath and lent toward me as I nonchalantly sipped coffee.

"It was a metaphor, Monica."

"Oh, you mean like the dangling carrots?"

"Carrots? What are you on woman? I'm sensing a romance of the year, one by the way you deserve, and we're talking about carrots and kebabs?"

"You started it."

"Gah! You're a real pain in the arse at times," he replied walking away to rattle bottles in one of the fridges.

"Don't have a paddy over it," I said, following him behind the bar to the fridges lining the back. "I appreciate what you're trying to do but the timing sucks and he's not my type of guy. It's that simple. Here…"

I pulled out the letter from my bag addressed to the hat and placed it on the countertop. Informing him, I had replied to Lenny's request, and could he pass it on to him when he next saw him. Bootsy began to grin like a toddler who's finally gotten his way before frowning at me in suspicion.

"Do I need to vet this," he said, picking up the letter, "I don't trust what you've written."

"Just give it to him," I said.

Back at home out on the balcony, my tape deck played a limited edition of a Van Halen album as I considered a dance with the devil. It was tempting to re-enter the digital jungle and read the slew of articles and social media posts about Lenny. I don't know much about him other than his latest film I haven't seen. Scrolling the internet would be an easy way to discover more about the enigma over the road if only it didn't feel the same as searching symptoms of illness and finding all roads lead to the worst scenarios. After glaring at the laptop screen with hesitant fingertips over the keyboard for a while, I chose not to make the mistake of dipping a toe into the waters of Lenny James because a) it's more out of nosiness than interest, b) from my experience, it's best to find out for yourself who someone is from them… and c) the media is not a reliable source of information.

I hadn't heard of Lenny before, why would I? All of this talk had dragged up the love issue within me and had got me thinking about boyfriends. The vagina power gurus say to write to find your dream person, I must write a list detailing all the qualities I desire him to have and be. So, fuck it. Might as well write what MB's heart deeply wishes for in that department because I've little else to do right now. My last boyfriend loudly and proudly dumped me in the middle of a wine bar as soon as my gothic coat and I greeted him. He had given me an ultimatum on our previous date about how I needed to change the way I dressed, or we would be over. It required no conscious effort on my part at all to ignore his garbage. I was more astounded that my style was such a huge problem to him. He knew what I looked like before we dated. After staring me up and down as though he had to tarnish me with his repulsion, he stormed out of the wine bar and left me standing on my own. I became instant entertainment for the onlooking crowd and shortly afterward I marched my cowboy boots right on out too. Flipping my finger at all the gawkers as I did… I went to bars full of wine and Prosecco-drinking people for him. Dickhead.

Proper Man List

- Old-school gentleman.
- Bit of grit and metal about him.
- Knows who he is.
- Loves his work.
- Strong yet romantic.
- Claims me like a king and adores me.
- Has a love of travel.

- Passionate, loyal, funny and kind (obvious traits I don't think I should have to clarify about my special person. However, I am not leaving it to chance in case cosmic cupid bypasses these because I didn't put them on the list).
- A man with shoulders wide enough to deal with life.
- Hands big enough to hold me.
- A heart so full he can love me silly.
- Supports and believes in me and what I do.
- Is my friend.
- Doesn't mind all the above from me to him in return.

I'm not sure if men who are *all of the above* exist, or maybe they do, but I believe they exist for other people and not for me. Either way, I will accept nothing less, and it does not bother me in the slightest to eat alone.

No. 11

Friday 11th July

1.30 a.m.

An idea for my magazine-slash-life crisis interrupted a hazy dream about Martha and her tarot cards, and it stirred me to consciousness. I didn't want the idea vanishing back into the same place sleeping dreams faded out to and forcing myself awake, I noted down what had been delivered into my head. It was bare bones. Half a skeleton at best, but as I sat there dwelling in it, the larger and more magnetic its presence became. One thought brought another and then the next and the next. They filled my mind quickly and I scribbled down each one, whether they made sense or not. Some were old hopes I'd long laid to rest. Others were wishes still to be acknowledged, yet this summer night's writing sprint appeared to be magically blending them all into one big plan. I'm almost glad my first three attempts failed, as this was shaping up to be interesting rather than a castle in the sky. I've written a lot in the middle of the night, thinking I was the new Hemingway, only to discover the following day, when I re-read my masterpieces, they were little more than diarrhoea. This time around, I'm connected to the energy of the words I am noting down as always, but it's different. To the point, I'm not entirely sure if it is me writing.

By the time I felt complete, and I knew the flurry of thoughts had ceased, it was 2am The time reminded me of the late-night smoke with Lenny. It's a peculiar feeling, calling him by his name and not *him*. Which is stupid. It's only a boy's name. *Lenny*, I repeated the name out loud and softly smiled to myself. *Lenny. Lenny.* I noticed peculiar was turning into twinkly, and I quit repeating his name before I got carried away with the feeling. I still went out onto the balcony to see if he would be loafing about all the same. All I saw were stars, Bootsy's bar all in darkness, streetlights and the glow of the hotel entrance. No evidence of Lenny. I sat down on the lounger and lit a cigarette anyway, blowing smoke out in thick clouds toward the moon.

I adore the moon, it's my favourite thing in the sky.

"I'm just on the other side of it. Talk to the magic night pearl, I'll hear it."

My dad used to say this to me when I was a young girl, and he was away travelling with his company. Globetrotting for work accounted for a lot of Dad's parenting… you know the type, here but not here. I think his partial absence bothers me more now than when I was little. Back then, it didn't matter as much. His work captivated me like a sweet shop would, travelling became normalised and my interest in a bigger world became a natural by-product. I often think wanderlust will always be a component in my blood.

In the same way I used to do all those years ago, I sat there in pyjamas shielded by a silver-studded sky enjoying the coolness of the air on my skin, wondering if the moon really does hear our wishes.

"Hey, magic night pearl," I whispered. "Been a while… I've got this mad idea, and –" *Shit, shit.* Half asleep and semi-concentrating, the cigarette fell from my fingers, hit the lounger, burning a hole in the cushion and rolled onto the floor and underneath. When I leant down and under the lounger to fish it back out, my hand hit the shoebox I'd shoved under it when Bootsy called round, and I was relieved it hadn't rained the last few days. The Barcelona book was back in the cave room and still prevalent in my mind, but with everything going on, I'd forgotten about the box.

I located the cigarette and stuck it in my mouth, letting it hang down, and lifted the battered lid off the box. Thoughts of Barcelona creeping in to add another bone to the skeletal frame I'd noted down earlier. Rather than stomping in with my cocksure opinion about Barcelona being wrong – hell – inappropriate, I let it roll. I let images be added to the previous ideas until they could have been scenes on the screen I was observing. Little lights were turning on inside me and I couldn't help but dare to feel anxiously excited.

I opened a few of the envelopes to read the letters and cards, but it was too dark to see clearly. Cigarette ash was falling into the box, causing me to create grey smudges on the stationary as I brushed it away. I knew what they all said. I'd read every single one. Replied to none.

I put out the half-smoked cigarette in the ashtray and took myself and my box back into the cave room. I love to sit in there in search of a personal holy grail, enamoured with my books and oddities. All of them contain truths, mysteries and fantasies about our world, blurring the line between where truth ends and fantasy begins and, somewhere in the middle of it, is me.

The ancient Egyptians reminded me of the deep enquiry we must take of our hearts. It is here answers lie, not in logical land. For as much as I run my mouth and speak my mind, there's a secret chamber within my heart where I banish the unspeakable and unthinkable to. I'm unsure if it's me who fears the cargo of personal truths I stuff in my secret chamber, or if it's others I fear knowing them. Either way, it's enough to make me cough. There's a lump rising in my throat, and it wants to be voiced and I don't know what to do with it. It makes me embarrassed.

By the time dawn broke, I knew delving into the inner abysses was a prerequisite to the solidarity of the self. Only then can a phoenix rise. I curled up on the red carpeted floor under the window. Threw a blanket over me still surrounded by open books on Barcelona, cave houses, fairy tales, Greek architecture and ancient Egypt, coming to understand it is only when one is pure and sincere in their demands of life, is the truth not withheld. I close with final thoughts of an unexpected deep night.

Thoughts from the Cave Room

The ancient Egyptians believed the heart, not the brain, is the vessel containing our human personalities, emotions, memory, imagination, creativity and wisdom. The heart *is* the true voice. The ancient Egyptians knew what those who would live after them would search for, what they would need. The big answers to life and creation. They left clues and wisdom everywhere; much of it beyond our reptilian brain's ability to comprehend how they did, but when you're ready to know, you discover their guise and the secrets they hold.

We must learn to trust ourselves over others and our insidious brains. To trust the subtlety of the inner voice and release the spirit of it. And perhaps today is a good day to sit the fuck down, shut up, and listen to what it has to say.

No. 12

Saturday 12th July

Late Morning

Days are moving on and after last night's ideas and excavation, I'm trying to accept the journey of my magazine may stand a greater chance of making it by launching it as a digital one. This means lower production costs. I can include certain content in it which wouldn't be possible in a print publication, for example video. There would be less chance of print mishaps and less risk generally, plus it's instantly available to worldwide readers (worldwide!) who don't have to wander far from their digital devices. I can travel Europe while I write it. It enables me to combine them all. It's a no-brainer, right? I can see why an angel would wake me in the night and tip me off to move my idea this way, instead of trying to force an expensive project into being in a competitive city with a high chance of it flopping. What is troubling me about this altered version of my vision is not all its benefits and ideals, they're great, it's that I cannot bear all this digital nonsense. Books, music, newspapers, photographs, paintings, all these precious pieces need to be held, felt, collected and appreciated. Not mindlessly scrolled through, or a next button pressed only to be forgotten five minutes later. Every wannabe in the land thinks they can spit out a digital publication or channel of some variety. Many of them, unfortunately, only achieve poor quality or content and they drown out the good ones. I am frightened I'll be classed as one of those and not worthy of proper print, just as much as I detest the medium.

I am not my reader; Viv has said this to me many times. I recognise the need for a digital presence. I'm far from stupid and, although more feasible, the marketing is still problematic due to the funding required. I don't want my work to hold a meaningless vibe, my readers are important to me. How ironic it is I am using a digital platform to write this blog, but no one else is reading this. For the first time in my life, I'm dithering, and I don't fucking dither… actually I'm incorrect. It's the second time I've dithered in my life. The first time was when Dad was leaving. It's a different yet same scenario… I am indecisive at a fork in the road, and I don't like it.

This is becoming messed up and convoluted. All I wanted to do was start up a magazine and publishing company. Produce authentic publications readers would be refreshed and excited to find. To remind them of their identity or create it if they'd lost it or never found it all, not enter a rabbit hole.

Remember the song Stick to Your Guns, Bon Jovi, Monica.

Remember what Dad taught you…

Creating from the heart and acting on it will always love you forward, he would say.

I condemned the hurricane Dad caused. I condemn I ended up as collateral damage, but I have to believe there is truth to his words. Truth to the dream seeds he talked to me about as soon as I could understand English. I watched Dad live his successful life this way. I believed it for him I believe for others, my old editor and Martha are other examples of people following their dream seeds. It's harder to do for oneself, especially when a detour I'm not sure I'm ready to face is thrown into my original plan.

It's on my mind I need to let la-di-da mother know. I don't want to ring her about current events until I have eliminated any bullet holes in my plan and wobble within me. She will hate I have left my magazine job and will despise more what I'm trying to do, and God forbid I make a fool of her in the process of trying to make a successful life. I am coming to resent my dependency on Mum for living and eating arrangements and it's turning into resentment. She expects me to fill a mould I simply don't fit into, and she wastes no time issuing guilt for this. Making me out to be less than because I walk a different path to her. It's a subtle control I need to shake and if I can eradicate my dependency on her, then my mother can no longer hold power over me. Mum doesn't let me forget she owns the house and pays for food and bills. I should have more understanding for her, she'll tell me.

"Do you know how tough it has been for me with your father? How foolish he made me look?" I am also reminded of frequently by her.

I don't know how long sympathy for your mum should last. Forever? I've lost count of the number of times

I've heard those lines. I wonder if she considers how tough it's been for me...

I rang Viv to check if she was still coming round to mine later for our night in after she finished work. When we were younger, we used to go to Smokes every Saturday and every Sunday and go to each other's houses during the week. Recently I've noticed Viv doing this less and less. Take tonight, for example. When I rang, she asked to re-schedule for tomorrow. She needed to sort out Ronnie's electric meter and wanted to finish a drawing on a new pendant and ring set, inspired by one of Ronnie's former band's songs. The tired part of me, from being awake most of the night, was silently pleased, and I didn't argue back for changing at the last minute, again. I wondered though, if she would have remembered to let me know had I not called her? And can't Ronnie deal with his own electric me-ter? Viv doesn't live at his house.

There's always something as to why our nights out or nights in are thinning out and it is generally laced with coke or Ronnie.

"Am I allowed to see it?" I asked, Viv. "The drawing?"

"Maybe, depends on if I finish it. Ronnie says it's a good one. Best yet. If I do, I'll bring it with me tomorrow and you can tell me all about your magazine 2.0 or is it 5.0?"

"Ha freaking ha. How many times do you –"

I was interrupted by happy knocking sounds coming from the main hallway. "I'll have to go; someone is at the door. See you tomorrow."

I legged it downstairs and peeped through the spy hole. Bootsy was standing on the doorstep. In his work attire, one hand in his pocket, about to rap the door again with the other, but I opened it before he could knuckle another tune on it.

"I have post," he said, waving a letter in the air with a grin reaching his eyes.

"Well done. Why do I need to know this? Oh oh oh, are the hotel reconsidering your offer to buy the bar?"

"Fat chance. No, you dumbo, it's for you. From Lenny."

Lenny wrote back? A familiar fluttery of something I couldn't identify, nor control moved across my abdomen. It was the same when another letter arrived from Barcelona. Both make me want to run as fast as I can from the unrest and seek the secret chamber.

"I shut this down. Why has he replied?"

"Oh, I don't know, let's see." He wiggle-tapped his fingers on his stubbled cheek in sarcasm, gazing into beyond. "Maybe, contrary to your opinion, he does already have a pair and doesn't need to grow them as you delightfully mentioned." My eyes rolled upward at Bootsy as I clenched my teeth together and twisted my mouth to the side, snatching the envelope. "But let's move on from balls and open the letter," he said.

"Bootsy. Out. Go back to work. I'll see you later."

"Come on! What's he said?"

"Out," I said, opening the door and holding it out wide.

I shuffled him across the threshold, nearly trapping his hand and neck in the door when I closed it because he was curling himself around it.

"Make sure you read it!"

"Out!"

I leaned my back against the door, opened the envelope and pulled out a letter written on hotel stationery. Sitting down in the middle of the hallway to read it, the coldness of the tiles was a stark contrast to the warmth skimming my skin as though the letter had Reiki skills.

Dear Monica,

My hat and I apologise for not asking you personally. The bar is an awkward place for me to come over to you without an audience watching and listening. Then you left. I wished I'd come after you.

I've had a gruelling schedule lately and jet lag messes with me for days. Sleep can disappear along with privacy in my job. When you saw me that night in the bar, I'd already done a 12-hour day and needed to stay awake to do an interview at 1 a.m. (our time), for the West Coast across the pond. Bootsy did an impeccable job of ploughing me with espressos but none of that matters I guess, it's all an excuse, because I wasn't sure how or when to ask you.

As you weren't too busy to write a letter, perhaps you could RSVP to this one?

Lenny

P.S. I hear you're into rock music. I literally hear it from your balcony when I come and go at the hotel. I'm into country music at the moment – does a rock girl approve?

P.P.S. How long is the foreseeable future?

What the hell just happened here?

I was quite happy, shitting it about sorting my life out with a machete blade and a rock angel. Then this-this-*this* MAN teleports out from the fucking cosmos adding another unknown quantity, I seriously don't need, to my embryonic phoenix.

I can't deny a part of me found him interesting for a few seconds when I let myself get the better of me, but I shouldn't find him interesting. I turned him down for good reason and thought he'd go away. Instead, he stepped up with an engaging, handwritten, no less, letter in return.

I'm sure he'll get over his jet lag messing with him, the poor lamb, but I have become very attached to this bird I'm trying to fly. It needs my undivided attention and nurturing… not my eye being taken off the game by a mirage.

Lenny is not only bad timing but also not my sort and let's be honest, he's a whole other level of potential carrot or kebab. Know what I'm saying?

Organised pretentious dating bores me tremendously, and I am not breaking my self-promise of no men and distractions. Finding out he's rom-com's latest golden boy also gives me a sense of distrust. Whilst probably judgemental of me, it's how I honestly feel. Shouldn't someone like Lenny be chasing the city's cocktail dresses and duck lips? What if I am a bet? It wouldn't be the first time. Monica Blue is not going to be left blue again. Besides, I'm ready to deal with a more thrilling matter. A flight I needed to book.

I returned upstairs to my bedroom for the laptop charger, placed Lenny's letter in the desk drawer, and closed it sharply. Problem fixed.

No. 13

Saturday 12th July

Afternoon

Booking a one-way flight ticket to Barcelona is symbolic as it is a committing move forward. No going back after I do it. My decision to head out to Barcelona took me a long time to arrive at, but once I'd finally listened to my heart, and entertained the idea of it, the decision to go was made in seconds. It's funny how long yet quick a one-eighty move can occur and the freedom of realising I can do what I want to, that I'm not answerable to anyone, deserved a cheer and a coffee. A cheap filter coffee at Smokes wouldn't empty my purse.

I'd left my hair as it had woken up earlier, a wavy messy mane hanging loose. I pulled on my biker boots and matched a layer of burgundy lipstick to the colour of my mini skirt. Good enough for a daytime Smokes visit. When I turned the corner to walk towards Smokes, disappointment halted me and made me groan. Martha's bike was parked outside. I turned around and left.

Half an hour of wandering with no direction had me back in the centre of South Kensington, by all the museums and eateries. The cafes are expensive, but to avoid a completely unproductive and pointless trip out, I gave in to the cute crêperie place. The one with a French design and atmosphere. It's owned, oddly, by a British chap, not a Frenchman. I've gone there for years and still don't know his name. I can only ever afford his coffee here and there. Although his bakery goods are tempting, they come with tourist prices. As I was handing my money over to pay, I overheard a group of young people with backpacks huddled around a table near the window talking about Lenny's film. How they believe he's back in London... possibly staying in Notting Hill, Camden or Chiswick, because that's where his dad lives.

He's about half a mile up the road, loves. Do people seriously discuss this stuff? Over waffles and pancakes?

"Oi. Hello." I realised the man who took my order was talking to me, "Don't be forgetting your change, Miss."

"Oh yeah...cheers. Was elsewhere," I replied, preoccupied with the talk on the shop floor.

I pushed the main door open with the side of my body and weaved through the rivers of people and the nutty road system. Red buses which chugged around every ten seconds beeped at me repeatedly. Three of them (THREE) were wrapped with posters of Lenny's film. A week ago, I wouldn't have noticed any of this. It bugs me I do now. He was beginning to be everywhere, but I made it home with no more run-ins about Lenny or the rest of the cast. Distancing myself from the surprise of his popularity, I plonked myself on the kitchen bar stool, retrieved a cinnamon bun and got back to work.

I'd already researched Barcelona as an area and picked a date, no rhyme or reason to the departure day, other than when I thought I might be ready. As I clicked my way through the airline's booking process, it wasn't long before I rubbed my hand over my half sleeve and blew out impatient sighs. Does my bag meet the dimension requirements? Do I want to reserve a seat, and which seat? Do I need priority boarding, and a fast track through security? Do I want to check extra bags in? Would I like text updates? Another fiver here, a tenner there. *Fucking hell, I just want to book a cheap ticket…* I say cheap, but it isn't. The £40 air ticket advertised all over town doesn't exist, unless you don't mind taking ten different flights all around Europe to finally arrive in Spain nine hours later, when it's only two hours away from London in the first place. If you want to take things with you, like clothes, be prepared for all the sneaky addons.

Eventually, I stopped complaining and talking at the website and hit the confirm and pay button. One minute later, it was done. Committed.

"I'm off. Outta here. Adios Big Smoke and Hola Espana."

I raided the fridge for nothing in particular and paced around the kitchen, clenching and unclenching my hands. Happy and excited energy brimmed out of me and wouldn't let me sit still. I kept reviewing my digital ticket and paperwork filed in my inbox, but I wanted to print them off to keep them as memories. I traipsed back up to my bedroom where I'd left the printer the other day, after churning out reams of information about digital magazines and printed off my ticket. I stared at it for a while in disbelief, as if it was the winning lotto ticket.

I may be far from my destination, literally and metaphorically, but I am on my way and this is the best feeling I have had in my life. It was all mine, and I had created it myself. I folded up the printed ticket and opened my desk drawer to place it with other Monica B keepsakes and there it was. Bootsy's note with Lenny's request and Lenny's subsequent letter smack in the middle of it all.

No. 14

Sunday 15th July

I debated.

I debated with drumming nails on the desk in my bedroom.

I debated in the cave room selecting a tape. There are many, many good albums.

I moved downstairs to stare out of the balcony window doors and twiddle hair.

I debated more whilst biting my lip and sat at the bureau in the sitting room.

Right…

Are you at work? I texted Bootsy.
Yes, why?
Is Lenny in the bar?

No 😦
Good. I'll be over in the next half hour.
A normal person would come over when he's in.
Guess a normal person would x.

Perfect.
I hit play on my tape deck and Poison by Alice Cooper,
played out at full volume.

Dear Hat,

I accept your apology. I'm surprised you had the time to write back amidst your gruelling schedule and jet lag turmoil. Country music is acceptable. I bet you listen to it on your phone or on some other subhuman digital device with wireless earphones. I do too at times, only out of convenience. Nothing beats hand-picking a tape from an extensive collection and playing it on a big ole boom box… my dad is a music producer or at least he was the last I heard. However, there will be no chance of hearing rock music from my balcony today as it's raining spears.

Whilst writing this has been a pleasant-ish ten minutes out of my own turmoil, I leave for Barcelona on the 15th of September. I have much to accomplish before then. Therefore, the foreseeable future is without end.

Good day to you (and hat),
Monica

I nipped across the road to the bar and placed the envelope
down in front of Bootsy on the bar counter. Turned around,
and ignoring the late afternoon drinkers, walked back out

instructing Bootsy whilst I held my hand up in the air, punctuating my points.

"No comment. I'm not taking questions. Please can you deliver it? *ThankyaBootsyLoveyaBootsyByeeeeBootsy*."

I heard him giggle to himself as I yanked the door open and promptly walked over the road home. Pouring a glass of vodka and orange, I could now return to the work in hand and wrote down tomorrow's schedule before Viv arrived.

No. 15

Sunday Evening

Viv sank onto my bed next to me and the holdall as the night sky rose outside.

"How many pairs of shorts do you think I'll need?" I asked, shaking out the holdall to examine its capacity.

"I can't believe you're going. Doing this," Viv said, looking in the empty bag. "Five maybe? I don't know. I've only ever been to Brighton."

"Any insights are helpful; I haven't travelled as a digital nomad before… It's stressing me out. I'm not quite sure what and how much to take."

Viv moved her eyes from the holdall and focused on the duvet as though she were on the wrong side of being equal to me. My joy began to feel awkward around her. I've noticed myself a few times recently, attempting to find the right level of happiness or excitement to exude which doesn't irritate her. This remains undiscovered, and most likely doesn't have a clear answer. It's tiring and confusing. Do I ignore her attitude? Slow mine down, stop and pick her up (again) or let her catch up? Regardless, I am wondering more each day how badly she wants her jewellery dream.

It panics me more not to take a real shot at changing my life than it does Viv being miffed that I am.

I looped around again to continue with packing dilemmas. I truly don't know the type of belongings to take, what electrics to carry or if I need washing powder. It appears simple in films... throw some stuff in a bag and go.

"I'll figure it out as I go along. Don't worry about it," I said and returned the conversation to her favourite topic, Ronnie and the bleakness of her life.

After some persistent probing, Viv admitted Ronnie was having nosebleeds and repeatedly disappearing. More than once she has had to use her jewellery business money to bail him out, the electric meter for example, she explained. Although Viv found him a paying drumming gig opportunity – someone at Smokes knew someone – Ronnie didn't show up to the audition, despite Viv thinking having a proper gig would help him. To her, these are more important problems requiring constant attention and deep discussion. Me changing my life around is all too princess and selfish.

"What do you think I should do?" she asked as I tossed the holdall onto the chair and sat down next to her on the bed.

"If it was me, I'd leave him, and set up your jewellery line as a side hustle. As you've planned to do for how many years now?" I smiled, flicking her forehead.

Viv glared coldly at me. Declaring her concern over ending their relationship would mess Ronnie up more, and how devastated she would be as she loves him with all her being.

I get it but what answer would she prefer I give her, a dishonest one? I don't know how to do that.

"I can't cut and run with no feelings like you can. I admire it, but a long-term relationship is different. You wouldn't understand."

"Low shot, Viv … I'll let it go on the basis I know this is difficult for you, but you did ask me what I think you should do. I've been warning you for weeks he's in too deep, and you need to slow up on the snow too."

She fiddled with the zipper and buckle on the holdall, her face gaunter than I'd known it to be since meeting her. Her eyes have become increasingly despondent, as though her soul is no longer at home. It's crept on gradually, and I kept telling myself her ghost appearance was due to too much black hair dye and not the truth I knew deep down… too much coke. Too much Ronnie and not enough inspiration and living. I'm no longer sure what I'm supposed to say to her.

"I'm no liar. Take my opinion or leave it."

The conversation flagged rapidly until I told her the only thing a decent friend could, that I was here for her either way. Whatever she decided about Ronnie.

"Via Facetime or Zoom," she replied.

A switch flipped. The empathetic smile I was directing at her instantly dropped and I saw red.

"Don't make me out to be a motherfucker for doing my thing. I can't apologise for being me because you daren't be who you are," I retorted, tired of her snarky.

"That's unfair. Not everyone is as ballsy or lucky as you,

Monica. Try some understanding for a change."

"You think I was born ballsy and a lucky one?... Oh my God, your self-pity is offensive."

We continued spitting like cats at each other until we decided neither of us knew how many pairs of shorts I should take, and what we needed were tequila slammers and Guns N' Roses.

Out on the balcony, Paradise City blared out, and we waved at Bootsy who stood outside refusing to serve a customer any more drinks or let him back in. The drunk stumbled off and Bootsy walked to the hotel, not back into the bar. He often warns the staff in the hotel's reception about obnoxious or suss guests. I had no doubt he was informing them about the drunken man. I kept glancing over at the hotel, thinking about the letter I'd sent earlier and about Lenny. Had he read it yet? I may not want to meet up with him, but our letter thing lit me up more than dealing with Viv tonight. She's beginning to feel like a harsh abrasive. Lenny's letter didn't. I'm not sure if this should mean anything, but I did notice the difference. Zoning back in, I turned to the distant voice of Viv, sprawled on the other lounger.

"Sorry, what was that?" I asked.

"How are you affording to do all this? Travel, setting up the maga –" she slurred and stopped mid-sentence, as she heaved herself slowly forward, missing the rattan mini table, her glass smashing to the floor.

"The ticket came out of my last wage. I'm bootstrapping the rest; most people do at this early stage. You know, using free platforms, free marketing, learning new skills and systems."

"I'd stay away from free programmes and tactics. They're free because they're not good enough for what you need."

"I'll do the best I can with what I can," I grimaced, "and if I must, I'll sell my collection. It's worth a tidy sum."

"Noooo! Not the clothes?"

"Don't be stupid, they're worth fuck all to anyone else. The cassette tapes. They're all originals, some are rare editions… Dad left some value behind, after all."

"Noooo. Shit. Monica! Shit." She smacked the table and broke into hysterics.

"You can't sell those," she said, swinging her legs over to sit up and knocking the tape deck over so Axl was singing into the balcony floor. Viv preached about how the cave room thing, my clothes, the tapes are all me and I can't sell a part of myself.

"Cassette tapes can be re-bought. Life can't."

"Huh?"

"Forget it."

"You're officially bonkers. Promise me we'll go to one last gig at Smokes before you leave?"

"I've got their latest list upstairs. I'll go get it," I replied, and sent Viv to retrieve the bottle of tequila from the kitchen along with a dustpan and brush to clean her mess up.

"I'll be back in a minute... and pick Axl up too," I shouted, pointing at the tape deck as I wandered off.

The ground beneath me felt unstable as I swayed my way inside and zigzagged up to my bedroom. Opening the top drawer by my bed, I took out a small brochure and slid all the way back downstairs, thinking I would surely be dead by the bottom one. When I returned to the balcony, the tequila bottle was balanced on the rattan table and Viv was hugging a long sweeping brush in one arm and holding a letter in the other hand. Unable to find the dustpan in the kitchen, she retrieved the big brush out of the cupboard in the hallway and found a letter on the floor by the door. I recognised the writing immediately as Viv quizzed me on who would post a letter at this time of night and why.

"It's probably one of those politicians pretending to send a personalised letter for my vote," I replied, reaching to take it from her, but she flipped the envelope over.

"Why would a polick… a polio… a, whatever they're called write 'only open if you love rock n roll on the back'?"

Bollocks.

I said I had no idea and snatched the letter, shoving it in the back pocket of my fringed leather trousers and quickly moved on.

"Here," I said, handing her the Smokes' gig programme, "who do you want to see?"

No. 16

Still Sunday

After bundling Viv on the bus home...

Dear Monica,

Pen pals it is then.

I had a day off today. Visited my dad and younger sister, they live in Chiswick. I don't get to see them nearly enough.

I noticed (heard) you were in when I returned and wanted to write to you. It's a new experience I'm enjoying, and I plan to sneak over and post it though your letterbox, like a normal person. If not, I'll rope Bootsy in. He's working to-night.

I'm an actor but I believe you know this or do now. Bootsy told me you're a writer, you have the presence of a writer. Magazines he said? He's a good guy Bootsy. Known him long?

I and the cast have much-needed time off in the coming weeks. Most are off to tropical places, but I miss British bacon, proper tea and August in London. I fly back to New York on the 14th of September as filming begins on the sequel in early October.

Why Barcelona? Is this the turmoil?

Your letter indicated you don't see your dad. Sorry to read that. I don't see my mum either – she left when I was ten and haven't seen her since. I don't usually tell people this unless they are my friends. It's a fine line knowing who to trust these days, but I think being pen pals makes you a friend. Maybe pages written between strangers who are so near yet so far away provide a safe closeness.

I'm in Manchester all day tomorrow, with interviews and lunches which require me to smile a lot. If you want to write me a note back, leave it outside your house. I'll swing by around 4 am to pick it up. Put it in the wishing well feature, the one with the roof in case it rains. No one will be around at that time. It will help the drive up north be less tedious. Oh, and sorry I do listen to country music on a device called a phone. Does this make me subhuman?

Lenny

A text pinged from Viv to say she was home and about to pass out in bed. I texted a reply letting her know I'm glad she's back at her place and asked her about the drawing of the jewellery set. It wasn't mentioned earlier tonight, and I didn't want her to think I wasn't interested in it when I am. I didn't get a reply.

Instead of calling me to bed, the late hour and my inebriated state had me on fire with energy and creativity. I began to upload a few videos I'd edited to my magazine template as a practice run to see how they would turn out. I set it all going doing its thing and whilst I waited, it led me to think about responding to Lenny. I re-read his letter swig-ing on the tequila bottle until it naturally moved me to fish out a pen and sheet of paper from the bureau. The laptop whirred busily on the sofa uploading content, as I considered the idea more. It would be rude not to reply, wouldn't it? Or it could be a huge mistake if I do. I decided only the holy would know the best answer.

"If the laptop has finished uploading, it means I don't reply. If it hasn't finished uploading, that means I need to reply," I said to myself.

I checked the laptop screen too fast for my liking. I'd expected to find the uploaded videos waiting to be watched, instead the uploading had been paused midway due to a pop-up notification from my blog platform interfering with it. Some rubbish about agreeing to a new blog system update occurring next month. 'Press here to be reminded,' it said. I clicked it to make it go away grumbling about updates here, updates there and not seeing the point of half of them.

I wasn't sure I believed fully in signs. We say we do, of course, but when one happens, we question if it's truly real and can it be trusted. It had to be a definite signal to reply

to Lenny though, it was too specific for it to be a coincidence. Yet how could the almighty power of the universe,
who executed it, think engaging with him is a good idea.
Befriending Lenny is in opposition to the plan. Lenny is
also very much not my type. Underneath my confusion I
knew a part of me was smiling and pleased about *the sign*.
I wondered about him and seated myself at the bureau
with the tequila bottle and a pen.

Dear Lenny,

*It's past midnight. I am drunk on tequila and it's unclear
how legible this letter will turn out to be. You are persistent
in your quest. I'll give you that, but don't be deluded. It's
possible I will regret having written this in the morning, but
the company of you tonight is a charm.*

*I shall say I'm impressed you take the time to write, I cannot
bear a text message saying only Hey. How does one respond
to hey? There is nothing to hold on to. It's lazy communication.*

*Are you a Chiswick boy or a New Yorker? Having not spo-
ken to you or watched your film (films? They're not my
thing – sorry) your accent never occurred to me, and Bootsy
didn't mention your nationality.*

*As you asked, I've known Bootsy for three years. We met
when he took over managing the bar. I told him the music in
there was dire and he said I was a liability, but we've become
the siblings neither of us has. He's tried to buy the bar twice
from the hotel, but the scoundrels refuse. It was on its knees
three years ago. It's a gold mine today because of Bootsy's*

light. He loves the place, Lord knows why; I only go in to see him. I tell Bootsy he should purchase another, hardly a shortage of bars in London and he's perfect at it, but he won't. I think the hotel's bar is his version of a home he finally found after a long search. He made it into a special part of South Kensington I've weirdly come to cherish too.

Parents are overrated. The situation with your mum sounds tough for you and your sister to navigate. I respect you felt able to tell me about it. Is this why you act? I ask because I believe I write and create, hoping someone might hear me. I used to write for the glossies. Until I began writing for myself and the new zeitgeist emerging, one, they at the magazine, have yet to understand. A turmoil I do not wish to waste further ink and paper on.
I don't recall the last time I spoke to my dad; he lives in Barcelona. He is not the reason for my travels commencing in the City of Prodigies; I'm going for Gothic architecture, mystical stories and caves converted into properties. All the authenticity of life in Europe I've so far only read about in books. Soon, I will be able to experience it for real. Wouldn't it be rock 'n' roll to own a cave and transform it into a house, or better yet, a library and publishing house? I don't know if these things are feasible, they simply exist nicely in my mind.

My wandering music lord of a dad was right about one thing, if little else. He taught me each of us have dream seeds planted within, containing our purposes and assignments in life to complete and live. I learned recently how smart my dad was to know about these. They might be unseen, but they are real… they're just bastards to sprout.

Sincerely,
Monica

   P.S. I'm not sure what you are, but I don't think it's subhu-man.

I addressed the envelope to Lenny, went to the kitchen and rummaged about in the cupboard filled with the carrier bags my mother insists on keeping. I found one from Martha's shop and placed Lenny's letter in it in case it rained during the night. I wrote his name with a marker pen on the front, and at 1 a.m. left it in the wishing well.

No. 17

Monday 14th July

The duvet kept ringing. I patted both my arms around and couldn't find my phone. The duvet rang again. I sat up, eventually finding the phone lost between duvet folds, last night's underwear, fringed leather pants and a green velvet top with a snake on the arm. The scene inside my head resembled Guy Fawkes night as I considered how great the snake top is. I bought it at Martha's last year. The snake winds up the sleeve and appears to bite into my shoulder with its wide-open mouth. This is what I was thinking about when I answered the phone with barely an audible hello. It hurt to talk.

"You sound horrific. Shouldn't you be on your way to work? Are you alright?"

A call from my mother at 7.30 a.m., hyperactive about

her day ahead, made me wish I had left the phone lost in the duvet. She's spending it with her new friend, whose house has a pool. I tried to palm her off with an 'I'm coming down with a flu bug' story, but it seldom works. Nor does saying I ate a dodgy pizza, or an infected curry causing explosive diarrhoea or my tonsils, which I had long had removed, are playing up again. Everyone, including bosses, knows - you are hungover.

I had to hold the phone away from my ear as she blasted me for pulling a sickie at work because of my – once again – irresponsible behaviour. I can rarely bluff a hangover past her these days, but worth a shot. I needed to steer the conversation away from my magazine job, where she thinks I'm supposed to be.

"You're lucky to have been given that job and if it wasn't for me, you wouldn't have it. Yet you spend more time drinking and smoking the devil's lettuce."

I spend more time writing and creating if you hadn't noticed but ok.

"For the record, Mother, I don't smoke weed. It's boring."

"Ugh, this is what I'm talking about! You need to get a grip on yourself. You can make something of yourself and this career if you try."

"That's exactly what I'm doing. Don't slip in the pool. Goodbye, Mum."

I'd fallen asleep with all my jewellery on, and I couldn't get it off fast enough. All the clasps and hooks to undo were infuriating. I found the darkest pair of sunglasses I had. Tied my hair up with no care, made tea with extra sugar and wondered if I could take four paracetamol tablets instead of two. Four tablets might stand a better chance of providing pain relief.

I leaned over the island in the kitchen and laid my head

next to the fruit bowl with no fruit in it and thought about lying down on the worktop completely. Reminders of how I'm meant to be working on business plans today left me uncertain about what to do about myself, until I rose suddenly with a short gasp. *The wishing well.*

I unlocked the front door to check outside, and the bag had gone. It made me smile involuntarily but the fuzzies didn't last. Within seconds, I critiqued the letter I had happily written to him whilst unarmed with alcohol. It reduced me to cringing about myself. I shouldn't have been so open. I shouldn't have replied, and definitely not when drunk.

I returned to the kitchen and stuck my head against the drawers in the freezer because I didn't know what else to do with it and stayed there.

No. 18

Tuesday 15th July

I don't care I'd lied to Viv about how selling the tapes wouldn't half kill me. Whilst the money will cover the initial setup and travel costs and a new tape collection could be rebuilt later, it would take years. It would break my heart all over again…if my heart did heal at all after Dad blew my world up.

I don't want Viv, Bootsy or anyone to know I'm not making any money and have none saved up. It makes me feel unsuccessful and not good enough, and it's a big enough issue to be slowly bringing my life to a grinding halt and have me surrender my dream as a pipe one. I'll have no choice soon, and it's dragging me down quicker than I can lift myself at times.

I thought sweeping change was possible if I stayed true

and remained focused, but it's not working. I'm scared I will have to return to the life I fought to leave, yet it's confusing as I can't turn my back on this new path either. When is it the right decision to give up an unrealistic idea, and when is it the right decision to hold on and push past the fear?

When my head finally gave up hurting last night, I prayed to her in my candle-lit bedroom. Holding an Ankh between clasped hands, dragon's blood incense smoked out from a backflow burner on my desk, permeating the air. The rock angel is silent in voice but never-ending in the ear and I sense her unearthly presence around me more every day. It's comforting. I don't feel wrong when I speak or write these daily accounts to her with the vomit of my life. If she was a visible being, I imagine she would have big black ass wings with a piercing in each. Wear an extravagant black dress straight out of a historical drama, whilst fanning herself and auburn hair cool with a handheld wooden. She's no witch from the dark side walking the devil's strides. She's the fucking light.

I talked to her for the longest time. My prayer time started with the debacle about my father, and it brought me to my knees. Years have passed since the day he left. I vividly remember standing in the hallway watching him go, yet it's as raw now as it was when I slammed the front door shut on him. I am supposed to despise this man, aren't I? Maintain the bitterness, as Mum does to demonstrate my disgust and hurt at what he did.

How does anybody live another life with other people and homes for two years, when they are supposed to love you and take care of you? He played the part brilliantly. I believed everything about him. Everything he said. Dad must know what it is like to be a spy, living life with two identities. Which one was my real dad? The one he was around me or the one he was with paella woman. I'll never know for sure, but why do I think I still love him? I moved on to talking about my travels and problematic magazine, before she had a chance to condemn my heart for being unable to let my dad, who didn't consider mine, go.

I'm convinced it was my rock angel who magically gave me the idea to travel. This is a goal I had written off as one to aspire to, not a possibility I can have now. We are led to believe travel is a rationed gift or for the wealthy. To me though, it's not a dreamy idea. I want it to be my normal way of life and living. I have witnessed many people confined to only a package holiday once or twice a year. I've never wanted that.

The simple addition of going digital and travelling combines multiple wants and needs into one. I can explore my passion for lands and seas far and wide *and* set up and run my own magazine. I will not give up on print, but the digital version slices the costs massively whilst not tying me to any location. It's perfect really. My travels could become stories in themselves. It might not be how my old editor did it, it might not be my first choice as a formal and I might not understand those who prefer digital reading to print. It doesn't matter. I need those people who love e-reading and the modern way. It's not my right to cut them off and it lifts my spirit to realise they too, are the ones who will enjoy my content. It's inspiring me to create the best magazine more than ever. Who knows, I might fall in love with e-book reading one day too... pushing it, but never say never, hey.

I do know, after spending time with the digital idea and watching a few inspirational stories from rock musicians to writers, I shouldn't be damning the subhuman sign of the times. Rather work with it and try to accept this, albeit hard, concept for me. By default, travelling also places distance between me and my mother, which can only be a good thing. I will no longer be bound to her passive hold. I can live the experience of the books I've devoured for years and, if I should be so inclined, in a time far from now, swing by dads. If I wanted to. Only from a distance and only to take a secret nosey at where he is living. I'm not sure if I'd react kindly if I saw him or *her*. The point is, being open to a few degrees of change, provides more crazy options and possibilities. Without writing this blog, I don't believe I would have ever thought of this combination.

I remained in the safe space of talking to a rock angel until the last of the ash dropped from the incense stick and a burning heat within me took over. It grew and grew, encouraging me to get up off the bedroom floor and move forward. I can ask and whine in prayer only for so long, before it is me who becomes the problem, not life.

I recall speaking with the bank this morning when I made an appointment to see the business manager to apply for a start-up loan. Creating a solid business plan would be more helpful right now than being a mess on the floor. This loan would provide the support and encouragement I need. It gives me funds I desperately require. Allows me to keep my tape collection and shows evidence another believes in me and that I can deliver the magazine the world has been missing.

I opened the first of the business books I'd borrowed from the library with a sense of dread that my current notes were far from the mark bank people expect.

No. 19

Wednesday 16th July

What's with early morning disturbances? First, it was the duvet ringing waking me up early. Today the doorbell did the honours. Three times it jarred, reverberating around the house.

I threw the covers off, charged across my bedroom, shoved the sash window up and leaned out shouting hello. I couldn't see anyone from my skewed angle. I don't have a full view of the front entrance from my window, only a partial one. Apart from the usual humming of cars driving down the road, silence governed the 6 a.m. morning hues of South Kensington.

"Oi. Who's there? Don't wake me up then fuck off."

Nothing. No response.

"If it's a parcel, leave it there. You have permission to

sign. If it's not a parcel, go away."

I slid the window back down and returned to bed. Disgruntled and fiery, I couldn't re-find a comfortable position and took it out on the duvet, throwing it from side to side. Serious thought began pecking my mind, like a bird lived in there, to resume an orderly work routine. I couldn't be successful by staying in bed all morning, and reluctantly, I pulled myself out of my pit and went downstairs to make a strong coffee.

I'd assumed the mystery doorbell ringer had gone, but better to check, it was too early for the normal daily post, but delivery drivers rock up at all times. There was no post through the letterbox and nothing outside on the doorstep. Wrong address presumably. There are multiple combinations of building numbers, numbers with letters and names of buildings on the street, it's surprising anybody gets the correct mail. *The delivery people must* – I was halted mid-thought on my opinions about the postal services because that's when I saw it. A small white paper bag in the wishing well. Monica Blue scrawled across the front of it in what had become familiar handwriting. That's when I felt it. Again. A salmon flipping in my belly as I tried to reject a smile.

Leaving the open business books on the island in the kitchen, next to a bowl of soggy cereal, I took my mug of coffee, a pack of cigarettes and the white paper bag and sat outside on the balcony. Perched on the end of the lounger, I tapped my lip repeatedly. Why? Why is this happening? The bright sunlight in my face had me squinting my eyes as I struck the wheel of the Zippo lighter to light my cigarette. The lighter's flame raged uncontrollably, nearly singeing my eyebrows, and I had to close and relight it a few times before it returned to a calm normal state. I've singed my hair a few times due to mischievous lighters behaving in this manner. Once, sitting in Smokes, I set the sleeve arm of my top on fire because all the hairspray I used had also coated my fishnet top. I resembled a human-sized flaming Sambuca, until Ronnie saved the moment by rolling me against the wall and handing me a pint.

I chuckled to myself at the memory of it as I delved into the bag of temptation. It contained a letter and food.

Good morning, Monica,

100 percent I'm a Chiswick boy. How could you mistake a Londoner for a New Yorker?!

To repair your hard night on the liquor, I had the hotel prepare an extra breakfast. I'm leaving early for a meeting in Soho with my UK agent. I ate mine in my suite but I will drop yours off before my driver arrives.

I might see my old mates after my meeting. We were always known as the Chiswick charmers; three actors and two singers. I managed to make it out of there. Whilst we meet up for dinner or days out when I'm here, it's becoming harder. I keep thinking my best friends I've known for years are slipping away, and I don't like it or want to face it. Distance, fame, or nothing stays the same. I don't like any of these answers and I don't know the reason why, only that it's there. I ended up staying in New York after landing the part of Sammy, the lead in the film you haven't seen, and everything changed. Anyway, I'm back in town for the summer. Maybe it's me who is feeling left out and nothing is wrong with the Chiswick charmers at all.

The house I was meant to be renting for the summer got messed up. My new assistant booked it all wrong, hence why I'm staying in a hotel. It would be better if it had a second unseen entrance. I don't have to come and go out of the main one that way, and it maintains privacy, but the new assistant didn't know about this tact either. I got annoyed with him as a hotel isn't a home, but now I'm thinking, perhaps my new assistant had a role in fate and not a mistake I hired.

No parents are normal. I have come to this conclusion. God knows my mother wasn't/isn't/wasn't – unsure of the correct term, as she's not dead, but may as well be. Deep talk from me for a mid-week early morning!

I don't want to spoil our writings, but what do you reckon about moving to email? I set up a private account. This way, we are not at the mercy of Bootsy's postal services or need to behave like thieves in the night.

thehat@coffeemail.com

Your call.
Lenny

Oh, for pity's sake. Emailing? Shit.

What do I do now?

I folded the letter back up into the envelope and pulled out a fluffy croissant and a clear plastic bowl of fruit salad bright as a rainbow from the paper bag.

I understand his logic, clearly, life isn't understanding mine. I'm proving myself right already. I'm meant to be reading business books and continuing with my business plan ready for the bank and doing a thousand other things – and yet – what I AM doing, is sitting outside in the sun, reading letters, eating fucking kiwis.

No. 20

Thursday 17th July

3 a.m. Witching hour…

Martha had taught me about witching hour the more I became intrigued by her back room at the shop and fortune-telling. I'm on the fence about whether the readings she rambles out to people are indeed a person's real past, present and future, or made-up stories from inside her head. Prompted by a bunch of peculiar drawings on a set of cards. I mean, where does Martha pull her information from if the readings are true?

All her happy clientele can't be wrong though. The more intrigued I become, the more I can't explain certain events and outcomes with logic. I'm leaning toward believing a mystical realm invisible to the human eye is in fact all around us. With *things* in it. *Things* I don't understand.

Martha doesn't advertise her tarot readings. It's all word of mouth, and she's renowned for accuracy, apparently. I used to question her ability and call her *special gift* story time for life's hopefuls. I enjoyed ripping her about it until one day, having had enough of me disrespecting her, an unnerving glint in her violet eyes altered me. She stared into my soul with a power I can never forget. As though she struck me with inner lightning. Seconds later, the swinging birdcage fell without rhyme or reason to the floor and the main light bulb blew out. I haven't roasted the subject since.

The weird event led me to wonder further about the supernatural world. How can I dis the tarot and psychic minds, questioning if they are real, but not the strange powers behind the building of the Pyramids and the Sphinx? What kind of ancient Egyptian raconteur would I be if I didn't believe in at least a slice of a phenomenon beyond what I can comprehend? I don't have answers yet other than I do not think we reside alone on this earth. I've stopped ridiculing the supernatural and those who converse with it, it bothers me too much. I don't worry about offending a few humans here and there, but otherworldly energies, who could locate me during witching hour to demonstrate their presence, I do. A friendly encounter scares me as much as one that may not be. Until I have more answers than queries about this realm, I'd rather not meet anyone or anything from it. A rock angel is all I need.

The time of witching hour can vary depending on who is asked. Most agree the hours between 3 a.m. and 4 a.m. is the time of night when witches, ghosts, supernatural beings and other weird shit are at their most powerful and visible. It's haunted me since Martha taught me about it, it's only fascinating until I wake up at this time. Convinced one of them had been standing next to me, watching me, and therefore the reason I was awoken. I am not certain of the truth of this statement, but it scares the bats out of me, nonetheless.

As I write this blog, communicating with a non-existent rock angel I've befriended, I consider again if this is any different from reading tarot cards or having witchy vibes? I believe in something that isn't visibly there, yet feels like it is, with a knowing the connection is more than wishful thinking. Is it all one and the same?

I couldn't return to sleep, given the time. I shot out of bed and ran around the house turning on every light and lamp. Playing the radio with the TV on in the kitchen but muted, I sat at the island with hot tea and picked up my business plan and attempted to make my first draft of it. Reading business books and writing corporate language are activities which do not come easy to me. The start-up loan people or investors claim to want unique and stand out ideas with driven people behind them. Yet they don't. What they want are the same ideas, with people not too far out there. They back what they've seen done before. Unique, the great and stand out people come at risk. It's a degrading experience for a person like me, trying to fit into their required box. After a while, it was enough to zone me out and, repeatedly, I had to re-read paragraphs and re-write my answers with yawns and crumpled eyebrows.

Somewhere around 5 a.m. I couldn't take it anymore. I closed the books and my thoughts returned to the latest problem. I opened my email and switched the radio over to play a tape, pressing play on the song, These Dreams by Heart, letting the whole Heart album roll because each song is perfect and genius.

To: thehat@coffeemail.com
From: monicablue@coffeemail.com
Subject: Thanks for breakfast

Dear Hat,

An email has no style. It's a corner shop. A letter is like an original fashion house in Paris but I'm trying to find love for a digital world. I thought I'd start here, with a digital letter to you.

Does this make me subhuman now? Please no.

Monica

No. 21

Thursday 17th July
Lunchtime

> **To:** monicablue@coffeemail.com
> **From:** thehat@coffeemail.com
> **Subject:** Digital Love

Monica,

If it helps, I'll print out your emails and when I read them, I'll imagine them written on your fine stationery delivered from across the road. How does that sound?

It was me ringing your doorbell yesterday. I heard you yelling out your window as I was spinning myself around in the hotel door to go back to my suite. So much for a low-key drop off! I'd tried to hide my amusement as I walked past the receptionists, but I couldn't. They gave me a standard professional smile and pretended not to notice I was laughing for no reason.

You asked me if I act because of the trouble with my mum. I thought about this and the dream seeds you mentioned…. I watched a lot of TV and films growing up. A. LOT. My dad used to hate it. That's all I did. Especially after she left for the last time. Escapism turned into wanting to be those guys on the tele. Not the one lying in bed wondering why my mother couldn't love me and my sister enough to sort herself out. I still don't understand. I've given up trying. I guess, as you wanted to be heard, I wanted to be seen. Now I hope to be the inspiration and support for some other young lad or teen girl going through it, you know? I don't know if an acting career was pre-destined for me, only I knew it was what I wanted to do. Still is. Is this the same as a dream seed?

I didn't see my mates the other day ☹ *. The meeting dragged on… the powers that be decided to extend it with new scripts for me to consider and contracts to discuss. I had to reschedule the boys, they said it was cool, but they sounded annoyed. I'm catching up with them another night* ☺

Lenny

I always knew, should I have the chance to travel, the first place I'd visit would be Barcelona. For all my reasons cited, but now it's muddled with the thought of Dad and the idea won't leave. It's growing bigger and all this talk about dream seeds with Lenny, as brief as it's been, is making it more potent. It isn't the only place I want to visit; I want this odyssey to take me everywhere. See everything, write and publish as I trek but, Barcelona is, and always has been, a priority. This makes a difference. Is it an ulterior motive of my subconscious to be an inch closer to Dad? I Can't say other than I accept I can no longer ignore what is going down here.

Taking the shoebox out of its cupboard in the cave room, I emptied the box of letters and cards onto the sitting room floor. I scoured the sprawling heap until I found the latest communication with Dad's details in Barcelona. He writes many times a year and has done since he left. Hadn't missed a birthday or Christmas. I made a note of his address, phone number and email, which he writes on each letter or card and stuffed it into the pocket of my bell-bottom jeans. I hummed quietly as I carefully stacked all the contents and placed them in their box and back in the cupboard but felt I had committed a sin.

When I break the news to Mum, how I have left the magazine and will be leaving her, London and managing my own publications whilst travelling, I have no intention of keeping my first destination from her. Each part of my plan she will despise regardless, but visiting Barcelona would be gasoline for her fire. For reasons unknown to me, Barcelona (to Mum) doesn't mean a thriving, lively city of over a million people steeped in history and Gothic elegance. No Barcelona means my dad. The way she carries on at times you'd think my dad owned the city. She proudly scoffs at the name if it's merely mentioned in friendly conversation or on the TV, as though the person talking about the forbidden city is on Dad's side. What the chuff is that about? She won't even go to Spain! Why is their marriage disaster Spain's fault?

I'm dreading discussing any of this with Mum. More awkwardly, it will have to be over the phone. No doubt whilst she swims in a pool, with a flute of champagne, eating weird French things. She isn't due back from the South of France until the middle of September and I can't dump a huge change on her with only a couple of weeks' warning. Time will be required for both of us to process this unexpected development since she's been gone. She would not, though, and could not, find out I was contemplating calling Dad or considering walking past his house. It would drive the chisel through the widening crack between us into a full break. I don't want to hurt her, but I can't hurt myself either. Which one of us is more important? Until today, the answer had always been her.

No. 22

Friday 18th July

I printed out the latest version of my business plan to read through for the one-hundredth time and make any final changes over the weekend. The last few days I'd found it necessary to abandon writing the columns and features for the debut issue I had wanted to write. I didn't care much for the life force within, prompting me to focus on the much-needed bank loan, which means I *can* continue doing what I love and offering it to others. It made me uncomfortable and annoyed, but I ignored it and cracked on with the work in hand.

"I've excelled myself," I declared to the ethers, the home of any rock angel, "are you seeing this?" I said, waving the papers upward to the ceiling. "I bloody hope you are. A month ago, I didn't even know what a business plan was."

Feeling organised and accomplished after having completed it, I am uplifted and motivated to continue. It's changed my inner talk to one of being more positive. That I too, like the big fish of the industry, operate on a professional level, not an amateur one. Working from *it*, not looking at *it*, wishing I could have it. I can almost say I'm excited about the appointment with the bank next week and I will wear an outfit to punctuate myself. I rang Viv to tell her about my excitement over the progress I'd made and asked if she wanted to go to Smokes tonight, but her phone rang out to voicemail. I texted her instead, to which I received no response either. I gave up checking my phone, discounting the slight deflation I had because of being unable to tell my friend the good news. I retreated to the sofa with the Hollywood Vampires album. I hadn't listened to it before and sat for half an hour clicking through their songs on my phone. Not letting one fully finish playing before skipping to the next. When I'd played them all, I clicked my phone off and remained motionless, staring at the sitting room wall. A free yet hemmed in bird. At least fifteen minutes of dull silence had passed before I realised this would not do, and karate chopped my way out of the escalating downward spiral. Literal pretend karate chops and kung fu-y moves. Nothing like the real sport, but it was liberating to move and express. I needed to be me, grounded in my own power, which had waned in recent days. I will not be tossed around by life; I'm in charge of my universe and my universe takes care of me.

I needed a drink.

I curled and back-combed my hair. The bigger, the better and changed into a green and gold embroidered military blazer, ripped denim hot pants, black tights with my trusty thigh-high boots. I added reams of chains and rings and pinned a dragon broach onto my shorts. I drew a small pattern on the side of my left eye in black liner and green eyeshadow.

Line one up I'm coming over, I texted Bootsy over at the bar.

Friday Night

Feeling more certain about the future, I decided tonight was the night to tell Bootsy about the magazine and travel venture. I was ready. I want him to know. It's fun talking to Bootsy, and I hate keeping secrets from him. Even if he is overprotective like an elder brother whose heart is in the right place but finds it necessary to point out all the obvious what-ifs. It's an exceptionally annoying habit of Bootsy's. I seldom listen to him. It beggars belief how easily he finds these obstacles, when logic is no friend of mine and I simply don't see them in the first place, or I try to ignore the beasties vying for my attention to stop me on my path. Negative beasts are the highwaymen of the mind. Yet this had become such an important project and life mission for me, I knew I had an element of doubt within me about it working out successfully, one someone like Bootsy, a person I love and trust, could reach and bring to life. I braced myself for impact.

I drank firmly seated at the bar; the latest London Newspaper lay on top, and an interview with Lenny and his co-star about the film dominated the front page. I was becoming accepting of seeing Lenny everywhere as a normal occurrence. I turned my focus to Bootsy, refusing to let him interrupt the monologue I delivered about my vision of the magazine, travelling and issues with my mother, Dad and Viv.

With his chin propped in his hand and elbows balanced on the bar, he didn't mansplain a single pothole. Not one. Despite my sitting there waiting for the onslaught. His eagerness for listening and offering genuine support for me became quite a surreal shake-up of the evening. He did offer to read through my business plan if it helped. He knows more than me about business, there is no question, but I don't need the words of others meddling with my creation and knocking it sideways. I declined his assistance. Bootsy, the guy I know as much as I do rock music, blindsided me with his cheerleading and encouragement, and was that a freckle of awe I'd observed? I believe I have turned a corner on my track to nirvana.

"Proud of you," he said, ruffling my hair.

"You know I hate that. Stop it."

"Never. I also think, for what it's worth, there is unfinished business with you and your dad," he said, holding his hands up in surrender. "Just saying before you come at me."

I didn't respond but pinkie promised to always keep him abreast of my whereabouts and gossip and agreed to his only request... taking me to the airport. We both thought a second too long about the idea of an impending emotional goodbye and sadness dropped like a mic.

"How's you and Marco?" I asked, turning the mood.

He beamed a thrilling account of an upcoming minibreak they are taking. Complete with a posh picnic in a park – Bootsy's dream place for a marriage proposal and one he's held forever. I mirrored a broad grin back at him in anticipation of his dream of marrying Marco coming true for him. Bootsy is a real-life love bug who adores romance, Marco and the happy ever after. All he has wanted his whole life is his own bar, a fly husband and happy family life. He's on the verge of having it all or at least half of it. The more he talked about it, and all the trimmings of a romantic trip, the more I noticed a strange fogginess about it all. It tainted my joy for him and I couldn't pinpoint why. Marco is organising it, following Bootsy's discussion with him about Marco cancelling yet another dinner date at the last minute. He used air quotes for the word discussion. I assume; therefore, he meant arguing. I've met Marco many times. He loves fine dining with panoramic views of the city with dinner plates the size of a planet… not eating mini triangle sandwiches from a wicker basket sitting on posh grass but, you know, compromise and all that. The puzzlement I was feeling was not about Marco, however, it was Booty's overdone excitement about the lush break which struck me as odd.

My eyes slanted. "I don't believe you," I replied suspiciously.

"Forget Marco, I want to know about Lenny!" he exclaimed. "Is romance in the air? I'm right, aren't I? He generally pops in on weekends, I'll text you when he comes in."

"Nothing to report. We're pen pals."

"Pen pals? He's living across the street!"

"We were paper, but we've gone digital now. Gimme another vodka, then I'm off to Smokes."

"Emailing you mean?"

"I feel that word lowers the tone."

"Why don't you give him your number?! I don't understand your mind at times."

"It's not meant to be understood, my friend."

To: thehat@coffeemail.com
From: monicablue@coffeemail.com
Subject: Dream seeds

Lenny,

I am sitting on the bus. Bored. Listening to country songs on my way to Smokes, a rock club I go to all the time and became inspired to hear something different. I'm meeting my friends Viv and Ronnie there, or I'm supposed to be. Haven't got hold of either of them all day, but I'm in the mood for decent drinking, rocking out and playing pool. Don't ring my doorbell in the morning.

If I were to ask my dad, he would say yes. Entertaining others through acting is your dream seed — but only one of them. Don't let it be the only one you recognise. There's a whole universe within you full of them. I think the strife you endured, and I sense you still wrestle with, became the hammer to crack the acting seed open. Nothing, however difficult, is wasted. If none of it had happened, what fodder would you have to be able to give to other people? Why did your mum leave? You don't have to answer that if you prefer.

Monica

P.S. Your work is hardly a 9-5 job… why should friends be annoyed over a reschedule?? I'd make a note of that.

To: monicablue@coffeemail.com
From: thehat@coffeemail.com
Subject: Smokes Club

Monica,

Noted.

I could meet you at Smoke's Club? I don't care if people recognise me or if the dark side approves of me or not.

To: thehat@coffeemail.com
From: monicablue@coffeemail.com
Subject: Smokes Club

It's not your scene, golden boy.

To: monicablue@coffeemail.com
From: thehat@coffeemail.com
Subject: Smokes Club

Again. I don't care. How do you know what my scene is, anyway?

To: thehat@coffeemail.com
From: monicablue@coffeemail.com
Subject: Smokes Club

You're not coming. Good night, hat.

No. 23

Saturday 19th July

I'd expected a usual Friday night at Smokes – drinks, talking and trying not to be sick on the way home. Except I ran into Martha near the pool table not long after I arrived. I'd been searching the building for Viv and Ronnie, who were nowhere to be seen and not answering their phones and began to wish I hadn't gone. I thought they would have been there. They forgot they were meeting me, as I learned in a text message this morning.

"Haven't seen you around for a while," Martha said to me.

"Can't think why," I replied, walking away and knocking a pool ball out of place from their game on the table. Martha blocked my path. "I'm not interested in a fight, move outta my way… please," I said to her.

Martha responded with a soft laugh and a twitch of her head, as though she was shaking a thought out. As usual with her, it was tricky to read if this was good or bad. All I knew was I didn't want to deal with her and end up in a big argument or fight, resulting in me being barred from Smokes. This happened to me once before, when an argument with one of the biker's ex-girlfriends got out of hand. They lifted the ban eventually after I promised not to cause any future trouble.

"We're not fighters here. What makes you think I want to fight you? Come on, Monica, this is madness found in the playground. Find it in your heart to bury the hatchet and let's start again."

Martha missed seeing me in the shop, she said, and had hoped she'd bump into me at Smokes to iron out our differences. As I had done a spectacular job, up until tonight, of avoiding her, she hadn't seen me to be able to discuss it.

"You could have texted me," I said.

"Would you have replied? Anyway, I'm more of an in-person person," Martha responded. I couldn't fault that.

My stubbornness can be infinite. I'm not one to go back on myself when another has done a number on me, yet she spoke with such sense and kindness I couldn't help thinking I'd misjudged her. It was relieving, distinctly different and easier than continuing to keep fighting the fight with fire. Normally I would have done that, egged on by Viv but the difference between Viv and Martha is miles, as I am discovering. We agreed in the end, the job incident in question did not warrant attacking jugulars.

"I'm not giving you those clothes back though," I said.

Martha smiled and wafted a hand tipped with black and orange long nails, saying she likely would have done the same thing.

"Keep them. A present from my leather-covered soul," she said.

"I was planning on doing. Can't stop though, I'm meant to be meeting Viv and Ronnie," I replied, craning my neck around her to see if they had shown up.

"Viv was in earlier, picking up gear from those two idiots," Wookie, one of Martha's biker friends, leaning on the pool table, said. He nodded over to two slick guys sitting in the corner who didn't fit the normal mould for Smokes. "You don't send ya woman to pick up gear," he added, shaking his head at the act. Wookie threw a spare pool cue over to me, which I caught one-handed. Impressive given I wasn't expecting a long pole to be chucked at me suddenly. "Stay with us. You can take my place against queen Martha. I'm off outside to the others."

From out of nowhere, that conversation, which may appear irrelevant on the surface, turned out to be a transformational moment taking me from reality to another.

One day, I'm on the outside of the older cool circle and in a split second, I'm one of their hood. I still had no idea what had gone down with Viv and Ronnie, I only knew they hadn't shown up and as the evening got underway, I hoped it would stay that way. They would both be high, argumentative and disruptive, and I felt on edge checking my surroundings for them every ten minutes. I surprisingly quickly became comfortable with Martha, Wookie and the other bikers. It wasn't until experiencing this dynamic with them that I realised my time with Viv and Ronnie, particularly of late, had been the opposite.

"Loser buys the next drinks," I smirked. I knew I'd beat her.

"Winner gets a free tarot reading," Martha retorted.

"Lose-lose situ for some then," I replied.

"Don't be knocking the cards… they know stuff, or I do. Can't decide which one it is," she said, tossing her long hair to the side, eyeing up the layout of the balls on the pool table. "I still remember the messages I gave you the last time we spoke. How might they be playing out, Miss?" Martha said it with an air of cockiness.

The faith she held in the cards and herself I'd never known to wane, it only strengthened. I recalled the two simple messages she randomly gave me back then, and I'd paid no mind to them. Revisiting that scene tonight, Martha wasn't far off the mark with her psychic senses and cards. Maybe it's the cards I need to consult with and not the bank…

"Interesting," I replied, striking the white ball. "Interesting."

To: monicablue@coffeemail.com
From: thehat@coffeemail.com
Subject: Opinion needed

Monica,

I've been offered a few roles for after the next film. One is a complex character I'd love to play, good plot too but I have to ride a horse in it. I'd need to learn how to ride… I don't like horses. They scare the shit out of me.

Rosie (my sister, she's 22) used to have a horse when we

were younger. It kicked me in the ribs, breaking three of them and bruising half my face for weeks. I was in a bad state for weeks, my ribs still give me gyp today. Rosie never lets me live it down how I ignored equestrian etiquette 101. A swishing tail and pinned back ears mean an unsettled horse, but I didn't care about stupid horse rules or if I was making the giant thing mad or frightened. I was a 15-year-old cocky bro, chasing after Rosie trying to trip her up (she'd thrown manure-covered hay at me). Getting her back was more important. Didn't anticipate ending up in A and E with a lecture from dad and the hospital staff. Never been near the pretentious pedantic creatures since.

What would you do?

I don't mind telling you about my mother, but I do mind the world knowing... She's a junkie. I prefer to keep that private and out of public gossip. Last I heard, she'd stayed clean after the fifty-seven thousandth rehab attempt and was travelling around the US in a camper van with a friend. A new age hippie or something like that. She wasn't a scruffy street addict type. Mum is the opposite. A smart-dresser, well-spoken, had a great job in tech... and unfortunately, a secret addiction which helped her spin all the plates of her demanding life. Until it didn't. I see it in my industry all the time. Me, Dad and Rosie became a unit after she left. TV became my friend; the violent horse became Rosie's. I'm always torn about whether to move back to London. I can't stand the distance sometimes.

Why don't you speak to your dad?

Lenny

To: thehat@coffeemail.com
From: monicablue@coffeemail.com
Subject: Opinion Enclosed

Dearest Lenny,

So you got beat up by a horse.

Get over it.

If it's the role you want above all the others, I suggest you saddle up and learn. I do hope it's a black horse in the film. There's a magnificence about a man riding a stunning black horse, don't you think?

Does this answer your question?

Dad lived a double life with a Spanish woman for two years and then moved to Barcelona with her. I remember him leaving, vividly. He was at the front door, leaving for good after Mum kicked him out upon discovering his other secret life. I remember the pain tormenting Dad's face as he begged me to reconsider staying in touch. I hesitated while hovering by the half-shut door. I despised him yet didn't want to lose him. Wailing coming from my distraught mother in the kitchen also pulled at me and I didn't know which side to fall too. Stay in touch with him or cut him off like a dead head on a plant and stand united with Mum. He could sense my torment.

"In silence, one voice — the true voice — will always be louder," Dad had said, "whatever you decide, even if it's not the decision I wish for, it's your truth, and I can ask no more of you."

DEAR ROCK ANGEL

I called him a bastard and slammed the door in his face.

You are right though. It's easier to be yourself on the page with a stranger than with someone you've known for years. My friend Viv comes to mind as I write that…

Sincerely,
Monica

No. 24

Sunday 20th July

The church clock across the road from Viv's flat struck six. I thought how beautifully Gothic the trees were in full bloom. How they framed the old stone and windows of the church perfectly. Viv clattered in the kitchen making another round of coffee and I ignored my phone ringing, as I continued staring out of Viv's sitting room window. My phone rang again, then again. After the third, I answered. I couldn't stand it any longer.

"I've finished at the bar early. It's quiet and over-staffed. I'll come over if you want. I can help you sort packing out. I'm a genius minimalist packer," Bootsy said.

"I'm not in. I'm at Viv's. Role-playing banker and unworthy loan applicant... guess which one I am?"

"I was hoping to hear about exciting itineraries, not play a game of guess who."

"We're being productive businesswomen whilst Ronnie is out. I'll be back in a couple of hours."

"Viv is no such thing. Speaking of which, how are the two bottom feeders of west London?"

"Don't be a knob. They're good people at heart."

At that moment, Viv's front door, onto the communal stairway, opened, followed by Ronnie. Groaning as he collapsed on the floor of the tiny kitchen, his face bloody with patches of purple. Viv's chatter turned to screaming and the coffee mugs smashed to the floor. Hot coffee burned both Viv and Ronnie. Not that they noticed. I watched on from the sofa at the unfolding carnage, with Bootsy fretting down the phone, asking if I was okay.

"I'm fine," I said, lowering my voice. "It's just Ronnie arriving. Looks like he's had a beating. I'll phone you later."

"I'm sending a cab for you. Both of them are trouble. Wake up, woman."

"No, I can sort it. I need to check she's ok," I hung up, watching her smother Ronnie as he rolled about the floor. But the mirror above the worktop, opposite the front door, showed me two men standing on the threshold. The same guys from Smokes Club on Friday. I froze at their drug dealer's ugliness and shifted in a ninja silence from the sofa to the far corner of the sitting room between the old gas fire and the window. The furthest point away from them yet still giving me a side view into the kitchen. The men demanded Ronnie pay up his tab or Viv was next.

Tab? Shit. I was churning through ideas of what I could do, or whom I could call. Martha? The bikers? Possibly. One of the bad but good guys I know? I couldn't decide for panic, and I hadn't seen any of the bad good guys in a while. Martha and I had just reconnected again and my reluctance to drop this at her feet so soon stopped me.

Viv, ashen, curled her neck up, taking her gaze off Ronnie and placing it on the open door and the men. She disentangled her arms from Ronnie and scuttled back to her feet, scrambling into the sitting room. She couldn't acknowledge me as I tried to breathe as little as possible after discovering how loud breathing can sound. Viv yanked her savings tin from the DVD drawer and, with dithering arms, handed it over to them.

"It's all I got," she said to the two men.

"No, babe, don't do that. I'm sorting it out," Ronnie groaned more deeply, curling into a ball.

The two men counted Viv's money meant for her jewellery business, wafted what must have been a few hundred in the air and left smugly. Not without landing another kick on Ronnie's arse.

I heard the men walk down the stairs and then the main door slammed shut, and exhaling never felt as good as it did at that moment. I peeked out the side of the blind half covering the window and watched them casually turn left and walk down the main road toward the centre of Hammersmith. Adrenaline on the run around my body, bothered me greatly. This whole situation – Viv, Ronnie, all of it – had frightened me. Why? Why has this changed? It wouldn't have shell shocked before, I would have dealt with and not turned daunted. When I think about it, my stomach has dropped most times I've been with Viv recently, which, for a close friend, is surely wrong.

"Shouldn't have done that, babe. We didn't owe em that much," Ronnie spluttered.

I wanted to beat the shit out of the idiot myself. I tried to shove down the sneaking suspicion that Bootsy could be right, and she'd become baggage I didn't know how to un-pack. A friend I've spent years with has, overnight, it seems, been letting off a warning flare every time I see her, instead of a vibe of the sisterhood. Maybe she always car-ried a warning sign, and I didn't notice it until I stepped off the boat for a minute.

I stuffed the papers scrawled with half-finished an-swers into my blazer pocket and called out to her as she walked through the sitting room to fetch the first aid kit from the bathroom.

"Don't start on me now," she hissed.

"I wasn't. I was going to ask if you want me to stay over, but clearly, you got this." I replied. "You know where I am," I added before stepping over Ronnie and leaving.

Once out of the main door, I turned the opposite way to the dealers. I ran toward Chiswick in mid-calf win-klepickers until I found a busy bar to stand in front of and called for a cab, my hair now half unpinned and sticking to the sweat around my neck. Makeup had run. A burning sensation swamped my feet and calves, and they wanted to burst out of my winkle-picker boots. The balls of my feet throbbed with pain as I lit another cigarette and noticed various groups of people congregating outside. One guy yelled out to me whilst I checked my cab arrival every five seconds.

"Which lock up did you get out from?"

He and his buddies all roared with drunken laughter. I was going to ignore him until I found myself slowly walk-ing through a parting crowd toward him and the rest of the toffs. I paused for a second in front of him. Flipped him the finger, stubbed my cigarette out on his pompous boat shoes, turned and dived into the cab, which pulled up in the nick of time.

Change of plan, I texted Bootsy. *On my way back. Come over.*

Later, out on the balcony...

I cradled a mug of hot water, whiskey, lemon and honey Bootsy had made for us both. We sat on the same lounger, the bar and hotel radiating brightness as I rested my head against his.

Normally, I would have stayed or helped or done something... not walked out! But Ronnie's drama had become more dangerous than worrying. He'd brought it home with him. Not even to his own home – to Viv's, placing her in jeopardy too and, by default, me. Her dream of the jewellery business had gone with it. I feel sad for her. I feel sad when it came down to that one defining moment identifying your real values and truth, she chose Ronnie. She chose familiar unhappiness and a darkening path. It's not about her choosing me, it's about her choosing her – Viv choosing herself over anything else. I'm sad she can't find the place within her to do that. I'm sad I was put in danger, with no remorse from either of them.

"She's no intention of doing anything that she says, other than riding on your coattails," Bootsy said.

"Oh, that's unfair, don't you think?"

"Is it? Have you asked yourself why you're still friends with her?"

I shook my head.

"I'm loyal. I care, I stand by people I love... as friends do," I replied.

Bootsy's head lowered and his eyebrows ticked up with each word I said.

"And do you feel her love and support for you?"

I turned to watch the twinkling street, the bar and the hotel. All were busy, a delightfully friendly corner of South Ken, I am a part of, not excluded from. I considered for a moment how random pieces of my life, like my South Kensington Street, Bootsy, and cinnamon buns are a natural comfy fit within my body. Had good vibrations. Fuck, did those feelings vanish when I brought Viv into the picture. My stomach whoshed downwards and muscles tightened.

"Honestly? I'm finding her draining. Ronnie too. I've been in dicey situations before, but tonight, I was scared."

He lifted my chin and our eyes met as he riffed…

"Stop searching for the things you need and want in people who don't have the capacity and ability to give them to you. You can't blame them for it, but you can't carry them either. You deserve people who can match what's in your own heart. We all do."

I swore to us both I would remember his words, as I kissed him goodnight on the cheek at the front door.

"I love you, Boots."

"I love you too," he replied, with his hand on my shoulder. "Sure you don't want me to stay over? We can watch an old black-and-white film. Bring out the duvet and snacks?"

I smiled warmly at our memories of watching films until all hours and I thought of Lenny, and imagined this must have been an activity he'd spent most of his life doing.

"Cheers, but it's late and I'm done in. Off to bed."

"Okay. Call me if you need me."

I'm going to miss Bootsy terribly when I go. I cannot contemplate the idea of leaving him without it turning my throat into shreds of achy flesh. I harshly said to myself I'm doing the right thing regardless, as I closed the door on the night, shut off all the lights and slumped into bed.

To: thehat@coffeemail.com
From: monicablue@coffeemail.com
Subject: Unknown

Are you there?

To: monicablue@coffeemail.com
From: thehat@coffeemail.com
Subject: Unknown

Yes. What's up?

To: thehat@coffeemail.com
From: monicablue@coffeemail.com
Subject: Unknown

Nothing. That's all I needed to know.

No. 25

Monday 21st July

I would love a hand to hold. I have done for longer than I care to admit. Would I still know how to hold one back? Is it wrong to need another's hand in a world where those with only a machete to make it, are meant to be warriors alone?

Listening to Pat Benatar – Shadows of the Night.

No. 26

Tuesday 22nd July

I woke early. Without any alarms, phones calling or doorbells ringing.

No word from Viv either. I considered texting her this morning when her well-being popped into my head. Bootsy's words from the other night shortly followed, causing a redirection in my mind.

Shouldn't she also be asking if I am ok? I know Viv, she'll be sitting at home or at work assuming I'll contact her to check in on her, with no effort from her side of the street. As Viv sees it, her life is far more stressful and difficult than mine… automatically assigning her and her drama to first in the queue and first dibs on attention. It's been the way of our world in hindsight, and I hadn't clocked on until now.

It won't have crossed her mind how I am feeling because 'Monica is always alright.' This is a new path I am treading for myself and decided not to reach out, but to wait to see how long it takes her to get in touch with me.

Frustration is slowly forming into resentment towards Viv, and towards myself for behaving in a way I preach against. The longer I stewed on the imbalance in our relationship, the harder I picked my bottom lip until gradually it dawned on me, we were different people. It's a sad time. A large part of me knows my friend Viv and I are not the duo we once were. I'm unclear if she has been suspecting the same, but I think she is clueless about this issue. For too long I have been blind. For too long I've tried to be the person I was not the one I am now. For too long I felt bad, as a friend, if I did not rally to her every disaster and console her.

There are only so many times one can do that, and this isn't how I roll, but what I say to her or how I handle the situation is beyond me. Heat spread across my upper back, like a lit bonfire of dread and fear. I turned the TV on in my bedroom to watch something, anything to distract me. The time of day limited me to watching morning breakfast shows… one with a distinctly wasted-looking Lenny on it being interviewed.

"I know a hangover when I see one," I Said out loud to the TV, thoughts of Viv became replaced with amusement about Lenny. 'This is going to be worth watching," I said, as I sat upright and turned up the volume.

Lenny and two other cast members were being interviewed on the morning show's purple sofa. Lenny fidgeted, trying to sit still and be perky. I could see a fragile yet unmistakable clamminess coating his face which could have easily been the poster of a new shade of paint, off-white with a hint of sage green and grey. I could tell he was relying on his co-stars to do most of the talking, and he repeatedly ran his hand through his blond waves and rubbed his thighs. Only moving his head if needed. When the presenter asked him direct questions, he stammered his way through with short answers.

But it got better. A surprise judging request was thrown into the ring – the three of them were to taste a range of scrambled eggs to decide the winner of the show's wannabe chef competition. The winner would land a one-month stint at a top London hotel as a commis chef as the prize. As Lenny peeled himself up and off the sofa to head over to the staged kitchen area, I recognised, from experience, the subtle forward-leaning curved body shape as he walked tentatively over to the counter. It's an effective posture to avoid standing up too straight and disrupting a volatile stomach, and I was roaring with laughter under the covers about the ordeal. I know this scenario all too well, but at least I don't have millions watching me cope with it.

The stainless-steel cover was lifted off the first plate to reveal the sloppiest serving of scrambled egg I'd seen. A hit with fancy hotels, apparently. It made me want to barf, let alone Lenny. I'm convinced I heard a desperate quiet groan via his pinned-on mic as I watched him squirm, barely tasting the disgusting-looking gruel. They had three more dishes to go and whilst my heart did go out to him, it was the most entertaining ten-minute tele slot I'd watched in months. When I flicked the TV off, only then did it click. It was the first time I'd heard his voice. I didn't think a voice to hear more though it had been in my life forever. A sound which made me feel safe.

To: thehat@coffeemail.com
From: monicablue@coffeemail.com
Subject: Over easy or sunny side up?

Good morning,

I have an important meeting tomorrow about my new work venture. It's troubling my head, enough for it to be taking over my eagerness for it. I'm hopeful for a good outcome, yet another holds my fate in their hands. Why is it always some-one else who gets to decide whether to make a dream come true or not. Shouldn't it be the dreamer's choice? Are auditions this way?

However, I wanted to write to you and let you know, by accident, I saw your morning breakfast show interview. It distracted me completely from my thoughts about tomorrow's meeting. I am assuming you are hungover and not ill, as I'm sure the presenter would have mentioned if you were poorly. I hope the hangover has gone, ghastly inconveniences that don't improve with experience or age. Eggs aren't much better.

Rosie sounds fun and my type of girl. How can I not rate someone who throws manure-covered hay at you? But I am truly sorry for what happened to your mum. I sometimes think it must be harder when it's a mother (as opposed to a father) who betrays their children. Mums aren't meant to do such things, are they? Except they are human too. Their minds can be taken over by the dark as easily as anyone else's. We all have a story.

I'm not saying I condone bad behaviour or that I understand your mum. I don't. Nor do I understand my dad or my mother. Trying to can be wasted time, when our focus should be on ourselves. Breaking patterns and expanding beyond what is. I think what I am trying to say is, we don't need to burn in the night because we ended up as collateral damage for their demons.

No.
We are the zeitgeist.
A rising tide lifts all boats, as they say. That's what we are.

Monica

To: monicablue@coffeemail.com
From: thehat@coffeemail.com
Subject: Hate horses and now eggs

Good evening,

I survived. Just.

Can't believe you watched it. Of all the work I've done, that shitshow is the one thing you saw... I promise my films are better. Aha.

I was with my mates last night for curry and drinks at one of their houses, and they convinced me to stay on drinking and playing cards. I knew I had to be up at 4 a.m. for the show, but it was nice to be normal for a while. I didn't get back to the hotel till past one. Thought I was gonna die live on air this morning. The original judge for the cooking contest dropped out that morning due to a family emergency (I found out later) and they landed it on us. It was not fun.

I'm in Edinburgh now, after having my knuckles rapped for turning up in a bad state. More of the same talky talk, smiles and signatures for the next couple of days… the home run of promo is in sight! I'm shattered. Managed to escape the hotel and life for an hour, wearing an 'I love Edinburgh' T-shirt, sunglasses and a baseball hat with a Scottish flag on the front. I looked ridiculous but it worked. I had fun dressed like that. No one bothered me. I wanted to sit and drink coffee in one of the bustling cafes as I used to in times gone by. I would bounce around coffee shops drinking tap water and cheap coffee. Write up my latest actor's CV whilst dreaming and planning of being where I am now unable to do these things anymore – ironic, hey. Now I can't café hop. I appreciate those times in a different light.

I was not disappointed though, I wandered about the city for as long as I could. It's a memorising place, it almost beats London. Almost. I've attached a picture I took of The Writers' Museum on the Royal Mile; it made me think of you.

Good luck with the meeting tomorrow. If you need anything, I'm here, on the other side of the screen.

Lenny

To: thehat@coffeemail.com
From: monicablue@coffeemail.com
Subject: Picture perfect

Lenny,

You don't come across as a curry and card player. Had you pinned as more of a cowboy with a bottle of beer sitting on a fence lost in the view.

Thanks for the picture. I haven't visited there, but it looks like a place I should. I printed it out and took a polaroid of it, which I will keep in my pocket when I have my meeting tomorrow. It represents my intentions rather well. I figure taking the building with me to the meeting will bring me the golden touch.

Enjoy sleeping under the mystical skies of Edinburgh.
Good night, hat.

Monica

No. 27

Wednesday 23rd July

The building the bank operates out of has existed since time became a creation. It has maintained its original architecture of white outer stonework, high ceilings, oversized chandeliers and vast floor space with a grand staircase. Its opulence reminded me of films from times past when banks featured in the story were as glamorous as today's modern hotels. I'd arrived early for my appointment and peered around an oversized poster hanging in the entrance window. Sitting in the waiting area, exposed and fretting over my pitch, didn't appeal to me. I wanted to feel larger than life, not question my worthiness whilst I waited. Spending a few minutes window shopping, listening to Get The Funk Out by Extreme on repeat would prevent the latter. Books, clothes, kitchen-ware, electronics, more clothes, mini supermarkets, tea shops, gifts, musical instruments on and on the stores go. A Londoner simply wants for nothing. I came across a jewellery shop soon enough, and I cannot pass a jewellery store without investigating. Even traditional jewellers with tacky ornaments in the window have hidden gems if one looks for them. I rested my forehead on the window, placing my hand at the top of my brow to block the sun, deciding whether it enticed me enough to go in. Whilst it stocked a collection of interesting pieces, I wouldn't be entering into the place, not today. Not because I feared losing track of time, Marco was inside. Standing at the counter. Gushing over rings. Indicating to the assistant to bring out various trays from a display cabinet. I rolled myself to the side of the window, leaning against the wall. OMG, he's doing it. Marco *is* going to ask Bootsy to marry him! Trying to remain unseen, I covered my mouth with my hand to prevent a giddy shrill escaping, but being inconspicuous isn't easy for me.

Wait... I dropped my hand and squinted quizzically toward the sky.

Bootsy couldn't have been lying about his mini-break as I had thought from our previous conversation. Yet some parts of Bootsy's account of the upcoming trip carried an *off* vibe. It had a suspicious edge to it. I can't fathom what exactly, only that I wish I didn't feel these things. I sneaked another peek from the side of the window. Gasping to myself. He's done it. Marco bought a ring. Bootsy will be made up! Marco and the assistant grinned widely as he handed his card over to pay, and the man boxed it all up pretty. I walked off quickly to avoid bumping into Marco and went straight to the bank; it was time anyway and not my place to interfere with Bootsy and Marco.

I walked into the bank, pulling my earphones from my ears as people sat in tub chairs dotted around the central waiting area, nodding their crossed legs.

My full tulle black maxi skirt bounced, and a daring burgundy bodice hugged my chest. All eyeballs watched me click my way across the marble floor to the reception desk. A man and a lady busied themselves with papers and computers, pretending not to see me. People do it all the time and think I don't notice. I didn't wait long before raising my hand high and banging it down on the brass bell, making my wrist cuffs and bangles jingle with the bell's ting.

"Can I help you, madame?" the man asked, baffled, if not offended, by my back-combed hair and the heavy eyeliner pattern off the corner of one eye.

"Oh. Hello," I said, with a respectable level of sarcasm. "I have a meeting at 1 p.m. My name is Monica Blue."

He clicked the keyboard as his eyes searched across the computer screen, taking his time and my patience with it. I'm quite certain if I dressed mainstream and acted a little quieter, I would have been dealt with nicely and not as though I am a second-class citizen. With no sign of a friendly face anywhere, I heaved out a loud sigh informing him it was with a lady called Janine in the business department.

Janine, it turned out, is off sick and my meeting has been moved to a chap who is the manager of the business team.

Great.

Feeling like a black forest gâteau on display at the wrong event, I quickly discussed with my mind if the heads of departments were easier or harder to impress. I didn't want to fall at the first hurdle by delivering my practiced spiel to the wrong person, but I couldn't decide which one would be my better bet. Janine is a fellow female fond of the arts. The head of the department, on the other hand, holds more authority. Whether the head will be tougher to impress or, due to years of experience, be more open-minded and able to spot my potential easily was an unknown factor. Irrelevant too, as the meeting was happening now either way. That was until –

A blond haired man glided across the floor and came to a halt in front of me.

"Monica Blue, I assume. I'm Michael," he breezed. "We've met in passing before, I believe. You have an, erm, unforgettable presence," he added with a half-smile, offering his hand out to me.

"Thank you kindly, Michael. Fortunately, you do," I replied.

The head of the department was the entitled buffoon from the bar – the same night I saw Lenny and his hat. His sleazy aura was as much apparent in the day as it had been that evening … buffoon man, not Lenny. The thought of sitting opposite him for the next, however long start-up loan meetings take, made my skin feel like ants were creeping around in it. I could feel my abdomen prickling on the inside. My internal objection was instantaneous. It spoke loud and obvious to me… having to prove my worth along with the value and viability of my magazine to him, repulsed me.

"Excuse me," I said, turning to the reception man, ignoring Michael's outstretched hand. "I cannot see him," I said, pointing at Michael whilst my gaze fixed upon the reception dude. "I insist upon someone else."

"There is no one else, and the first appointment with

Janine will be in three weeks. Short-staffed," he smirked.

"No, you don't understand," I said.

"I'm afraid I can't help you, miss," he said, refusing to try further.

"Fine." I glared hard at him, wanting him to think my eyes held spell wielding powers. They didn't but he didn't know. He fidgeted with his and shuffled himself further away from me as I swivelled and turned to walk out. When my inner voice reappeared again and rushed to speak with me. *Stay on your line*, I heard it say. Instantly, I knew a smarmy slick suit would not – and should not – get the better of me.

"Ok," I yelled to Michael, who too was walking away in the opposite direction. "Oi!" I yelled louder. "I'll take the meeting," I added, flicking my hand to the side.

The man and the lady behind the desk raised their eyebrows at each other. I smiled sweetly at them both and banged the bell as I passed by the desk. The people in the waiting area watched the scene intently as if they weren't nosing at the saga already, as I followed speedy Michael to one of the offices lining the far wall.

"I'm the branch's business manager. Nice to meet you, officially," he said. "Take a seat," holding the door open to a small side room with a round desk and two chairs.

God, he was awful. It intimated me being alone with him in what was the most depressingly decorated room I've been in since school.

"Uh-huh," I replied, pulling out the file containing my business plan and letting it fall onto the table as he clicked the door shut. Knowing I can make a lot of noise quickly should I need to bring attention to an unwanted situation.

No. 28

Thursday 29th July

To: thehat@coffeemail.com
From: monicablue@coffeemail.com
Subject: Meeting

Cute.

That's what the bank man said yesterday about my magazine and publishing business.
Cute.

Does anything about me suggest to you – cute?

I've invested everything in this magazine and my work. I

know it's good too. It's been my dream for years, not that he was bothered about either of these, only the viability of it (or did he mean me?) making money, which he doesn't think it has. He trashed it all. Am I overreacting to feel like official red lettering, reading declined, has been stamped all over me? I Failed.

He told me to go back to working in the industry, learn more, get some mileage with my keyboard, and start writing official features. Then branch out on my own when I have a better track record. I told him he was the arse end of the male species who knew nothing about intuition, entertainment or the media industries and left. But what if he's right, hat? What if he is right?

Despite defeat, I am still going to Barcelona. I feel happy when I think of investigating it and writing there. Maybe the time out of London will give me proper time with my soul. My soul doesn't mind me being a misfit. I have spent many hours recently trying to visit that unknown place be-yond our human shell where an all knowing angel exists. To tap her for advice. We all have a magical part within us. Guiding and supporting our personal truths, don't you think? It doesn't worry me if you disagree. Perhaps the real question I should be asking is, how do I continue to believe with both feet when it appears impossible. Risky? Nothing works with one foot in and one foot out... we are either fit for purpose or not. I pray I am not the latter.

Sincerely blue,
Monica

To: monicablue@coffeemail.com
From: thehat@coffeemail.com
Subject: Meeting

Monica,

Banks only loan money if you can prove you don't need it. Worst places for creatives and entertainers to go to for help. Do not let the decision of one man or one bank deter you. You don't strike me as a woman who gives up easily, and you shouldn't… setbacks can get a grip on you if you let them, and I forbid it! But man, I do know how you feel. It reminds me of those days I wrote about to you… sitting in cafes wondering if my career had a hope in hell of taking off and if that flight would ever arrive. I can't tell you how many times I was told no. Still am. The torment doesn't leave you, even if it appears to the world you've made it. I can say though, the day it will turn around for you, will begin like any other day. Out of the blue, you get a call, a letter (aha), an offer, a random event happens, or something occurs changing your course of life for the better. In an instant, the old harder way of being is gone and replaced by those dreams YOU had the nerve to keep dreaming.

What if I had given up? I wouldn't be doing the work I love; people wouldn't be entertained, and I wouldn't be able to give myself, my dad and Rosie the life we all deserve.

What if the icons you admire had given up?
Persist.

There are many places and ways to get funding other than banks. I haven't seen your work, but it will likely be far from what the bank man described and it's only a case of finding the right home for it. I'd be happy to read it and give my opinion if it would help?

Lenny

P.S. Do I think there is anything cute about you? Yes. I do. You're a lot cute. Just not in the way the dick at the bank meant.

P.P.S. Don't send hate mail for the P.S.

I finished reading his email digital letter again by the balcony doors watching the hotel frontage wondering if he was looking over here. Then remembered he's Edinburgh. Hundreds of miles away. I presumed he was still there; I didn't know, and it didn't matter. He's edging closer and closer from over the road each day and it's both tempting and bothersome to me.

I shut my phone off and returned to my pity party.

I take Lenny's point. There are many roads to raise money, but those roads take time. Nor do they eradicate the need to prove your salt in some form to others, either. I don't have time and cobbling together explanations and proof of my value, so another believes I am enough, turns my stomach to lead. It's depleting. 'Help' is best found in your own hands… and in a tape collection worth enough to initially fund pretty much everything.

It's a devastating solution, but I am determined to make my plan work. I tried to stop thinking about selling the tapes and rested in the idea of walking onto the plane to Barcelona instead. Thoughts of my new life took over and filled the afternoon.

Thursday Evening

To: thehat@coffeemail.com
From: monicablue@coffeemail.com
Subject: Meeting

New levels bring new devils I am finding. I don't need your money or influence. Are you thinking you are the way for me to break in? Thank you for the advice but I may have found a way forward, allowing me to continue. If I need to delay launching until I am in Spain, then I will accept it as a reason fate and fortune understands but I, as of yet, do not.

Sincerely not as blue as before on the balcony with a vodka, cigarette and listening to SIXX: A.M "Maybe it's Time."

Monica

To: monicablue@coffeemail.com
From: thehat@coffeemail.com
Subject: No drama here

I wasn't offering money or my influence. Sometimes another pair of eyes and mind on a subject or problem is the support we all need – even you. Monica Blue.

Good night.

Lenny

I think I've offended him. I sensed a sharp tone in his reply. He should be clearer about what he meant by help. What did he expect me to think? I opened the vodka bottle and typed a reply on my phone explaining this and how I appreciate his talent and wisdom. It still doesn't change my final response to his offer.

Two hours later...

I blame vodka. And rock music, which never lets me down... I caved in and messaged Viv.

Not once have I been in a situation or in any of the emotional states humans experience, where a rock song, somewhere, didn't perfectly reflect it or advise me. Lyricists of rock music are some of the most underrated writers on this planet.

Back to Viv.

I hadn't heard from her. The idea she might be in real trouble, in a hospital or in dire need of help, not abandonment, plagued me daily. The friend I know myself to be would, at any other time, contact a person to check in with them. I couldn't let my own values slide purely because Viv is shapeshifting into a person I once knew. I received a blunt response back saying she's OK, going through a difficult time but sorting it out.

At least you're not dead. I'm alright too Viv by the way, thanks for asking.

I wished I hadn't bothered messaging after reading her reply. I'd fallen for it again. I couldn't stand myself today. I poured the remaining vodka from my glass down the kitchen sink, opened my phone and deleted the earlier unsent email to Lenny.

No. 29

Friday 25th July

I still can't stand myself; I am a stalled car whose engine refuses to do anything other than turn over and over despite how many times I turn the key and press the pedals. Frustration weighs my body down and my wonderful imagination is nowhere to be found. I am becoming lost in my pursuits, out of my depth – normal occurrences according to business and mind experts. I disagree. There's a chance I have temporarily misplaced my balls, creating a fake booby trap I've stuck in. There's a bigger chance I'm not cut out for this and my work is rubbish. Intellectually, I know I need to persist, as Lenny suggested – in reality – I feel fruitless.

The bank man's opinion struck deeper than I care to

admit. After some consideration, my frustration is more about what to do next, rather than about a buffoon managing to offend me. Everybody else is changing and creating their success, except me. What if I'm still sitting here in a year, in solitude, telling my life story to a rock angel on a blog only I can read? No further forward other than I have typed more words that don't pay.

Viv, a good friend of years, bears only a question mark after her name, which saddens me. Bootsy is about to be engaged and all loved up, Martha has her own swag going on, as per, and what have I done? Created half a magazine and met a guy called Lenny who knocked on my heart. I'm a cliché and I'm thinking about him more with each day. I glance and gaze at the hotel out the windows all the time as though I'm sixteen again. What the fuck for? It's a hotel. I've seen it every day of my life, or has this act become the equivalent of driving past a crush's house? It's got me checking my email numerous times a day to see if *hat* has landed in my inbox. Today there was no hat in my inbox. Is he still mincing over my reply about his offer of help? Who knows. This is precisely the type of behaviour I absolutely did not want myself doing, yet our writings have become special and a comfort I didn't know I needed. From a guy I suspect I might need more than I think and want more than I dare to write. I banned myself from checking phones and laptops and sat in the cave room.

Sitting with all my tapes, I traced over each one with loving fingers. Memories flooded out as I mourned their impending sale. I'm not sure if I can bring myself to do it and returned to my original yellow legal notepad, where all this writing to a rock angel began, wondering if I had created a mess, not my destiny. In secrecy, I will tell you I am enjoying this blog writing process. It's like writing regular articles or a column for the newspaper or magazine I was never given the chance to do. Any publication I applied for, or pitched to, delivered either a rapid *no* or more commonly graced me with no response at all. The worst.

I worked at a magazine for a while, I'm aware. I am more aware I was little else than a glorified paper pusher, button presser and phone answerer. Not a proper writer. Maybe this is what writing my blog has taught me without knowing. I now feel like a proper writer, and I'll take this small self-revelation as my win today.

I thumbed the first page of the notepad revealing the scribble about finding my nirvana. It helped me recall myself and why I started this journey. I mustered up a few words and with a self-kick up my rear, the literary cogs turned once more.

Thoughts from the Cave Room

The compass. The kind used in math class to stab boys' hands was created in ancient medieval times, before the magnetic compass used for direction. What math teachers don't explain, however, is the symbolic representation of it, well documented in old texts. The sharp end is the stable point of divinity, creation, the big bang or the human imagination… the workhouse of the human mind. The compass' other leg draws a perfect circle expanding and expressing outwards from that one central point. Few notice the compass' structure and operation match that of the universe at large. We *are* the central point – *our own opus* – to which, if we remain rooted in, and expand outwards from, we can bring order to chaos. Widen our existence and create our own extraordinary worlds within the circle of life.

Listening to:

Def Leppard – Run Riot
Bon Jovi – These Days
Skid Row – Youth Gone Wild

No. 30

Saturday 26th July

To: thehat@coffeemail.com
From: monicablue@coffeemail.com
Subject: Cities on a Saturday Night

Dear Lenny,

Are you offended by my response over the offer of your help? I sense I've nettled you. It's not intentional, I've come to rely on myself and prefer to sort matters out the same way. When the magazine is finished, out there rocking it, and success is mine not nigh, I will know it's down to what I did, what I created. Not because of another. I told Bootsy the same when he offered to read my business plan. I'm seeing him later. I'm popping into the bar before I go to Smokes.

A lady I know called Martha texted me earlier and I'm meeting her at Smokes tonight, she's not my usual going-out friend.

Martha offered to pick me up on her cruiser motorcycle… I don't like riding on bikes and I can't deal with helmets. They're claustrophobic and cause flattened hair. How does one cope with a wide machine, thigh-high boots and too much chrome without resembling a superhero character trying to be on the right side of female empowerment? Don't the writers of those shows or films know strong empowered females use completely different energies and mindsets to a man?? I don't understand these people and their portrayals of what they think strong bad ass females are.

I digress with my pet peeve about screenwriters. I'll stick to writing magazines and London's public transport. My bouffant and I are quite happy with the tube and buses.

My normal Smokes friend, Viv, is slipping down a dark alley led by her boyfriend, Ronnie. Both are currently MIA. I've kept trying to save her, which I have failed to do, and now I don't know how to.

This is a lot of words when I simply wanted to ask what are you doing tonight?

I wonder how different a Saturday night in New York is compared to London. I imagine it faster with buildings that intimidate and big slices of pizza. New York is mysterious, a secret world where only those with a special badge can enter through its portal.

… I must ask. Is there a girl in New York? I don't follow your socials or trust entertainment news, but I must know for myself. Being pen pals feels wrong if there is.

Monica

Later, at the bar talking to Bootsy, it was tempting to ask him about the girlfriend situation with Lenny. I trust Bootsy would have covered such an important piece of information before he involved himself with matchmaking. Questioning Lenny's heart is slowly turning into compulsive thinking. It started out of curiosity, then I wanted to know, now I need to know… Does his heart belong to another? Is he on the rebound? Is he only a surf and turf guy? A lot of questions about the golden boy I could dwell on further, but then that would make me properly interested in him and I'm only intrigued. We all have a story and bags we carry, but I'd rather some New Yorker or Londoner beauty wasn't one of them.

"Beats me how you can think he's not all that hot," Bootsy said when asking me if we were still 'communicating' with an eye roll. "He's a genuine guy. A great catch, like you. Cares a lot about people, although I reckon, he becomes lost about where to draw the line on it."

"He's an actor," I replied. "He could tell you anything and you wouldn't know if it was real or not. Lenny is a million stars away from my world… he listens to country music in white joggers and eats kiwi for breakfast. We get along on paper, which is very fine, but that is all it is. You keep trying to pair me up with him, but what happens when he moves back to New York hey? What's cupid's plan then?"

"A lot can happen in a week, Monica. Let alone a month, but you're not even prepared to find out," he snapped, taking my glass and placing it in the stainless sink at the back. "And you're not having another if you're heading over to Smokes either," he added, returning to the bar with a straight face. Bartender's prerogative."

Something silent told me this wasn't about me but about him, or Marco, or him *and* Marco. I had to bite the inside of my cheek to stop myself from blabbing and telling him not to worry as I saw Marco buy the ring. I'm certain he is going to pop the question on their mini-break. Bootsy has yearned to marry Marco for over a year and now his dream is a couple of weeks away, and he doesn't even know it.

"Didn't want one anyway… you are a grumpy gerbil tonight. What's wrong?"

"Nothing. Just don't let love slip away if you find it," he said.

I left shortly after, bound for Smokes. Bootsy was no fun tonight and we couldn't talk properly. He was distracted with work and clammed up about whatever he was stewing over, and I left him to it. When I met up with Martha and the bikers at Smokes, a pint was waiting for me on one of the three picnic tables outside, surrounded by a bunch of metal machines and black helmets. A small gesture which touched me unexpectedly.

Hope you're ok. Here for you cupid. Always x, I texted Bootsy as I downed my pint.

No. 31

Sunday 27th July

Wanting to locate Dad's house, and possibly him, when I reach Barcelona is the most surprising discovery of my journey to nirvana so far. I know it's moved from an idea to something sitting in the pipeline, but it still wasn't enough to shut the voice up of my soul. It wasn't satisfied with the answer of a drive-by.

I noticed my fight against Dad had become futile if indeed it was ever my fight in the first place. Now the shrapnel had settled, and this summer had allowed me to find a rare space in my busy dusty mind, I'd considered my desires with an honest heart. From my perspective. No one else's. Mine. No more sticking up for another upon principle or flying the flag of righteousness under the illusion of love. I was holding the torch Mum had passed to me to carry and feared thunder would strike me down if I dropped it. It's only now I have thought about his matter with Dad more deeply I realise the opinions I uphold about him are mere lies. Incorrect feelings I have fed myself for years to hide the truth. I believed the feelings and choices I made were what I wanted. I truly believed them to be true and didn't take the time to nurse the opposite. What I've discovered is, personal truths are obvious if one dares to ask for it, and it is revealed quickly once we do. It doesn't require a drawn-out duel at dawn. The truth just *is*… the answer is right there. It's lies that take energy and effort.

I sat in silence, cross-legged on the carpet in the sitting room in front of the closed balcony doors. Rain stabbed the glass at speed as I tried to ignore the view of the hotel. I had caught it a minute earlier as Lenny was arriving back. A man trailed behind him carrying two holdalls and I presumed Lenny must be back from his latest trip. It was tempting to throw the doors open and whistle to give him a wave. Instead, I propped up the polaroid of The Writer's Museum on the floor and leaned it against the glass of the doors as I reorganised myself. My back against the glass also, I faced away from the hotel and sat polka straight. The polaroid to the right of me and the folded bit of paper with Dad's details I'd kept since making note of them, in front.

I smoothed the piece of paper out with the palm of my hand and placed it back to my side and ignored it. I did nothing but side-eye it and then rolled my head against the glass to look at the hotel. Quickly switching back to check the paper as though it would have grown legs and walked away.

"In silence, one voice – the true voice – will always be

louder," Dad had said. "Whichever you decide, even if it's not the one I wish for, it's your truth, and I can ask no more of you." I repeated his words out loud to myself again. Hot damn that man was smart. Unlike me.

I'm older and wiser now. Having studied and embodied the teachings of ancient Egyptians, I'd taken heed of the still voice of the heart. A voice I'd gagged as a young teen. I'd done the same with Viv recently, to mask my real feelings about her. Viv has always been a person I was convinced was a good friend and an asset to my life. I sadly knew she no longer was. Once I took a minute to listen, I understood why Bootsy had never taken to her. It hurts this has happened to a close friendship bond but also because I fooled myself. I would have gone to war for Viv and for what? I understood more than ever today what Dad had meant all those years ago. Understanding the *feeling* of one's own truth is the key to knowing the right answer for any situation. It sits comfortably in the body like relief, and it's obvious once when I pay attention.

There was one other action I could take. I didn't know if I had the nerve to or if it amounted to a bad move or the right answer. I listened for the voice.

"This is useless," I said, a few moments later, unwrapping my legs. "All I can hear is Iron Maiden lyrics reciting in my head."

I paced the floor and rampaged my questions believing movement and noise would reveal answers where the silence hadn't. I had been fixated on my magazine and website to be complete, all perfect and launched before I left. I could therefore arrive in Barcelona a fully-fledged business and creative woman. Show up all about town and at dads, as the phoenix who had risen. How important and brilliant he and my non-existent readers (and let's throw my ex-magazine buddies in there too) would think I am. The professional approach to this was to admit the schedule is frankly not practicable if I want to do the job right. The rigid plan was hopeful at best, but having hope is not dope. Hope is not faith in yourself. Hope is tepid and timid, the result of pain from indecision and lack of action. I am not a hopeful woman; I am a passionate, bold woman who knows hope – is fucking overrated.

I picked up the paper with Dad's details and cradled my phone, my hands trembling slightly. My eyes focused hard on the hotel across the road. In an obscure world, it felt like support. *I need to do this. I should, right?* My hands started shaking. *I can do this. I can d–*

"Oh, for pity's sake. Shit or get off the pot, Monica."

I tapped the Spanish phone number on the screen's keypad and waited for the strange European ringtone. It was answered after two rings.

"Hello," Dad said. My mouth bobbed like a goldfish as I melted into the sound I hadn't heard for far too long, and it caught my throat.

His voice hadn't changed, still as warm and generous as I had remembered it, before the tapas third-party saga. He always had the knack of cosy every time we talked, as though I was listening to story-time being told by a master, sitting around a campfire with soul friends. I tightened the back of my throat to speak and then promptly hung up.

No. 32

Monday 28th July

To: monicablue@coffeemail.com
From: thehat@coffeemail.com
Subject: Don't assume

Monica,

If I thought you were after money and connections, I wouldn't have offered to read your work. I'm annoyed your mind even went there.

It's been full-on the last few days, making me question many things about myself, you, the Chiswick charmers. Life in general. The success and fame I longed for, and others encouraged for me, sure does seem to change people when it's real.

I'm meeting the boys tonight. Taking them to a private party in central… they feel left out of my life, I've learned. Decided to try and make up for it because part of what they say is true. There'll be lots of names, free drinks and gifts going on, which they'll love. It makes me happy knowing they will be happy. I become engrossed in what I'm doing or tied up with heavy schedules. It skews life and relationships at times. I'm not the best at being a friend or partner a lot of the time.

Lenny

To: thehat@coffeemail.com
From: monicablue@coffeemail.com
Subject: Sorry about the wrong thought stuff

Maybe it's your friends who are skewed, Lenny, and not you.

M

I don't know Lenny. I've never had a conversation with him in person. Despite these formalities, I feel close to him, even a little protective over him. Nothing about us makes sense yet makes perfect sense at the same time. I've noticed my body is relaxed and not tense since communicating with Lenny. I didn't even know my body was tense, but I do know, I don't like the sound of his friends one bit.

No. 33

Tuesday 29th July

3 a.m.

I bolted upright in bed, rigid. The doorbell jarring around the house. Angst froze my muscles, my breathing short and rapid. I hate this time of night. Why is my doorbell ringing? I tried to slow my panic and picked up my phone, unlocked the screen ready to dial 999 as I glanced out of my bedroom window. I couldn't see the door entrance, only the stillness of South Kensington. I wish we had a video intercom gizmo for the front door. Why has my mother not done this? It's a big house. It hadn't crossed my mind before; naivety or bravery I'm not sure. Not that it matters as I appear to no longer have either, given I am considering security devices need to be on the to-do list.

It rang again.

Dithering on the spot between pressing the call button on my phone and checking out of the window again, tightness returned to my chest. It gripped my stomach harder as nerves whirled.

I didn't know what to do. Is someone ringing your doorbell at 3 a.m. a 999 emergency?

It rang again and this time, whoever it was, didn't remove their finger from the buzzer or let up. The continual noise of the bell rasped and vibrated throughout the house until a thought hit me. I dropped my shoulders and huffed out a breath the size of an inflated beach ball.

"Fricking Viv. That's who it will be," and I marched downstairs, still gripping my phone tight.

My hand poised on the lock to open the door as I peeped through the spy hole.

It wasn't Viv.

I left my hand on the lock but didn't open it and scanned the person leaning forward with one hand outstretched on the door, the other pressing the bell, his head hanging low.

It was Lenny.

I turned away and leaned my back against the door to face the hallway and not him. Why is Lenny here? What do I do? I stared through the spyglass again but couldn't stand to hear the scratchy bell noise anymore. Evidently, he wasn't stopping any time soon and I flung open the door.

"Lenny," he prized his eyes away from the floor and toward me, they were wild and unsettled, "I thought you were the fucking witches coming for me."

"Witches?" He replied between deep forceful breaths, which felt like distress. "What are you on about?" he added, not interested in one word of my welcoming line.

"Yeah, it's the time of night and… never mind. Why are you here?"

"Can I come in?"

By streetlight his pallor looked pale, his energy stressed enough it needed no words, and it began to concern me as he subtly rocked from side to side.

"Not really. Why are you here? You have a suite over the road, remember?"

"Please," he said, leaning closer to me.

"Yo, you can take your finger off the bell now. Are you alright? You don't look like normal, Lenny?"

He lurched across the doorway, wandering aimlessly around the spacious hallway he stared excessively up the staircase and all around before finding a spare piece of wall next to the hall dresser. He slid down its cream-painted surface and slumped onto the floor, knocking the vase of red daisies I'd dotingly dyed yesterday off the dresser, sending them crashing to the ground. The vase was obliterated and my softer sense of wonder about him from earlier along with it.

"OI. Don't walk in here uninvited and then trash my stuff. What's happened?"

Suspicion promptly overtook my concern as the dots of Lenny's oddness began to link together, reminding me of Viv, Ronnie and too many people I've hung out with. Every week the three of us would find ourselves in somebody's cold and hazy flat after Smokes until the early hours. The worn carpets would be littered with empty bottles, a lone coffee table always covered in flakes of ash from overflowing ashtrays, and the kitchen cupboards would contain nothing but tins of cheap, orange-coloured vegetable soup. No matter whom the flat belonged to or where it was, they were all the same. I would be too drunk to care, of course, other than what rock song was to be played at full volume. I was always the drunk bitch in charge of the music systems pressing buttons. Finding the most perfect song for whatever my mood would be at the time, and making sure people didn't snort themselves into comas.

I used to think it was fun back in the day. Tried the white stuff a few times myself, only to learn it made the shadow side of me rise, and I would turn into an out of control person. I loathed the comedown too. Now I can't bear to look at tins of vegetable soup on the supermarket shelves without it wanting to make my stomach heave. The smell of drugs, empty nights and the ache for my proper place in life only became a repetitive server from the dark side and a reminder of how, somewhere within, I knew this wasn't the sum total of my life.

I crouched down in front of him, Insisting he focus his glazed eyes upon mine to anchor him. He couldn't manage more than two seconds, yet it was long enough for me to be encapsulated by them. They were like cornflowers and summertime and in that moment, as though magic had reached out and touched me, I recognised how much like cornflowers and the summertime. Lenny does too, and despite his accolades and world following, I am not convinced he feels his own warmth.

I smacked my hand down hard on the tiled floor, which stung my palm, but did the job of returning us both to the present moment.

"I'm willing to place my bet on this… most delightful version of you, is not from eating too many kiwis?" I stated.

"Correct, Monica Bluuuue… whiskey, bit of blow earlier, and I got in a fight. I'm doing great, how are you," he said, tipping his head up to watch the ceiling, his neck smooth, solid and much like the rest of him blessed with an

American tan.

"What is this," I said, losing my patience, "you trying to be some sort of rockstar?"

He dropped his head as though his neck was made of rubber and, in a messy sprawl of legs and arms, pushed himself upright. I rose too, grasping his lower arm to prevent him from walking away toward the door.

"You know what, Monica?" he said, glancing down at my hand, "I'm glad you turned me down. You're too hard work. An open and closed shop sign… your heart is weird, man."

"Is it really? And yet here you are."

Lenny didn't respond, only rubbed his thigh up and down with his spare arm in no rush to remove my hand from his other. I couldn't remove my hard glare from him. Nor bring myself to throw him out. He had gotten himself onto a ledge I suspected wasn't a place he had much experience with.

"First of all," I said, pulling him by his arm toward the kitchen, and my God did I enjoy touching him, "you don't get to speak to me like that in my house, or anywhere for that matter," we came to a halt by the island, and I dropped his arm. "Second, why are you here?"

Lenny picked random items up and down from the kitchen's worktops – Mum's post, the lid off the biscuit jar, my cigarette lighter in the fruit bowl and mindlessly pressed buttons on the coffee machine. Winching at his hand sporadically, he rambled on about an argument he and the Chiswick charmers had a few hours ago at the private party Lenny had invited them to. His narrative of the evening was disjointed and messy. I couldn't piece all the details together, other than the disagreement kicked off later in the night. Over girls and clubs and turned sour when his friends accused Lenny of selling out, forgetting his roots and them. After fists were thrown and received, he and the other charmers were asked to leave, and Lenny wound up at a late-night bar drinking whiskey alone.

"They don't mind being attached to your name when it suits," I said, "and let me guess, you paid for all the drinks... and snow?" he nodded with sad eyes staring through the opening of the kitchen door before gazing at the floor and finally at me. Nursing one hand with his other, he asked for a coffee to help sober up the alcohol. I filled a glass with tap water, slid it across to him on the island, and folded my arms across my chest.

"You don't need more stimulants,"

"Don't hate on my mates, they were enjoying themselves. It got out of hand, that's all," he said, ignoring the glass.

"Kind hard not to. They left you alone when you were wired. They're not friends. They're dicks."

"Sorry, didn't realise you knew them... to be fair, I told them to go after security threw us out."

"Stop defending them. I don't care. They should have put in you a cab or at the least made sure they knew where you were going."

"I'm not a kid, for God's sake. I can look after myself."

Clearly.

"Tell me again why you're here because I could use sleep more than this."

My eyes weren't sure if they were half awake or half asleep. I wanted my bed, I wanted to lay down and drift away. To Spain preferably. Some girls get the dream guy showing up at their door with flowers, or an invitation to meet a prince at a castle. I have a paradox blindsiding me in the middle of the night. The truth is, our pen pal relationship might have been bewitching me, offering a tempting branch from the tree of romance, but on reflection, I didn't know this guy at all. Could he have been sent to me by an angel from nirvana? Absolutely and equally unlikely, I considered, as I absorbed his presence as a real person in front of me, not a letter and an ideal. He's no better than the vegetable soup people, is he? Oh, for sure, Lenny is packaged better, but it's no different. The contents are the same. Disappointment dropped like realisation, hitting my soul so deeply and fast, I almost heard it thud. Our writings had been a secret reality consisting of nothing more than a Pollyanna script we'd concocted, and I had been distinctly foolish for having thought anything other.

No. 34

Tuesday 29th July

3.30 a.m.

For the love of all things holy, I asked my inner self to grant me a kind mouth and patience to deal with Lenny until I could send him back over the road. I turned the TV on to add a distraction whilst I left temporarily to fetch a blanket and cushion for him from the sitting room. Comfort can always be found by being wrapped in a blanket and hugging a cushion in front of one's abdomen, and I decided he wasn't the only one in need. Upon arriving back in the kitchen with two blankets and two throw cushions, I found Lenny sitting on one of the island chairs flicking through TV programmes. He didn't want to watch world news, police chases, tacky shopping channels and definitely not his film. He didn't want to watch anything.

"You want to know why I'm here?" he said, turning to me, still holding the remote. "I can't go to dads in this state. Bootsy is spending a romantic night in a hotel out of town. I didn't attempt to call him. I don't want to see the hotel staff or be in the hotel room and… I don't want to be alone."

"Right. That makes me what then… first choice or last resort?" I replied, placing the blanket around his shoulders and handing him the cushion to hold.

He paused his eyes on the puffy velvet cushion as though it was the first one he'd seen and promptly hugged it tight into his stomach.

"You really need me to answer that?"

As I sat next to him cocooning myself in the other blanket and cushion, I reached for Lenny's glass of water and downed a few gulps to wash away the nerves his unexpected comment gave me.

"I know what I would prefer to think. The thing is, I'm not sure what's true about you anymore… if I ever did. I am glad you had the sense to come here, at least. I erm –"

My sentence became intersected by a near miss in the face of Lenny's sudden flying blanket, which he'd thrown off abruptly as he clambered out of the chair. A pending moment of honesty between two people snatched in a second by Lenny's nervous system reverting to high alert mode. He paced back and forth and round and round the island, fretting over his pounding heart which was racing. Wiping his face every two seconds with his non-injured hand, fear took over him.

"Right. Follow me," I said, getting up and walking toward the kitchen window, letting the blanket trail behind me with my hair bouncing atop it.

"Where are we going? Don't call anyone, you can't call

anyone… or take me to the hospital. I don't need this getting out, I can't," he spewed in rapid fire, darting and jumping around in front of me.

"What do you take for me? I'm not calling anyone." Wafting my arm to move him out of the way. "You need to feel safe, not see a doctor." I yanked the side pulley of the kitchen blind all the way to the top, revealing a perfect night view of the garden and the properties behind the boundary stone wall. "Although please note, if I thought you needed the doc, I'd be dragging your sorry arse to accident and emergency, whether you liked it or not."

"Your sympathy is outstanding,"

"I know. Okay, stop staring at me and look out of the window," I instructed, keeping a forward gaze toward the view outside, ignoring the impulse to turn and meet his eyes head-on.

"I'd rather look at you," he said.

I knew by the warm air delicately drifting past my cheek he continued to be locked onto me and not the window. How easily I could have lost my words in the dark musky scent of him and give way to an entangled vision of him and I which simply won't leave my head. I sidestepped to the right, removing myself from his proximity instead.

"In the garden," I pointed, "right there, in the middle, is a tree. It's a pear tree, most of them go to waste… I prefer apples personally, and next to it by the climbing flowers are–"

"I can't see anything. It's bloody dark."

"Try," I said, my patience waning. "The houses over the wall are offices. That one straight in front is a travel company. Never been in though."

"Maybe you could give them the pears?" he said, playing some obscure hopscotch game with his hands on the windowpane. I sucked in a long stream of air filling my lungs fully and sighed. It was like trying to train a flipping monkey.

"Concentrate, because you see, soon the sun –"

"Why are you telling me all this shit? It's boring?"

"Stop being an arse. It's not meant to be a Hollywood story, it's meant to steady you. In a couple of hours," I repeated, "LOOK at what I'm pointing at, Lenny, the sun will rise and, if we are lucky, we might catch a sky of red and golden rays."

I don't recall the time I ran out of steam. I believe it coincided with Lenny when he finally became more stable shortly before dawn broke. His face appeared smoother and less taut as he shape-shifted back into a normal human being. Whilst I could have sent him packing out of my house and back across the road to the hotel, he was still fragile and vulnerable, and it would have been a shame to miss the rising sun together having gone about it at such length. I laid one of the blankets on the floor by the window with the cushions we had as pillows and we covered ourselves with the other. The daily transformation of a dark world into the light was not a glorious umbrella of purple, red and gold as hoped, but rather a standard palette of blues.

My tiredness could ignore the uncomfortableness of lying on a tiled floor more than it could the presence of Lenny next to me. Having another there, next to me, had been becoming an alien experience, but this wasn't just anyone it was Lenny. His energy encased me and it was all manly and secure. I can't recall the last time I could breathe out fully and feel safe. I didn't appreciate what I had seen or heard from him tonight, yet lying with him there on the floor was a part of me that wanted it to last forever. I watched him for a while, watching the view from the window, and I wondered if he was thinking about me and lulled myself into a semi-doze.

"Monica?"

"Yes?" I replied, not opening my eyes.

"I can't sleep, but don't stay awake on account of me."

"I'm not."

"Oh."

He shuffled around, and I sensed his eyes tunnelling into the back of me and no longer the morning view. I bit my bottom lip and squashed it around with my teeth before rolling over to meet his gaze. Once more stopped in my tracks by him, our eyes searched for one another. The energy in my body turned gooey, and I wanted to run my fingers around the outline of his darkening eyes. Tired and frozen with hidden pain they might have been, but they were still perfect to me.

"Monica," he said.

"What now?" I said with a smile I couldn't hide.

"I feel a bit floaty."

"Give me your hand."

He reached out his wounded hand to me and I laced my fingers with his. I soothingly rubbed the sore points and bruises with my other hand and, in a light voice, told him to try to shut his eyes. It wasn't the time to sort out matters of the heart and satisfy fires down below, and any attempt to do so would have backfired. He smiled back at me, our hands remained intertwined, and he moved a piece of hair from my face, telling me to fall asleep and how he was doing fine lying there and not shutting his eyes.

"You're incredible," he said, as I drifted downward in my mind and upward in my heart.

"Monica?"

"Yesssssss." I said, peeping an eye open.

"Do you mind if I play music super low? It's too quiet?"

"If it stops you from talking to me and waking me up, go ahead."

I turned the opposite way and focused on the kitchen cabinetry. It was less confusing and more solid. I let my eyelids have their way with me and reluctantly allowed them to shut.

"Lenny? What song is this?" I asked.

"'Safe in the Arms of Love' by Martina McBride. It's a country song."

"Haven't heard of it before. It's kinda nice. G'night, hat."

"Night, Monica Blue."

It couldn't have been a more perfectly awkward song to have played, as though he understood the importance music and lyrics had in my life. I'm guessing in his too. And shit me, what an attractive quality to me that is.

As the ballad lulled me to sleep, I asked Lenny one final question… if he preferred sunrise or sunset. He said he didn't know. I said, I thought he was a sunrise. Sunset is my bag; it reminds me of a powerful dragon letting out a breath of fire onto earth. Burning the day to ashes letting us rise again, new and reformed the next. Sunrises, in comparison, are more delicate, a gentle shake awake to life and loose tea leaves. And that is a distinction worth noting, I told myself, as I fell asleep in my own universe… are sunrises and sunsets the equivalent of Lenny and me? Both beautiful, both purposeful, both able to exist in the same universe only at opposite ends with opposite meanings, never together at the same time.

How can they be?

No. 35

Tuesday 29th July

Midnight

It was after lunchtime when I awoke, wincing at my aching body and stretching it out in strange octopus-like moves. Memories of the hours before quickly infiltrated my dozy mind, and I rolled over to find the space next to me was empty and cold. It didn't surprise me Lenny no longer lay there, but I wasn't happy about it either. I stared up at the ceiling, twiddling my hair and reasoning with myself… stay detached from him or dare to believe in the slice of happiness he brings me?

He could have been wandering around the house or in the loo I considered, scanning the kitchen and chucking off the blanket covering me. I knew he wasn't. The house's air held an emptiness, the same way the blanket den we'd made did. Like a vampire, he'd once again materialised from nowhere, caused turmoil and left. I hoped he was safe and finally human once more, and although I knew I would check in on him later, I didn't want to write to him right away. He's a grown man after all, who should have been man enough to face and wake me to say, "Hey, Monica, I need to go." Yet he wasn't. I can't help falling back into this tiresome alternating current I find myself in. Wondering if I should continue with our friendship or let it burn.

I couldn't answer my question and parked last night outta the way in my mind and vowed to enjoy the remainder of the day whilst wishing I had a can of air freshener I could spray inside my head to blow all this nonsense out and return to normal.

I found a rogue hair bobble on the floor, tied my hair back into a ponytail and made my way to the coffee machine and flicked it on. It gurgled and hissed as I glanced around, still fuzzy and a touch misplaced, when I spied a note from Lenny on the island worktop. He'd written on the back of one of the letters addressed to Mum. It pinged my eyes open and caused my stomach to flip-flop like a salmon. I picked up the envelope and read his message, leaning against the cooker, as coffee percolated next to me and chugged its way from the machine into my mug.

Morning Monica,

I didn't have the heart to wake you and disturb your sleep - again. I left around ten as I needed to shower and change before a meeting and script read this afternoon.

I'm not sure where to start about last night, and I don't

know what I'd have done without you. I wanted to leave you my cell number… I would love to take you out to dinner. To explain properly and to thank you (and NO, there is no girl back in New York to disapprove of us being friends) but at the risk of breaking any pen pal rules – I didn't. Maybe let me know in a coffeemail letter?

For the record, I don't normally behave like a moron. Maybe in the past I have. I've never claimed to be a saint, but I'm finding being back in London difficult. I always look forward to returning. It's the place I can call home, be safe and be myself. Not this time. This time it's all wrong, and I'm living in a hotel feeling like a tourist in my hometown. I wanted to have that normal part of my life with my boys and my family, and it hit me hard when I realised the original Chiswick Charmer era was gone. I can't reinvent it no matter how hard I try to. My life has changed, success and fame have changed it – changed me - whether I like it or not, and I fear I have lost more than I have gained.

I hope you have a great day of writing.

Lenny

P.S. Keep the pears from the tree for me, I prefer them to apples.

I folded the envelope and placed it back on the worktop, unable to remove my eyes and thinking from it. Feeling around for the mug under the coffee machine's spout, I slid out the chunky grey mug full of hot black coffee and read the note again, burning my mouth with boiling coffee. *God damn it, that hurt.* Of course, he'd prefer pears when I prefer *apples. I* shoved the letter bearing his note into my pyjama pocket and promptly retreated to a proper bed, feeling complicated.

No. 36

Wednesday 30th July

To: thehat@coffeemail.com
From: monicablue@coffeemail.com
Subject: Thoughts of the day

Morning Lenny,

I nearly wrote to you yesterday; I opened the laptop a few times. I wanted to check how you were doing and if you had heard from those people you call friends. However, part of you did behave like an arsehole, and I didn't care for it.

You don't need to explain the mechanics of last night. I will say you surprised me; you strike me as a guy who would walk away from fury not into it, brawling with old mates high on substances which wrecked your earlier years. I understand it's rough when the world farts at us, and you need a wingman. I'm glad I could be yours last night. I, too, am learning how people, places and things fall away without rhyme or reason. Despite the aching and disbelief it causes, we must learn to trust the process. That there is, after all, sense and justice in the nonsensical and unjust.

C'est la vie, I guess.

I'll return to the reason for writing. How are you feeling? How's the hand? You must have hit him hard? Did you manage your meeting? Will you continue to stay in London once work is finished?

Questions, questions, questions. I'll stop.

I hope London picks up for the rest of your trip. However, the two of us meeting is not a good idea. The offer of a posh dinner is appreciated, but not necessary to thank me. I'm not a fan of restaurants anyway. More of a cafe and festival girl. In any case, why would you want to wine and dine (and I quote) a heart that is weird, a person who is hard work, and who is an open and closed shop sign?

Regards,
Monica

To: monicablue@coffeemail.com
From: thehat@coffeemail.com
Subject: More thoughts of the day

Monica,

Whoa. Whoa. Hold on a second there.

I don't think you're any of those things! And I don't re-member saying any of that. Last night was a bit of a dark one for me. Monica, come on; you must believe me. If I did say anything hurtful, I am truly sorry and I can assure you I didn't mean it.

I recall saying you are incredible, or have you forgotten that part? Do you care how your kookiness has bewitched me and made me want to know someone more than I ever have in my life? Do you know how much I admire you? Do you care about any of this or just your judgy opinions?... I think you do care and are deliberately ignoring your feelings - and me. Give meeting up a chance, or me a second one, to show you I'm not an arsehole. Doesn't have to be dinner. I should have known a normal suggestion would have been wrong. Any-way, the location is completely irrelevant and not the point.

Last night, I tried to revive the bond between me and the boys. Treating them and partying as we used to years ago, and I regretted it instantly. The early part of the evening at the stupid event held little else than me being egged on with lines of coke, champagne, more lines of coke and fake people. I became madder and madder at myself whilst my mates leered after every free gift and woman in the place. I told them to knock it off and went outside for a smoke.

Joe, one of my mates, is an actor still hoping for his lucky break, but spends more time roaming around Chiswick in boat shoes. Chasing connections, being loud and cocky. He'd been throwing digs at me all evening. 'Look at Lenny here, too good for us now in his fancy clothes and cars,' he said shortly after arriving. 'You're forgetting who your real friends are.' 'All the times I supported you before you made it, and you won't try to help me break in.'

When I came back inside, instead of Joe being bored and done with his comments, as I thought he would be, he banged on more. Refusing to let it drop. It's the worst I've seen him, and the others only laughed and played along. All of them still eyeing up the women. It was embarrassing. I kept apologising to the ones they jeered after. Not because their behaviour would place a bad light on me, but because it's gross. I can't stand it.

In the end, I popped off at Joe. I told him that I had suggested him to a few acting agents before, but they weren't interested. I hadn't told him, as I knew he'd be upset. Truth is, he isn't as good as he thinks, and I felt like an idiot for putting him forward in the first place between you and me.

"No one wants to work with dickheads and blown-up egos," I said to Joe in anger.

"They work with you," he replied.

Wherever that last straw is inside of us he'd found it. I hated him at that moment and I flipped without warning.

I couldn't stop myself from throwing punches in his face.

The others stepped in, followed by security, and it was all over in five minutes. That's all it took to destroy years' worth of close, united friends. Five minutes.

I didn't hurt my hand hitting him. I punched the wall outside on my way to finding a cab, but then I stumbled on a quiet bar and sat there with my new friend whiskey and The Rolling Stones. Not the real Stones unfortunately, they were playing Ruby Tuesday on the wide-screen TV. I'd been staring at it trying to watch the video of them playing it live but it was more a focal point to keep me upright and I think that's when I thought of you.

I had the meeting with my agent and assistant. Both of them were annoyed with me the entire time for being awkward and blunt because all I wanted to do was leave.

I hate the thought of making you unhappy. If I said any of those things, it was drugs and alcohol talking, not me. Haven't you said and done dumb things you didn't mean when drunk?

Don't write off meeting up. We're meant to enjoy life, not keep it at arm's length and friends do meet from time to time, you know, aha.

Lenny

To: thehat@coffeemail.com
From: monicablue@coffeemail.com
Subject: The day is busy with thoughts

Lenny,

I believe when we are true to our dream seeds, we morph, overtime, into more of who we really are. I doubt you are what your friends claim; rather, your soul is shining, and those clowns are jealous. It's they who can't deal with it. Not you. Don't dismiss or downsize your wins and don't trust jerks who do either.

My friend Viv, a best pal of mine for years, has me facing a similar situation to yours with the Charmers. Viv and I are not the same anymore. Bootsy made me realise she causes me more pain than friendship and I know if I want to remain being me and to arrive at where I want to be in life – where I need to be – then I must cut off the fat. Viv has become fat. Fat is only helpful when we need insulating from wishes and dreams, we might want, but for reasons unknown, we are not quite ready for. But then one day we are, and the fat no longer protects or keeps us safe but hampers.

Cut off what needs to go.

I tell myself it's the act of a heart with mofo, the voice of spirit like the ancient Egyptians speak of. Not because I'm selfish or a bad person.

As far as disregarding what you spewed as it was substances talking smack about me not you, on the contrary. I think it is easier to speak true feelings when intoxicated.

… it's the same as there is always a little truth behind 'I'm only joking' or 'I'm just kidding.'

Look me in the eye – well – my inbox and tell me, deep down, you believe I am not any of those things? I bet you can't.

Monica

To: monicablue@coffeemail.com
From: thehat@coffeemail.com
Subject: Very very busy day of thoughts

I'd rather look you in the eye and tell you. And you're avoiding the meeting up question?

To: thehat@coffeemail.com
From: monicablue@coffeemail.com
Subject: Verdict

I'll add it to my list of considerations.
Let me know if you want to borrow my scissors to snip off the fat.

To: monicablue@coffeemail.com
From: thehat@coffeemail.com
Subject: Verdict's verdict

I can handle being considered.

I managed to cut off wobbly bits already without any sharp implements. In hindsight, it was a blowout bound to happen. Doesn't make it any easier, though.

To: thehat@coffeemail.com
From: monicablue@coffeemail.com
Subject: Solution – Fruit is the way forward

It doesn't. Stick to kiwis and rom-coms in the future, hey.

Monica

P.S. You know what? In support of the non-arsehole side of you, I'm going to watch your film tonight. It can be another moment in the strange meeting experiences of Monica and Lenny.

To: monicablue@coffeemail.com
From: thehat@coffeemail.com
Subject: Fruit is always a good idea

Not sure whether to feel honoured or nervous. There's a Lenny and Monica?? I'm intrigued.

L

P.S. In that case, in support of the cute side of you, I'll download a Metallica album and listen to it tonight in return.

To: thehat@coffeemail.com
From: monicablue@coffeemail.com
Subject: Brave choice for a newbie

Nothing intriguing about two people writing to each other, but I must go now. Whilst you might have managed to complete your meetings, my brain hasn't drummed up a single sentence for my magazine.

For reference, it's Monica and Lenny. As the great actor I am told you are, I thought you would at least get the words the correct way around.

Good day to you, hat.

Monica

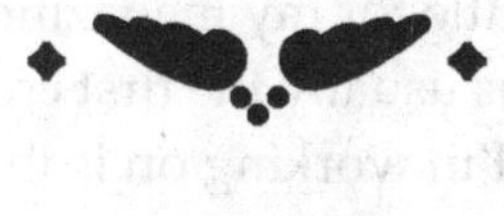

No. 37

Thursday 31st July

Out on the balcony, lying on my front, I kicked my legs in and out behind me on the lounger. The Scorpions whistled Wings of Change from my red tape deck on the floor and I dipped my sunglasses down. Dressed in a see-through mesh top and a red batik sarong, I'd hoped for a sunny working day outside, but it was more drab than sunshine. Cloudy days are boring and cast dour. Shivering from time to time, I searched different combinations for the branding and colours of my magazine, pausing periodically to peek over the balcony's ledge at the hotel. I didn't catch Lenny leaving or arriving once.

I lost hours of my life trying countless colours, failing to find the 'right fit inner click' letting me know I'd landed on the right assortment. The branding needed to work visually, match what I thought the public would connect with, and represent the magazine. Like a lot of things in my life I never know what I'm looking for, I only know when I've found it. These types of answers are not logical or calculated, they're experienced, felt as a moment of being in spirit for a split second.

I don't have a title for my magazine either. It's a problem harassing me, as usually the first creation for any story or piece of writing I'm working on is the title. I know each writer differs, but this has been my natural creative process since time began. It gives the project its point of focus and meaning. The foundational direction from which the theme and content flow, including colour ideas. My fingers skated about the mouse pad clicking endlessly with my face repeatedly vacant at the non-pleasing resultant colour combinations. I kept drifting back to last night, to the memory of being cocooned in my duvet on the sofa with coffee and a cinnamon bun. Several times I had caught myself with a soft smile, my eyes feeling a little glittery as I watched Lenny on the screen. It turned out to be the most surreal moment I've lived.

Whilst the movie was far removed from anything I would choose to watch, Lenny struck me as a more decent actor than I assumed young rom-com actors to be, and an odd sense of pride for him swept about me as it played. I didn't even pause it for cigarette breaks. I became wrapped up in a whole new world and I don't mean the film's storyline. The way Lenny and I have grown close so quickly is a breach of the logic we're taught about how friendships or any type of ship take time. Connection takes zero time with the right people, whether they be friends, coworkers or lovers…. If only he hadn't said those words to me. They are a hot iron branding his chest with suspicion as to who I thought my new friend was. If finding each other had happened a year ago or a year from now, I would run like a panther toward him. Perhaps he didn't mean them, but he did at the time. I can't shake off the disharmony I have over it or how different elements of this man seem to keep throwing me off my game. The thought of Lenny's chest was not helping me stay focused on magazine branding, the job I am meant to be doing... A case in point.

Then my mother rang.

"Hello, Mother," I said, twisting my head, grimacing at the screen and the *vaults of mauve* colour theme I'd been trying.

"I have an idea darling that you can pitch to your editor?" she replied.

"I don't need ideas; I have plenty of those," ... *and no editor to pitch to.*

"Yes, and she never runs with any of them. How about... finding love later in life? She's around my age too. She might resonate with it."

"And good morning to you, too."

"Don't be offended, I want you to get your own piece in the magazine. You deserve it. Finding love later in life might swing it for you. Everyone ignores us older people, yet we account for much of their readership."

Had I just detected sincerity in her voice? A heartfelt desire for her to see an article of mine in print, and not purely for the status. Quite bizarre, although she had a good point with her feature idea. Guilt wriggled around me. I can't keep hiding I'd left the magazine from her and how I am currently in mid-plans to leave London for Barcelona with my new digital nomad venture. And then there's Dad to tell her about. I dropped my forehead into my hand and banged it with the palm.

"Leave it with me, Mum. What glamorous plans do you have today?"

It involved shopping and lunch on a yacht. I switched off after the yacht was mentioned and her indecision over whether to wear a thong bikini or swimsuit, so I can't report any more on our conversation other than I hoped she'd chosen the swimsuit.

I slid the phone off and gave myself one last attempt at the colour scheme.

Burgundy and black.

An instant yes. The colours perfect. Stylish, sophisticatedly Gothic and I loved it. Still no title, but I have a colour scheme. The guilt about Mum and our call moments ago faded as I became more engrossed with the publication's design.

I clicked save, and it automatically changed all the pages to shades of burgundy and black. It was finally beginning to feel like my magazine was coming to life. A proper magazine, a real-life creature with a heartbeat ready for a future.

Revved up, I moved on to moving sections about on the pages, organising the placement of photos, text and the practice video from the other day. I played around with all the fonts, links and other clever gadgets available for digital publications that print simply cannot offer. Maybe this version will work out better than I first thought. I am warming to it more with each passing day. The trade-off with the free template, though, are the limitations. Fine for smaller publications, an event or for personal use. For a professional magazine burning to be the real deal not a wanabe, I needed to upgrade the account. All the decent fonts and technical abilities I require, including the full number of pages I need, aren't available on the free version of this system. Plus, when it comes to selling my magazine, I will need to upgrade to a paid level anyway. Only paid subscriptions allow me to embed it on my website and elsewhere to sell and deliver it to readers.

The phone call with Mother earlier reminded me why I started this and why I need to crack on and make it happen. Otherwise, I'll still be sitting here playing around with a pretend magazine when she returns home, and I'll have nothing to show for it. Nowhere to go and a lot of explaining to do. This is exactly why I shouldn't meet Lenny, wasting my time and summer days with a mirage.

Taking a review of my current position… needing to pay for the upgrades, marketing and the impending trip, I don't have another option if I wanted to pull this off.

I'm going to have to do it.

Sell my precious collection of cassette tapes.

And it's breaking my heart.

No. 38

Friday 1st August

In the cave room, I lingered over my cassette tape collection in a punk T-shirt dress, draped in sun and moon necklaces. I believe there was a skully key pendant thrown in for good measure too. I perched a headpiece Viv once made me, of black steel roses bearing a Gothic cross, on my head. Knowing this sacrifice would lead me to better places did little to stop the torment. I examined each tape lovingly, stacking them in alphabetical order into two flight cases. It was a goodbye I simply didn't want to go through with.

The wheelie flight cabin cases were the best idea I could think of to transport the tape collection to SK Music, a vintage and rare music store located on a narrow side street near the tube station. I had prepared myself all morning for a heavy-hearted journey, and, having already spoken to the owners at the shop a few times, they were expecting me this afternoon. In one of our previous conversations, as we ran through the details of each tape, I discovered the father of the family-run store knew my dad back in the day. My name gave the game away. The Blues are a well-known name on the music circuit. By which I mean my dad and his company, not me. My sudden panic over him knowing my dad was reprieved when the chap said he hadn't seen him in several years. I played along and let this man think he was indeed an old friend of my dad's when I knew he wouldn't be. Dad always had plenty of people hovering from the side lines who believed they were colleagues or friends of his. I don't know why I didn't think of this possible connection beforehand. It's obvious now he mentioned it. My dad knows or knows of most people who have any type of finger in the music industry and my music mogul father will certainly be mortified at my actions and displeased with me… Touché, Dad.

Should this somehow reach Dad's ears, I justify their sale because it is bringing me to the country where he lives and a step closer to him. Surely his beloved daughter is worth more than a library of music history.

I had stood by the front door, all set to leave with bursting cases standing by my side, but I couldn't. I became anchored to the hallway floor, unable to step outside into the day as though lead had filled my boots.

By the afternoon, I'd unpacked the cases and called SK Music with an excuse about how I couldn't make our appointment due to an emergency work meeting. They fully bought it and I ended the call abruptly rather than engaging in the man's never-ending chit-chat he thought I had an interest in. I must be clear to myself. Here in my private corner of the universe. I am not bailing on the task in hand. I just needed one more night with the music and my tape player. Some may laugh, believing selling belongings is not the same as a dramatic break up with a loved one. It is though. Love is love, right?

Rock bands from Mötley Crüe to Therapy, to Ozzy Osbourne to Whitesnake played continuously. Each band, each song, each rockstar completely understood me in different ways. The music gave a pulse to my house and life to my soul, and I can only hope I won't die or disappear without them. I took polaroid pictures of each cassette tape and their covers and made a huge collage of the collection on my bedroom wall. There would be no way to forget them.

I am making a pact, right here on this page, to not ever forget any of them and I will buy each one back from SK Music.

Tomorrow. Tomorrow I will go to the music store to sell them and then move the fuck on to nirvana.

By 9 p.m. my goodbye to the collection felt complete and I needed to escape.

I slumped my bag and leather jacket on the bar, my phone tumbling out of the coat pocket onto the floor as I slumped into my bar stool.

"No one is out tonight at Smokes. I need cheering up," I said to Bootsy as he floated about the public side of the bar collecting empties. The phone landed nearer him than me, and he stretched down to pick it up from the carpeted floor, balancing a tray with dirty glasses with the other arm. He placed the phone next to my bag on the bar and reappeared on his side of the bar in front of me. Grumbling in my throat, I swept my hair back over my shoulders then held it up in a ponytail before letting it fall and fluffing it out with my fingers, "and my hair is annoying me. It's all wrong."

"Miss Monica, what a delight to have you in the building again," he said, choosing a highball glass from a stack behind him before grabbing my vodka bottle from the cupboard.

"I know," I answered. I hadn't changed from before other than applying a new vampire eyeliner and throwing my leather and biker boots on. "Tell me something interesting."

"Your dress sense never fails to boggle my mind. Will that do?" he replied, pouring a stream of vodka into the glass for me.

I inflicted a black glare in silence at him, taking the filled glass firmly from him. Gulping a swig of the ice-cold vodka and orange warmed me more than any part of my day.

"I can literally feel the heat coming from those eyes," he said.

"Good," I replied, suddenly realising how quiet it was for a Friday evening. Only a few people dotted about with an older man trudging back from the toilets. I doubted tourist numbers were down this year, especially in this area but summer in London can be strange and unpredictable. Students return home, other transplants disappear elsewhere, and locals often zip off for the six-week school break to their summer locations. Certain parts of London are ghostly in the summertime.

"Ok, I'll try something else," Bootsy continued, "Lenny is coming in about half an hour. From what I hear that should lift your mood… or at least lift whatever that thing is on your head."

"Lenny? Why? How can he sit in here on a Friday night?"

"The same way you are. He's coming to hang with me for a while whilst I work. We might go for tacos after… he's a normal person you know and allowed to spend time with friends."

"Well, I won't be here… this day gets better. Maybe I'll hit Smokes on my own."

Meeting Lenny around Bootsy whilst random patrons chatted away their evening instantly dropped into it awkward and inappropriate. It was too much, an unnatural rendezvous. Our situation is, above all else, a secret one and private. I'm certain Lenny would agree. Not that there is a situation with Lenny and me, but Bootsy in cupid mode would make it a thing. I was thankful he'd mentioned it, rather than withholding the surprise encounter from me.

"This is my spot. Not his," I said, begrudging my evening had been hijacked, "and what do you mean from what you hear?"

"Oh, come on, you don't need to leave and it's my spot if anyone's."

"You're right I don't need to leave. I want to, there's a difference."

"Why? The vibe around you two is adding magic to the street. Lenny hasn't said much other than he can't stop thinking about you and I believe him. Do you think you two are going to move things on or..." he paused his inquiry holding a hand up to acknowledge a couple leaving, "continue passing notes?"

"I'm not answering that because I don't know how to. Stop overwhelming me."

"There's nothing overwhelming about it other than you are making it so. Stay! Chat a while, get to know him better. Get out of your head, it's not hard. I mean, you're wearing a bloody tiara for God's sake, how can you be concerned about giving Lenny a chance for five minutes?"

"We've been through this already. Leave it alone," I said with an un-amused force, drinking faster than I had in a while, which was, yes, to quell stress but also to leave quickly without wasting any.

Bootsy finally realising the conversation would not end happily ever after resigned in defeat. Siphoning the last of my drink and through a thick mood I relayed the whole cassette tape agony of tomorrow. Instantly all Lenny talk ceased as Bootsy dropped the pressure to stay and offered to come with me to SK Music tomorrow instead.

"Tempting offer," I told him, however, I needed to do the transaction on my own. It's my fight and as traumatic as it might be I have to do it by myself.

"Hate to be captain obvious here," he said, "but what if the music place sells the tapes, seeing as that is what they do?"

"Don't you think I thought of that? I'm going to have a word with Martha and get her to cast one of her spells over the cassettes. A protection one to prevent anyone from buying them until I can purchase them all back."

"Excellent. That ought to do it."

I screwed my face at him as he walked out from behind the bar and stood next to me and I fished about in my bag for a pack of cigarettes.

"Hang on, no friend would let you do this alone. If you won't let me come with you," he said, putting my pack of cigarettes back in my bag and placing his arm around my mid-back, "then I will come over when you're back. I'll cook dinner, and you can make me jealous about following your dreams. We can watch an old movie oooo... I have a new TV series you'll like. I'll text you the trailer. What do you think?"

"Monica likes that idea," I said, nesting my head onto his shoulder, "and don't touch the hair."

In our moment of comfortable silence, I remembered Lenny mentioning Bootsy being out of town on a romantic break, the night he'd shown up at my house. I'd forgotten about it until now but thought it odd at the time because Bootsy hadn't told me about the getaway. He always tells me everything. I wanted to probe him about this lovey-dovey night away, but I'd drop Lenny in it if I did. My mind raced to Marco, wondering if he had popped the question. A marriage proposal would explain the night out of town and Bootsy's more sparky mood recently, but again – odd. Bootsy would have hands down told me this piece of news immediately. I didn't want to dig if Marco hadn't pro-posed, and I'd ruin the special moment for when he did.

The old man was shaking his pint glass in the air at the end of the bar and I released Bootsy from our head cuddle to let him cater to the man's demands. I figured the myste-rious romantic night must be currently boy-only talk when my phone began ringing and vibrating against the bar's surface. We both peered down at it as Bootsy handed the man a new beer, and we saw Viv's name lightening up the screen. My stomach plummeted with a groan.

"Fake friend calling, fake friend calling," he sang.

I threw a bar mat at him and reached across the bar to answer it, but Bootsy snatched the phone first as I threw my arms about frantically. Stretching further over to reach him and my phone, I slipped off my bar stool and landed on the floor with a bang as his finger hovered over the accept button. Shaking my head madly and mouthing the word NO at him appeared to miss Bootsy's attention completely.

"Monica Blue's phone. Can I help?" He answered.

The thud onto the floor bounced through my stomach, and I glared at him holding my middle as I clambered upright and readjusted my headpiece.

"I'm sorry, she's unavailable," he said into the phone. I hit his arm as he smirked and I crawled back onto the bar stool pretending to slice my throat with my hand and then stabbing my finger at him.

"I'm fantastic, Viv, how are you? Oh, ah. I see. Oh, dear sorry to hear that. She's super busy at the moment, but she'll call back when she's able to. Toodle-oo," he said. wiggling his fingers in a sarcastic goodbye wave at the screen as he hung up and handed the phone back to me.

"What did she say?"

"Not much. She and the other bottom feeder have broken up, she wondered if you could call round at hers because she needs her friend. What do you fancy for dinner tomorrow?"

"You should have put me on!" I said loudly, the old man at the other end of the bar watched on, disgruntled by all the commotion. "Would you like a photo?" I said, he turned away blowing his cheeks out, muttering and sipping his drink, "I thought not."

"No, I shouldn't have," Bootsy said, "she hasn't called or texted you since that night at her place to see if you're ok. I need my friend… pahaha! Don't ring her back. You're not a free therapist – we're pirates sailing adventurous seas, you and I. Another vodka?"

Pirates?

"Are you feeling alright? Have you been drinking you're extra lively," I asked.

"Just enjoying life as I always do. Lenny will be here in ten by the way."

"I'm going to take that drink you're making me and go home; I don't want to bump into him. I am, though, up for being a badass girl pirate."

"Deal," he said, laughing and grinning to himself.

I leant over the bar and kissed him on his cheek. Holding my glass in one hand, I grabbed my bag and leather with the other and trotted out wondering whether anyone had changed their minds and gone to Smokes.

"To pirates," I said, raising my glass to passers-by as I crossed the road home.

Turning the key in the front door, I took in a last view over the road, catching Lenny and his hat arriving pushing open the bar's entrance door.

"Lenny," I shouted over, but it was too late. The glass door had already shut behind him and I watched him through the main window saunter toward Bootsy fist bumping him before sitting in my seat.

"G'night, hat," I whispered. "Have dreams of gold."

No. 39

Saturday, 2nd August

I chose to write today's entry in the kitchen as a nod to the journey I began one month ago sitting in this exact spot. Today marks the end of my first month of writing to a rock angel. My own magical attendant I found by accident and who only asks for unwavering faith in her power and invisibility in return. Can I prove she is there? No. Can you prove to me she isn't?

I don't know for certain how this journey will end up. My life, as always, resembles the kitchen of a potion witch making an unfinished enchantment. The only surety I can hold on to is these pages. This blog has become my version of the Book of Mirrors, a journal usually written by Wiccans, but writing to a rock angel has become a lifestyle. A personal religion I am realising will last forever more as the search for truth is infinite, and a rock doesn't bog off when the ships come in. She committed for life.

This morning could have been a replica of yesterday, only with a new outfit. I stood in the hallway and unclicked the latch of the front door, the flight cases once again on either side of me but, I knew, this time around, it was different. I had a fresh determination to follow through, and I knew I would not stop, pause or hesitate until I returned later having made bank. The only way through this was to switch off from what I was about to lose and concentrate on the gain.

Still not yet across the threshold, my phone inconveniently rang and rang. I struggled to wiggle the phone out of the tight pocket of the slate blue blazer I was wearing, calling the pocket all the profanity words I knew… I once had a mini scrap with a girl outside a club the magazine lot had taken me to on a work's 'bonding' night out and the bitch tore the pockets off my blazer. I couldn't bear to bin the jacket and enlisted Martha and her seamstress talents with scissors, a sewing machine and old-school fabric badges to mend my broken blazer. I see it as a twist of fate because I prefer the adapted version with badges. I've always wanted to tell the princess who tried to take me down that she didn't get one over on me, she did me a favour. Since then, I found new love with old American fabric badges and began collecting them. I asked Martha if she could stitch a few of my favourites on the left sleeve of the blazer. The trade-off with this iconic blazer means the pockets are half their original size. One fits my cigarettes, Zippo lighter and bank card perfectly, but fitting my phone in the other one is like putting a fitted sheet on a mattress.

I only wore the single-breasted jacket with denim shorts. It was too warm of a day to layer a top underneath it and spoil the display of the skull and bones clasp on the front of my bra band. Finally, the phone was out.

Viv.

Again.

It took the number of her missed calls to five, it was only 11 a.m. I thought about not answering again, refusing to fall for an obstacle sent from outer space to derail my cassette mission, but whether it was Viv, the frustratingly small pocket or a desire to debunk the derailment, I don't know, but it irritated my last nerve. I answered my phone with a n disgruntled –

"Hi. Can I call you back? I'm in the middle of something."

Viv heard the word hi and nothing else. Jumping into an intense rendition of her current despair. Out of thin air, according to Viv, and after three years of her and Ronnie being together and planning their futures, they'd split up. Ronnie called time on their relationship. For good, she'd reiterated, still stunned by events. I, on the other hand, was not shocked it had fallen apart, only that it was Ronnie who had done the leaving.

"I don't understand," she cried, "why has this happened? I hate life."

I rolled my eyes. I continued to listen about how Viv (now) believes she had it all wrong about Ronnie's vanishing acts being due to drug buying and consumption and has reason to think it's another woman.

"Another woman? Are you sure, that doesn't sound like Ronnie. Do you have evidence?"

"Yes. My gut! I need to tell you everything. Please can you come round later if that's ok. I'm a wreck, Ronnie and

I were soulmates."

"Were, is the operative word... you *were* soulmates, then you became coke-mates. You never know, it could be for the best, but I need to –"

"I can't believe how cold you are; this is hard. Ronnie broke it off over a week ago and he's blocked me. He hadn't kissed or touched me in over a month before that either... all the disappearing makes sense now. I'm such an idiot. What am I gonna do?" she sobbed.

"OK, yes. I agree it's suspicious, but do you know the full –" I stopped speaking when I realised I was letting myself become pulled into more drama and allowing the derail to raise its presence again and exhaust me further. I rerouted my mind. Not my circus, not my monkeys. "Erm, it's rubbish, I get that, and I'm sorry it's happened... to be honest, I'm caught up in a difficult task myself today. I'll see if I can make it over tomorrow. Gotta go, my bus is here," and ended the call.

Fuck me. I did not see that coming. Ronnie having an affair?!? He might be many things; he is many things, but I never had Ronnie pegged as a cheater.

With a rough hand, I pushed the phone back into the pocket in a rare one move, opened the door and stood at the top of my steps. Observing the world for a minute, I pulled out a cigarette from its packet from the easier pocket and lit it. Letting it hang from my mouth I puffed and wheeled the cases through South Kensington with a commanding stride to my first destination. Martha's.

"I'm calling in my tarot card reading win from the pool game," I said, wrestling with the cases as I yanked them up the steps and over the door frame at Martha's shop.

Martha, and a guy I was not familiar with, were poised

over an array of jeans and embellishments on the sewing machine table next to the cash register. An 80s poster of an American fuel station and vintage car covered a large part of the wall behind them. The two of them glanced up simultaneously from their work in discombobulation as Martha let my unannounced arrival sink in.

"Oh hi," I said to the man, as he took a seat at the sewing machine, "I'm Monica, you must be the chap who stole my job?"

"Ignore her," Martha said. Handing the assistant a bag of metal buttons and new threads, she advanced slowly towards me, still dressed in her squeaking biker trousers, "care to enlighten me," she said, eyeing up the over-packed cases circling a finger around them. "Why the fuck are you dragging cases about with you?"

"I'll explain later but I don't need a tarot reading; I need one of your spells."

The guy shrugged his shoulders at me and returned to his sewing, setting the needle thing bopping up and down on the machine making it whirr. Martha came closer and with firm warning told me spells aren't a fad product to buy off the shelf, "It's serious business. There's a process, a ritual... what's it for?" she asked with interest.

"Good because I'm not playing. I need a protection spell or one to stop things from being bought or picked out."

The machine whirred louder as the guy pressed the pedal speeding up the sewing machine.

"You sound like you're joining the ladies of the night; things can't be that bad surely," she said, tilting her head confused at my sudden interest in working with the esoteric side of life.

"No, not for me, you idiot. Jeeze. For these," I said pointing at the cases.

Turning her attention back to the guy, Martha raised her voice to speak over the racket of the machine and asked him if could hold the fort while she ducked in the back for a while. He held his thumb up in agreement and carried on sewing, turning material this way and that under the needle. Martha flicked her head toward the rear of the shop, indicating I should follow her with my cases to the back room. I trundled after her purposefully past the table to sneak an investigative glance at the new guy's work.

"I could do that," I said to him.

"Monica, drop it. And no, you couldn't. The back room now," she said. Stopping mid-walk, she pointed as firmly toward the purple beaded curtain. "If you quit being rude to Ben, and tell me what the hell is going on, then I might consider casting an appropriate spell. Sound fair?"

"Perfect."

"FYI. Your pool win was for tarot. Spells are extra," Martha added, her expression deadpan and a worry raised on my forehead, "but meh. I'm willing to do an exchange on this occasion," she said with a wink.

And with that, we set to work.

No. 40

Sunday 3rd August

To: thehat@coffeemail.com
From: monicablue@coffeemail.com
Subject: 2 a.m.

Dear Lenny,

I'm sitting in my cave room; I haven't written to you from here before. It's two in the morning and Bootsy hasn't long left. My mind needs downtime, I can't sleep immediately after being busy even if it is the middle of the night. I came in here to replace the Spanish and Greek books Bootsy and I had been consulting earlier, in their rightful spaces in my mini library. He helped me plan travel routes, find transport and banking apps. He wrote down instructions about what to do if I get lost, which is a given. Schedules and route planners are complicated, and I wish I'd learnt Spanish at school.

As I wedged the last book into place, a separate book about the Egyptians and their gods fell off the shelf. I felt called to leaf through the part documenting the sun God, Ra. These ancient people knew the importance and significance of the sun and Ra was said to be the creator of the world who embodied it. Legend says, he rolled the sun in his solar barque (boat) across the sky to light up the world. When he reached the other side, RA and his boat would sink into the underworld, forming the sunset. He would then make his way through the underground, leaving the moon in his place to illuminate the skies instead. When he made it across to the east, he would exit the underworld with his boat, creating the sunrise, and start over again.

These thoughts of the sun and the time of 2 a.m. made me think of you.

My brain has the 3 a.m. hour signed to witches and ghosts and now it's signed the 2 a.m. hour to you. I think this will remain a concept of mine forever. And, as it turns out, I enjoy talking with you. So hi. How you doing?

Bootsy cooked dinner. I'm banned from this burden. thank the Egyptian Gods, ever since I tried to boil milk in the kettle. He thought I needed support and a friend today. I would have been just fine without, but it sure was comforting to have him rattling around the house filling it with smells of proper cooking… tomatoes, garlic and prawns smell perfect. Who knew?

We spent nearly two hours plotting locations and a route around Spain. My plan after Spain was Greece, until Bootsy blew that idea out of the water by casually telling me about Verona in Italy. It's the place where the famous Romeo and Juliet balcony is and the Secretaries of Juliette. He visited a few years ago. How have I not known about this place of star-crossed lovers? With real people writing real letters and notes to Juliette, asking her for answers to their heartache and love ideals? The secretaries reply to the sender should they leave a return address. This makes my heart sing. I must go. I'm obsessed. Island hopping around Greece can wait.

I'm tired of waiting for this era of my life to materlise. My feet itch enough to burn me and I considered, why am I still here? Now I have more money, and my magazine is finally beginning to look like one, I'm thinking of bringing my flight date forward. I hear you wondering how I solved the money and funding issue…

I made a painful choice, to join the ranks of the subhumans by selling my full cassette tape collection. As of yesterday – gah, that word reminds me of the "Yesterdays" song by GnR – they are currently for sale in a vintage music store. I want to cry, but I have made sure they will be well taken care of.

I'm not sure if I am proud of myself for finding a way to more zeros in my bank account or if it makes me a sell-out. Although I can't lie, logging in and checking my bank balance has become a good experience for once. I keep doing it, like it's a text from a crush I keep re-reading. It is not the way I wanted funding to come to me, but it keeps other people, horrible forms and red tape, out of it. I don't respond well to society's rules and control. I was the same as a young girl, my parents lost count of the number of times I was sent home for wearing my leather instead of the school's blazer.

What does Sunday hold for you? Have you finished your work schedule? Surely the studio should be happy with the number of interviews and promo you've done by now?

My Sunday holds a challenge. I need to draw a line, even if it's a wiggly one, under the unfinished business I have with Viv. She and her long-term partner Ronnie have broken up, his choice and a bolt out of the blue for her. I sound callous rather than supportive when I say I'm pleased about their split, not sad for her. It's a blessing in disguise and hopefully, a way for her to find herself again. What Viv must understand is this is an opportunity for her to rebuild herself. I hope she takes it but it can't be with me carrying her. I can't do it anymore. I texted her to say I'll come over around five, I haven't heard back but I'm going, anyway. This ends today.

M

To: monicablue@coffeemail.com
From: thehat@coffeemail.com
Subject: How did it end?

Dear Rule Breaker,

Are you trying to say I'm a God? I'll take that one if you are. Fitting too as I am more at home in the heat and palm trees than I am in snowy and colder winters. I don't know why I live in New York and not Los Angeles. Many of my pals live in LA, not New York. You're making me view things differently. I think I need to be changing my life up to. I need to reconnect to me or to something. You're infectious and I admire what you are.

My friend played a role in a film which was set in Verona. The story surrounded the whole Romeo and Juliette balcony and letters thing. That's the only reason I know of it, but I thought YOU of all people would have known about it aha. You need to watch more rom-coms. ;)

I'll catch you later. Me and the cast are doing the last round of radio interviews and I'm due on air in five minutes. I'm writing to you from the toilet, by the way. I couldn't hold it in… the need to pee and the need to reply to you.

Byeeeeee!

P.S Why are you waiting then?

P.P.S. I'm sensing a budding secretary of Juliette emerging, you'd be perfect. If you go, I want a letter from you. By post, not email!

To: thehat@coffeemail.com
From: monicablue@coffeemail.com
Subject: Playing These Days by Bon Jovi

What a waste of bloody time. I'd readied myself for the second loss in my life on the same weekend; first my tapes and then a friend. I wore an outfit which, to me, is normal and comfortable. As usual, people who think it is OK to throw offensive comments at me about my over-the-top Gothic rock style came out in droves. Either by voice or a hint in their eyes, it gets said. I used to retaliate badly now it bores me. I don't ask for their opinion, and I don't care. I don't understand exaggerated dressing. There is no such thing as being overdressed or over the top. Normally, this doesn't bother me, but today it did.

"Departure from the status quo," I told one guy who asked what theatre show I'm starring in.

Viv wasn't in her flat when I arrived, the Polish guys in the Deli shop below it said they hadn't seen her. She didn't answer her phone. I went to Smokes, but Viv wasn't there either. Martha and Wookie, her biker friend, were though. They bought me a pint, and I lost at a game of pool. I never lose at pool. Now I'm here, writing to you, after a slow walk home in the rain thinking... do you want to meet?

Monica

No. 41

Monday 4th August

Lenny asks a good question, why am I waiting? Is there any need or point hanging around until 30th September?

I paced each floor of the house. Ran my hand over each wall and piece of furniture. Every part of the house has been a solid regular feature in my life. By the time I made it outside to the balcony, the sun beamed high in the sky, and its blaze burned my face nicely. I watched the street below. The balcony is one of my favourite areas of the house and it's seen some damage over the years too. With alcohol, friends, music and nightly chats with the moon no one knows about. I lowered myself into the lounger and my mind ebbed to the thought of co-existing with my mother once more. A ticking-bomb atmosphere I don't relish being in for longer than necessary. I don't wish to be around *her or that* anymore or my old life in London. It's over. It's time to move on and the parts I do love about my London life I will love deeply and forever.

I only booked 30th September believing I wouldn't be able to complete all the requirements before that date, but now I've stopped, and lifted my head for a minute, I can see the pieces falling into place. There's a whole world out there full of new best day ever-s and maybe Lenny, somehow, fits into all this because, despite my best efforts, he hasn't gone away and, though I tell my heart it should not, it is growing fonder of him each day.

To: monicablue@coffeemail.com
From: thehat@coffeemail.com
Subject: Meeting

It seems once more you have surprised me. Your suggestion shook me out of crawling about in the - I have no idea where my life is going - swamp.

Definitely. When? Where? I can move a few work things around and meet tomorrow??
Trust me. I can relate to bad comments being said to you and or about you. A LOT. Comes with the job or being original in your case. The more you shine or stand out the more they'll come for you.

Lenny

To: thehat@coffeemail.com
From: monicablue@coffeemail.com
Subject: Meeting

Not tomorrow. I need to do some Monica business first. When do you wrap up work and become a free man? Why do you have no idea about life, I think you do.

Let em come at me, I have a machete in my pocket and a dragon on my back.

Monica

To: monicablue@coffeemail.com
From: thehat@coffeemail.com
Subject: Meeting

After next Monday I am done!! How about Wednesday, the 13th?

If it helps, I trust your judgement of your friend Viv. You should too. You saw straight through my buddies. After accepting the fallout with the Charmers, I can recommend the split. I thought I needed them. I don't. I don't miss who they are or who we are now. I long for what we were, and I thought it would always be that way. I don't know how you got the measure of them as quickly as you did without so much as meeting them... There's no bullshit with you and that is a rare quality in my world. You remind me of my US friends.

I was excited about coming back to London, but it has not

turned out as I thought this time. London normally means home, safety and a re-set of the madness I live in. This summer has only made me question where I'm going and where is home if not here… I can't answer either of those.

Dad and Rosie would be devastated if they knew about the darker sides of my past. I'm pleased we didn't know each other before. I thought blow would help find the part of me which was missing, and I would discover the reason why 'that' life was a better choice for my mother than me, Dad and Rosie. I found neither. Only the isolation that being Lenny James brings me some days. And, I was a jerk to you for saying those things I said. I still don't remember, but I hope you give me a chance to show you it's not what I meant at all. My gentleman self would normally arrange where to take you and your outfits. With the aim of making it an un-forgettable evening, on the big chance I'm going to get that wrong, tell me where you would like to meet or what you would like to do. I'll sort all the rest out. Agreeable?

Lenny

To: thehat@coffeemail.com
From: monicablue@coffeemail.com
Subject: Wednesday it is

Dear Hat,

How about somewhere where we've both never been before?

Monica

I intended to write again to him today. I had wanted to take a little extra time before I did and ruminate on my response to his deeper troubles.

I'm discovering humans are dumb creatures, including me. It hurts when others don't think about or notice my needs… support, being cheered on and not questioning if I deserve what I truly desire, should be offered freely. Yet often it isn't, if one happens to be a person with a trait or quality they envy. It could be money, physical attractiveness, a magnetic personality, talent, living in the right location, the right connections, fame, the perfect peachy arse or whatever applies. Some fucker will use it against you. Let no one lecture another about how to live … that job is ours to do with the time slot we have on earth. Wish them well, pray they find their unique selves and go forth anyway.

I am grasping daily at deeper levels each time how important the dream seeds and standing firm to them are, because without those guiding lanterns and taking ownership of them, we will always be at the lost and found.

Viv texted me, breaking my concentration on my reply to Lenny. I should learn to turn my phone off. It removes me from my own world and peace, holds me hostage and causes me to be confused as to which reality is reality. The reality connected to the phone and all that comes with it, or this one. The one I'm writing here in the safety of Monica Blue?

I read Viv's message, and she said would call around after she finishes work.

Tomorrow.

Need a chat x, she added.

So do I, I replied.

No. 42

Tuesday 5th August

To: thehat@coffeemail.com
From: monicablue@coffeemail.com
Subject: Good morning

Hat,

I'm meeting Viv today. I'll write again later. I'm not ignoring your troubles and you are not alone.

Monica

To: monicablue@coffeemail.com
From: thehat@coffeemail.com
Subject: Good morning

You are not alone either.

Lenny

...and something about his last email touched me under my skin.

When I opened the door to Viv last night, it wasn't the Viv I used to know. Her presence had shrunken, making her appear smaller and what felt like a thick gloom pulsated out from her. I'm surprised it didn't glow around her. Her dyed black hair hung bedraggled around her blemished face, and I wondered when the last time was she had slept more than a few hours. At what point had her gusto for life been replaced by surviving until the next fix? Whether that fix is Ronnie, drugs, Smokes or me would interchange daily. I wondered again if she had always been this way and I hadn't seen it because maybe part of me had been similar to her too. I decided either way it doesn't matter anymore, as dragging myself through a defunct connection is no longer an option.

I didn't want her in my house. Her gloom was no longer welcome and if I let her stay, who knows when it would leave? According to Martha, bad energy sticks inside your house like tar from cigarette smoke infecting and affecting your own life.

"Let's drink over at Bootsy's," I said, pulling my denim dragon jacket off the bottom bannister pole, causing her to halt her presumptuous walk to the staircase to go up to our usual spot on the balcony.

"Why, we never go there?" she asked, twisting her face all confused.

"I've been inside all day. I need to get out, and you can tell me about Ronnie."

She dropped her shoulders and her face looked like a soap opera.

"You won't believe what's happened," she said, and, as if it were possible, the gloom grew brighter.

I locked the front door, muttering how nothing Ronnie does surprises me anymore or her as she messed about texting on her phone and rubbing her boney cheekbones. At least at Bootsy's, I have backup. He could send me an emergency text or nip over to our table with a calamity to break up the chat. We've done it before. I don't recall Viv's twittering as we crossed the street and into the bar.

We sat at a table by the window with a view of the main road and my house opposite. I didn't bother ordering drinks. Bootsy texted me from behind the bar as to why I had 'brought *that* in' and I smiled inwardly as I side-eyed him but ignored the message. I listened to her latest drama until my body automatically shuffled about in my seat. My brain had melted, and I couldn't hold my tongue any longer. Holding my palm up to her, I asked her to stop her hurricane. I riffed about how I felt our friendship had changed for a few minutes. We were going in opposite directions, and although I had tried to go with it, the truth was, unfortunately, obvious. Our friendship had reached its natural end, and I needed to move on. Viv didn't take it well; she didn't expect I'd ever break away from her, especially at the same time Ronnie had left and her life was crumbling. She spouted about how I am stone, both in her shoe and in my emotions, and how she is convinced people have a vendetta against her. I told her the drugs were making her paranoid, which triggered a slating of my magazine and unrealistic ideas After spending too long hurling her victim self all around the place, she leaned down to snatch her bag up from the floor. Several times she had to wrangle with it, as the strap had caught on the table leg until she finally yanked it free. Stropping out towards the main door, she called a selfish bitch loud enough to ensure all the bar heard.

"Am I? In that case, stick it on a big arse badge, and I'll wear it with pride," I yelled back to her, patting my chest.

She slammed the entrance door on her way out and I knelt up on the cushioned window seat, watching her walk away. I flipped her the finger. Thirty seconds later Bootsy slid in next to me on the poofy leather seating, sliding me a drink across the table.

"On the house. Do tell," he said, grinning.

"Obvious, isn't it?" I said, resuming a normal sitting position, noting I'd laddered my new fishnet nights. "I won't be hearing from her again. I know it."

"Good. Let her go. She'll find her way in life… if she wants to."

"You're probably right. Ronnie has, it seems," I said with a cheeky smile.

Bootsy raised his brow in curiosity as I explained the affair Viv thought Ronnie was having, was not, as it turned out, another woman. Ronnie's gone all namaste, cleaning himself up, cutting off people and places involved with his old ways. He's obsessed, according to Viv, with green tea and meditating in his house with his new pet. A goldfish. Called Tank. Had the VPGs reached the depths of Ronnie too, I wondered. A vision of Ronnie donning a new beard sitting in the lotus position isn't an image I ever thought would enter my head, but anything can change in an instant, I'm learning.

"It smacks though. Losing a friend, I thought would be lifelong."

"It's the best thing you could have done. New ones will arrive from out of nowhere, I promise," he said. Bootsy sounded sure of himself, too sure it almost felt safe to believe him.

"Is it better than agreeing to meet Lenny on Wednesday?" I said, rolling the sleeves of my Rolling Stones T-shirt back to the top of my shoulder. *I needed to get Martha to stitch these in place*, I thought, as Bootsy slapped the table with a flat palm, yelling an exaggerated yes, re-engaging the people around into staring over at me.

"Subtle," I said. "It's one meetup, cupid. That's all. I'm deciding whether to re-book my ticket to leave earlier and it seemed right to see him in person, before I go."

"I knew it! This is going to be the romance of both your lives,"

"It isn't. You need to get that into your rose-tinted skull. The new life I'm forging is the romance of my life… you need to stop watching all those love stories. La-la land isn't real, you know."

"I disagree. And what is so unreal about you and Lenny, anyway? There's no reason why he can't be a part of your new life also… don't be a dick and mess it up."

No. 43

Wednesday 6th August

To: thehat@coffeemail.com
From: monicablue@coffeemail.com
Subject: Striking the machete

Lenny,

I wielded the blade, and my friendship with Viv is severed.

I'm not sure how I feel about it yet, part better, part empty. The better half is relieved and feeling free. The empty half fears the new or fears my new future won't come at all and I will be friendless forever. I never expected to lose a good friend and be relieved about it. The unexpected keeps sneaking up and taking me by my cowboy boots this year.

I've been thinking about you today. I did try not to, but it unsettled me you are dispirited.

You're not lost in life, more looking in the wrong direction. Perhaps, you've tried to keep stoking an old fire, like me, but it's gone out. It's dead. Not even an ember glows. This is not to say London and old friends can't reignite in the future or won't always be special, but you don't belong in your old story anymore. You made a new and better life and you don't need to justify it by splitting yourself into two halves to serve both. You just need to pick a side.

If the pain with your family is a burden, why don't you tell them? Clear your ground? They sound caring and supportive, and it will release you most of all. Old hurts and wounds can't torment you if you call them out. I need to tell my mum about my new plans which will be a showdown too if this helps. I have been avoiding it and it's exhausting.

Telling your family is only an idea I thought I'd share. Equally, there may be no need to raise the dead. Only you know. You ought to be proud of who you are, all of it. I can understand your position must be a lot on your shoulders, and being a commodity for other people has to be draining, but can you see yourself doing anything else? Unlikely.

The advice my bones have for you is to get out of London until you return to the USA. Go learn how to ride horses, cook non-vile scrambled eggs (if that's possible), camp by a lake and meet yourself again. All of this will become the summer that was, and you'll find out you were perfect all along.

Monica

No. 44

Thursday 7th August

Today is a good day and I intended it to stay one. At mid-morning a bandanna kept my hair away from my face, and I lit a smoke out on the balcony and reflected on my progress thus far. I'm smiling as I write this entry because the machete wielding is working. Movement is occurring, and a space is being created to accommodate *me* and my dream seeds. The unseen does become seen. It will not withhold itself if you give it fire and a backbone.

I have a small lump of cash in the bank and the magazine is gradually formulating page by page. I have grown in the right direction on the scale from wannabe to professional and the two are entirely different states of mind. They are indeed different people who wear different shoes.

I haven't sold a damn thing or gained a reader. None of the so-called facts have changed, but I have changed. And that's the point, isn't it? The VPGs said in one of their videos, the facts change following a change of mind. I have gone within and been honest with myself about my father and feel grateful to have a rock angel, a plane ticket, a semi-plan, Bootsy, Martha and my new pen pal Lenny. Whatever happens, I have seen a wider view and better days must follow, because once you get a glimpse of nirvana, you can't go back.

Godspeed to the phoenix forming in the ashes…

To: monicablue@coffeemail.com
From: thehat@coffeemail.com
Subject: Wednesday

Monica,

Am I man enough to speak to the fam? I don't know. You're braver than me and your mum does need to know, in fairness. Dad and Rosie don't. All it'll do is hurt them and cause unnecessary drama, especially for my dad and he's my best pal. I can't risk destroying that. Maybe leaving London earlier than intended is the way to go.

Let's continue defeating the world on Wednesday! I'm looking forward to it a lot. Given our upcoming schedules, I thought we could make a day of it. How about we start with breakfast? I'll pick you up at seven? You're free to leave when you want, of course, although I'd rather you didn't.

Lenny

No. 45

Friday 8th August

To: thehat@coffeemail.com
From: monicablue@coffeemail.com
Subject: Wednesday 7 a.m.

Good morning,

You bring the hat. I'll bring cinnamon buns.

Do I wait outside for you, or do you knock on my door?? Or will your driver come to my door?? What are famous persons' rules'??

I have no problem walking away. I don't suffer fools gladly, but I'm willing to try, as I believe you. I told Bootsy I'm meeting you, hope that's OK. He won't tell anyone, but he's exceptionally giddy about it. Bootsy holds you in high regard and, usually, he's spot on about people even when I think he's wrong. Viv, for example. I'm taking a chance he is right about you too. He seems different recently, don't you think? More… pop-y. I can't put my finger on it.

Anyway, I thought about what you said about why I am waiting until the end of September to depart for Barcelona, and I couldn't find a single reason. I will end my letter here as I need to re-book the flight for the 1st of September.

Monica

They charge to change the date of booked flights! What a rip-off. Why? I'm still taking the flight to the same place only earlier, which means they get money earlier too! I wrote an email to the company with anger at their ethics and morals, hoping for a freebie but then paid the fee and rebooked, anyway. I didn't want to wait, and I know complaining, especially to big companies about prices, changes nothing. We used to come across these situations all the time at the magazine, either directly or via readers writing in. I didn't want to waste time over admin fees, however scammy it might feel, as I can't wait to go.

I attempted to call my dad at least four times today. Full of myself each time I might have been… but only until it came to tapping the call button to connect us. What would I say to him? What would he say to me, and then what would I say back to him? I rethought the situation, deciding I'm not good at talking on the phone in general. Ringing him on a random Friday after all these years of no contact is awkward and could kill any chance it might have of going well.

Instead, I did what I did best and wrote him a letter.

I kept it brief with no swearing or anger. I only informed him that I am arriving in Barcelona on 1st September, and if he is open to the idea, would he like to meet for coffee? That was all I wrote. I guess there is nothing else for me to say. I am almost certain he will be willing, but who knows, men can be unpredictable. I am in no way gullible enough to trust promises made in his letters and offerings until he is sitting in front of me putting his money where his mouth is. I sealed the letter in a cream envelope and immediately ripped it open again and added my mobile number underneath my signature. I could miss a written reply if it arrived after I left. The addition of my phone number also transfers the problem of… *to call or not to call* into his court, from mine.

I chose a new envelope and sealed the letter inside. Adding his address on the front, my letter was ready to post, which I will do on Monday at the main post office. I didn't want it to get lost over the weekend or for it to be sat alone in a pile of other mail waiting for a person to collect it. I placed it on my bedside table next to the picture of The Writers' Museum from Lenny.

Gazing down at the letter and the photograph, I felt content. Ease was surfacing, and I wanted to clear out the old and tie up loose ends. My mother, of course, is one such thread but one which could wait until tomorrow. After writing a groundbreaking letter to my dad, dealing with my mother in the same twenty-four hours was one situation too much.

I spent over an hour decluttering my room. I stored away candles, incense burners, old notes, half-used eye pencils, magazines, photographs and my red tape player in a flowery storage box I stole from the magazine office and placed it at the back of my wardrobe. I dusted and cleaned my bed, desk, wardrobe and drawers and hoovered the bedroom carpet until it felt fluffy under my bare feet. I even attached the narrow nozzle attachment to it and dragged it around the carpet edges. I opened the sash window and let the summer breeze blow through my room and remove mothy remnants of incense and old air. Within a short space of time, my bedroom had transformed into fresh and free, and I slid my phone off the desk opening the last text message from Ronnie and began typing.

I heard about your change in direction. I respect that and wanted to let you know me and Viv have broken up too. I wish you and Tank good luck and good times ahead. MB

Thanks, he texted back.

I don't think I'll be seeing him again either, which doesn't hurt my heart other than one more person I once thought a friend is another distant memory.

To: monicablue@coffeemail.com
From: thehat@coffeemail.com
Subject: Wednesday

Monica,

I'll make it all up to you. I'll be outside your house in a white Jeep at 7 a.m. Keep an eye out for me. I don't use a driver when I want to keep my life private – and you – under the radar. Not because I don't want to be seen with you, but so you aren't hassled, and we can enjoy the day in peace.

I agree, Bootsy is an excellent judge of character, aha. As far as him acting differently I'm not sure. You know him better than me. If he's happy, does it matter?

I spent the afternoon with Dad and Rosie, we drove by my old school reminiscing. The place still looks the same as it did all those years ago. I don't think school and college buildings ever change. The same fencing and main gates, the same stonework, and no doubt the same boring classes teaching the same crap nobody uses.

Dad cooked a roast dinner like back in the day (can't beat Dad's roasts!) and Rosie tried to enlighten me about horses… and failed miserably. My agent is pushing me to accept the role and I need to decide soon if I'm taking it or not. Why couldn't it have involved a friendly dog or a cute rabbit?

Rosie and I spoke about horses a lot. She fessed up she wants to drop out of uni and return to working with them. God knows why, worst job on the planet in my book. I told her not to ignore her passion and how a special person once told me we all have dream seeds contained within and we must follow them, or they'll haunt us. Dad will flip out of course. "All that money wasted on fees" he'll say. "She only has a year left. What a waste," he will also say. Is the whole world transforming or is the hocus pocus of Monica Blue silently working across town?

I spoke with Dad and Rosie about how my summer here has not been as I expected. I've lost something and now even London is no longer the same.

"You miss this," my dad said, circling his arm around the

three of us "and feeling at home. A place where you get to be Lenny without fear but that son," he said, tapping his chest, "is in here. Trust yourself and you'll find other people and places you can trust, but it starts with you. Don't think for one moment you don't have a circle of steel around you because you do."

I'm glad I didn't tell them about blow and booze and partying ways. It no longer matters. With one (nearly) honest chat with the fam, the Diablo disintegrated. I don't have all the answers to my future yet or know whether to stay in New York or move to Los Angeles or elsewhere, but I do know I am Lenny James and I can't wait to see you on Wednesday.

Lx

No. 46

Saturday 9th August

Telling Mum about my new venture has changed from a *need* to a *have* to. What was once an entry on the to-do list is now a pest, biting at me. Lenny believes I'm braver than him. I'm unsure of the truth of his assumption given I haven't exactly carried out the same unsolicited advice I told him to do. By lunchtime, I knew today had to be the day.

Today, I will ring my mother and tell her everything.

I spent the whole afternoon gassing myself up to reach a place of inner stability. Her response will either be vicious, a plaguing guilt trip or both. I had prepared myself for all events, telling myself none of these outcomes mattered or could hurt me as long as I stayed in my lane.

Shortly after four o'clock, I decided there was no time like the present, my mood was strong, the speech rehearsed, and I had no interest in chatting or swapping niceties.

I caught sight of the hotel through the balcony window doors en route to the kitchen, turning the downloaded version of Go Your Own Way by Fleetwood Mac off. I stood stiffly against the kitchen island with a strong coffee, my bones and roses bracelet tinkered against the mug as I stared down at my phone screen on the worktop. I grabbed it and rang her in one swift super-speed action. She'd been in the South of France for eight weeks at least; the length of her stays increased year on year.

"Monica! How funny. I was just talking about you to the girls and Rodger, how you work at a top magazine and—"

Rodger

"—Are you drunk? It's not even six o'clock there," I replied.

"Happy tipsy darling. We're celebrating. Can I ring you back in about an hour?"

Celebrating

"Sure."

Who am I to interrupt the South of France women?

A wobble returned, blobbing in the pit of my stomach. I needed to say what I had to now, not in an hour. I opened the blog on my laptop, because as daft as it may sound, my blog had become a form of support, a presence letting me know I wasn't completely alone. The stupid update message had returned. Flashing in the centre of the screen asking whether I agreed to the new updated terms and agreements or not, I couldn't continue without accepting or, if I disagreed, I needed to return to the platform's settings and alter my preferred choices.

"Oh, fuck off," I told the screen and hit yes to stop the message bugging me and make it go away. "What's the update, a new font? A bug fix which makes naff all difference? Pointless faff is what it is," I grumbled.

I figured a quick vodka and orange wouldn't hurt the situation and would give me a chance to remain grounded and keep my confidence alive. I exchanged my mug of coffee for a tall glass, threw a bunch of ice cubes into it and poured an ample mix of vodka and cold, fresh orange juice. The cold liquid soothed my tensing throat, cooled my chest and relaxed my shoulders.

I paraded around the kitchen, then the sitting room, ending up on the balcony smoking with Go Your Own Way playing again, waiting. And waiting. An hour felt like a day. By the time Mother rang, I'd knocked back a few more vodkas. I felt invincible. It was ideal.

"Before you say anything, Mum, I need to tell you something. And don't interrupt me until I've finished," I said.

She muttered a suspicious OK. Softening my abruptness, I launched into sermon, knowing it would wound, but remained poised as I shot four bullets… One—leaving the security and notoriety of the magazine; two—writing to my father and planning to restart contact; three—launching my own publication, inspired initially by watching my father in music production; and four—leaving for Barcelona in less than three weeks.

"I don't believe this," she said in a whisper. "I don't believe how hurtful and foolish you are being," the whisper grew in volume.

"I'm not doing any of this to anger you or to hurt you. It's for me, it's not about you," I said, cutting in.

"How could you?" her whispering escalated to screeching. "After everything I've been through! We've been through!"

I tried to switch off as she told me how ungrateful I am. How I'm throwing all that she has done for me in her face with a shovel. How Dad will do a number on me. Unsurprisingly, I was not to expect any further financial support from her because 'I'm a reckless girl.'

"You've chosen your side. You're a traitor; just like your father."

"Wow."

She'd brought me to silence and reduced me to rubble. Old weeds rapidly multiplied in my mind until there was no more room for me to think or a way to return to my power. I wanted to retreat and be far away from her, but at the point of hanging up the phone a mini miracle swept through me. Removing enough weeds to provide an inch of space, enough of a gap for the original me to return and hold on to my strength.

"Stop belittling me. I'm not here to continue *your* war that was over years ago…You bitter old jealous cow."

"How dare you speak to me like that and oh, I am not bitter, Monica," she spat. "I was going to tell you this when I got back but, seeing as you won't be there. Rodger and I have got engaged; he's coming back to London with me. I—was—excited about you meeting him."

"Wait. What? Who? I don't even know this guy."

Fuck me, I should have known. This is why she wanted me to pitch the feature to my editor at the magazine. To get her face and story in there for all to read, not for me to have my writing published in the glossies.

"Clearly, I have nothing to be bitter about, and I am definitely not jealous of you. I've found love again, unlike you, Monica, who walks around like some sort of witch with a steel heart. You'll never find a decent man or job behaving as you do."

I was about to explode; my eyes were practically out of their sockets. I squeezed my knee hard. I was certain crescent marks from my nails would be on my skin for days.

"You know what, Mother? I'm done. Spew your acid onto *Rodger* instead."

"Ugh!" she spat again and hung up.

I threw my phone onto the sofa, grabbed my glass off the coffee table, and hurled it at the wall across the other side of the sitting room. Glass shattered all around and orange liquid dribbled down the wall, much like the tears down my face. Her words were a blade to the chest and fury to the mind.

I played Civil War by Guns N' Roses on repeat on the main sound system, turning it up until it boomed around the entire house. I sang along loudly with it and, in a stupor, I took my phone and barged my wavy legs back to the kitchen. Snatched the vodka bottle from the island, swigged at it as though it was water, and rang her back. Of course, she let it go to voicemail. I couldn't leave as it was, and I didn't hang up.

"For your information, and please do pass it on to your entourage. I have an excellent career already. I don't need you to believe in it because I believe in it, and I will rock the world. Watch me. AND I've met a decent gentleman. He's more than decent, actually! We met, quite romantically in my opinion, and we write letters to each other. He's strong, certain and different from the herd. He's a talented misfit like me, interesting with a big heart! Sharing his passion for life with the world through his work, and I appreciate him more than I've cared to admit. And you know what, I was wary and unsure about being closer to him, but he never disregarded me. Not once. I am not the disaster you imply I am," I yelled down the phone, "and I have found something special both within me within my work and with him because he makes me feel safe and like, like, LIKE… FUCKING TINSEL and his name… his name," I slurred, taking another swig, "is Lenny James. That's right. The film star. So, sit down, bitch."

No. 47

Sunday 10th August

I awoke thinking I'd slept with an air conditioner on all night. *I don't have an air conditioner*. The skin on my face was all dry, taut and tight. Narrow slits accommodated my eyeballs in the centre of puffy sockets and a wrecking ball swung constantly from side to side inside my head, pounding the temples.

Between the thuds in my head and a severe thirst, my stomach began to heave, and I staggered my way to the bathroom. Bouncing off the hallway walls, I made it to the loo in the nick of time to throw up the toxic damage from last night. I couldn't move afterwards and lay with my arms over the toilet seat staring down at the white ceramic bowl. It was comfortably reliving for a while until I could take the sight no longer. I sat on the floor exhausted, leaning against the wall under the window and pushing the flush button. Wrung out emotionally, I clutched my concave stomach when I recalled how last night had ended with the voicemail to my mother.

Oh God, Oh God. This is bad. This is really bad. What the hell was I thinking? Half of France will know by now.

I crawled on all fours back to my bedroom, the journey guzzling what little energy I had, and I face-planted the floor next to my bed. Reaching up to the bedside table, I tapped my fingers around trying to find my phone. Lenny's picture of The Writers' Museum fluttered down with Dad's letter, followed by the phone landing on my head, and I groaned with regret and illness as I opened my email.

To: thehat@coffeemail.com
From: monicablue@coffeemail.com
Subject: About last night

Lenny,

It's me. I think I've made a very slight fuck up. Reply when you can, preferably today.

M

I heard the whooshing noise of the email ascending into thin air and then, reluctantly, phoned Mum. It went to voicemail.

"Can you pick up or call me back? It's urgent."

She did neither.

I rang again, leaving a second message insisting she not disclose the information I left on her voicemail about Lenny to anyone. It's private and I shouldn't have mentioned it in the first place. She still didn't call back.

"Just answer me," I mumbled into the carpet.

I was becoming hot, sweating alcohol out of my pores and stress was building, squeezing every muscle. I couldn't stay on the floor and began to manoeuvre my phone and me back into bed. This task became a mountaineering expedition as I scaled up the side and moved the pillows to the other end of the mattress. Focusing on the spotlights on the ceiling with my feet elevated against the headboard, I retrieved my phone and inhaled deeply. For the next hour, I frantically texted the same message I left on her voicemail to Mum's messaging and social platforms and emailed it to her for good measure too. Mum is constantly on her phone scrutinising the world so she can't play the 'I didn't receive it' or 'I missed it' card with the bundle of communication I'd sent.

No reply.

To any of the messages.

I could hear blood flow pulsating in my ears as I let out a long arrrghhhhh.

Midnight

I don't remember falling back asleep. I only knew I had woken at midnight, praying everything had been resolved, and the alcohol had vacated my body. The dread in my stomach told me neither had occurred. I suspected this hangover would be a grotty two-day job and I'll likely be awake till dawn feeling dreadful. I'm no stranger to the night hours and I pondered why, as I threw on my dressing gown and checked my phone in my darkened bedroom, the night skies and silence can be inspiring as much as it can be depressing.

Unless you are injured, ill, or there's an emergency with the house. Please stop calling and messaging while I deal with the hurt. I will ring you next week. Mum.

Fucking great.

A single text all about her: she hadn't mentioned anything about me or Lenny, and I am clueless if this is a good or bad sign.

12.30 a.m.

I stirred two heaped teaspoons of sugar into hot tea in the kitchen. I couldn't bear to switch the lights on and fumbled about using one of the white emergency candles Mum keeps in the cupboard in case of power cuts. I held up the lit candle to the cabinet above and slid out a side plate. Turning the candle at an angle, I let wax drip into a small pool in the centre of the plate and stuck the bottom of the candle to the hot liquid to secure it when a thought occurred to me. My mother's game playing might have led her to write me a response in an email. We seldom use email, but in an email, she had room to explain her point of view and at least offer me some reassurance about the Lenny situation. I perched on the laptop with a deficient amount of faith as I logged in.

But it wasn't faith I experienced when I opened my email and saw my updated inbox list. It was coldness washing down my body like an unwanted spirit had entered the room. I brought the candle closer to the screen to re-read the words Mail Delivery Failure sitting, highlighted in the sender section of new messages.

"What's the nutty bird done now," I whispered. Confused and losing my patience, I placed the plated candle back on the counter and rolled up the sleeves of my dressing gown.

"I can not deal with this woman anymore," I said louder, as I clicked on the message to expand it and read the error message.

The following message could not be sent to this address.

A string of computer talk and sentences rambled on after it. Code only nerds understand. It doesn't matter what it says, all of it pertains to the same thing. The message had bounced back. I continued scrolling through the jargon.

The following message could not be sent to the below recipient. Message delivery failed…
thehat@coffeemail.com

With my earlier message to Lenny typed underneath looking rejected.

No. 48

Monday, 11th August

I've resent my email to Lenny numerous times. All of them have bounced back. It punches me in the gut each time. Unrest is making my body fizz with anxiety. I can't sit still. I don't deal with unrest well when I care about something. I fiercely care or fiercely don't care, there is no middle ground. I don't understand what has happened or changed.

I read all our letters and emails this morning instead of working on my magazine and I don't consider anything I wrote would cause him to cut me off overnight… unless I have been foolish, and Lenny's real identity all along was a carrot. This is hardly my first rodeo, but he's gotten under my skin because I let myself entertain love for a minute. I entertained the idea of a Lenny and me, and now I'm not quite sure what to do with myself. I should have believed my thoughts about him in the first instant. I wonder how I've got to this… sitting out on the balcony overly concerned, I shan't see thehat@coffeemail.com in my inbox again or see him rolling around out of the hotel door, and I'll have to play Whitesnake Now You're Gone.

Running through the possibilities for being removed from his world at least distracted me from my hangover and, logically, there could be many legitimate reasons why this happened. I don't believe my mother has run her mouth. At first, I would have bet my life on it being the answer, but she is more concerned with herself and likely won't think my friendship with Lenny is real. I mean, who would? This stuff happens to other people or on the silver screen, not in real life. Not to me. No, as I dwelled on this further, my mother wouldn't have said a word about it, in case I had made it up, and she would be the butt of people's jokes for boasting about her daughter's new friend when it came out not to be true. Lenny's inbox can't be full unless he is using the email for various women, and *the hat* is not our private space at all.

Have I been played? Did agreeing to meet him mean Lenny had won his hunt or game and now it was over? Has his tech failed or the email provider down? I suppose all these scenarios are possible realities, yet none of them feel right either. While digital issues occur and devices don't always work, for the most part, they do. Human intervention is involved here, I'm certain of it. If his tech was down or stolen, someone such as Lenny, with a team of people around him, would have made magical moves and sorted any problems fast. He would have sent me a new email address if privacy had become dodgy or a message via

Bootsy. I did consider he'd done a Ronnie and taken himself off to a tent by a lake to disconnect. It would be good for him, yet hugely rude not to have told me if this is the case. Still, this version of events settled my lurching chest more than any of the other scenarios. Until I thought of the obvious and smacked my forehead with both hands several times.

I've been blocked. And what's the betting he lied…and he does have a girlfriend in New York. Probably a woman who is the complete opposite to me and why I was fascinating to him. Maybe she came over to London as a surprise and walked in on him as he was messaging me, or she could have found our communication by accident. Perhaps she grilled Lenny, suspicious something was afoot. Women are smart, rarely will they dismiss a hunch about their partner, especially if they fear being heartbroken. I could google if Lenny James has a girlfriend to back up my unfounded claims… but what media tells the truth and who the fuck cares anyway, I'm an idiot. Not him and not her. Me.

When one o'clock came around, I jolted across the road to the bar to see Bootsy. He would be the only person to shed light on this. Oddly he wasn't working, another guy I hadn't seen before was tending the bar and said Bootsy wasn't in as he had had to take annual leave. Emergency time off, by the way the chap spoke, he didn't know why only he was called in by his agency this morning to cover. It's most unlike Bootsy. He's rarely away from his first love – the bar but as he was my only way of contacting Lenny, I needed to speak to him.

I returned home and rang Bootsy, but it went to his voicemail. I immediately rang him back, and it went to voicemail again. On the third time, he declined my call. What is wrong with everybody?!

I called again, using the call feature on a social messaging platform as I could let it ring constantly until he answered, which after four minutes and forty seconds, he did.

"I don't want to talk to you right now," he said abruptly and ended the call.

"Oi!" I yelled, but the other end was already dead.

I stared at the phone in disbelief and then all around the walls in the sitting room with an open mouth. What the chuff was going on with him? He didn't sound sick, upset or happy to have a day off. He sounded angry. Venomous. I've never heard him angry before. Bootsy doesn't get angry.

I rang again, but he cut me off and now I had become bored with the game and texted him instead.

You sound at war but I don't appreciate you taking it out on me. It's uncalled for. I need a small favour, can you get a message to Lenny? His email must be down, and my messages are bouncing back. I can't get hold of him x.

He didn't respond.

I chose not to send my second text asking him for Lenny's number. I knew Bootsy wouldn't give it to me. He's a loyal friend and wouldn't pass his or anyone's information on without permission. I wish I'd taken Lenny's number when I had the chance. Way to go, Monica, making life more complicated instead of doing acts my future self would thank me for.

By 2 p.m. I had not had a call, text or email from Bootsy, Lenny or my mother. I passed it off as a coincidence but couldn't help thinking it was odd. However, I couldn't continue sending messages out to crickets because people woke up this morning throwing their toys out of their prams for reasons beyond me. The time had come to ignore petty drama and crack on with important matters, the countdown to Barcelona.

No. 49

A Strange Afternoon

At nearly thirty degrees, the city was sticky and unsettled. I kept my look simple, hair tied in a ponytail, mascara and a layer of matt burgundy lipstick. I wore basic witchy ankle boots, a printed Rara skirt and a vest with an array of necklaces, which I later came to regret as the back of my neck turned itchy and sweaty from the metal chains irritating the skin.

Carefully placing Dad's letter in my bag, I walked to the post office oblivious to my surroundings. Like the Pat Benetar album I was listening to, the vision of my future was more inviting. When I reached the front of the queue, I pulled out one earphone and handed the letter over to the lady behind the postal counter. I had noticed a few more extra stares from others as I had waited, hardly an unusual occurrence for me, but my appearance was tame today. It didn't quite make sense to me. I shook it off and asked the cashier how much it would be to send my letter to Spain using the fastest service. It was more expensive than I thought. I don't recall the amount because her comment of, "I hope you get the response you want," as I tapped my bank card caught me off guard and prickled me like I'd touched a cactus. I leaned forward an inch and examined her closer with narrowing eyes.

"You say that to all your customers?" I replied through the screen, stuffing the proof of postage receipt in my bag.

The lady didn't answer but continued her sympathetic smile, creasing her middle-aged eyes. I peered over my shoulder at her again as I left. Outside, I glared through the main glass doors, still perplexed by her, until she moved on to the next customer. I'd addressed the envelope to Warren Blue, not Dad, to keep it neutral and unannounced at his end. Surely, I couldn't have picked the only post office with the only cashier in London who knew my dad and family. I should have taken note of her name, but in any event, her comment unnerved me.

I'd hoped my unrest from earlier in the day would have diffused with the walk to the post office and sending my letter. Instead, it's growing, and at speed. First the post office incident and then, as I meandered back through central South Kensington overheating, I noticed more and more onlookers catching my eye with some doing double takes. It was most weird. I found myself retreating to the pancake and waffle place. I needed sugar and coffee to relieve the gnaw in my stomach. I couldn't tell if it was there due to the lingering hangover, genuine hunger or because I'd officially entered a foreign state of nervousness. The man, whose name I don't know and who has served me hundreds of times, seemed surprised to see me and the usual packed place of tourists appeared to hone its eyes on me. Especially the younger ones. I normally pay no attention, albeit notice it, but catty faces were in abundance along with extra stares, sneaky glances and whispering. An air of bitchiness fell around me and as soon as my order was ready, I left, flipping my finger to a table of teens whose eyes were full of an unpleasant force.

Is it always this way and I hadn't noticed until today? It's not normally this bad.

I didn't place my earphones back in my ears when outside, and I all but ran home to escape to what felt like a dark and cold city. I sunk my mouth around the now tepid crepe and had a word with myself to get over my paranoia. Monica Blue does not do paranoia nor care what muppets do and think. It's just a strange day with an extended hangover causing anxiety, I told myself.

It's midnight, as I type this entry and there are no messages anywhere. Bootsy still hasn't replied to me. This is unusual. I attempted one last time to email Lenny. It bounced back, and I collapsed into the back of my chair at my desk in my bedroom. Baffled, I surveyed the road and the lit hotel from my window chewing the end of a pen… I'm trying to ignore the feeling something is drastically wrong, but I can't. The day feels broken.

1 a.m.

I'm going to see Martha tomorrow and ask her if the planets are messed up in the universe. Perhaps they are turning around or going backward or something… taunting life on Earth. They do that. Martha told me all about it once. There has to be an explanation for the thunder in the air.

No. 50

Tuesday 12th August

Dear Rock Angel,

I am writing to you on my yellow legal notepad. I've
shut down the blog.
I am not in nirvana.
I AM IN HELL.

No. 51

Wednesday 13th August

7.30 a.m.

I didn't make it to Martha's yesterday. I didn't need to. I didn't need to ask her about the planets, not that I could leave the house, anyway. Jupiter and Co are fucking fine. It is me who is not, and I wish there was a black hole closer to London I could disappear into.

I should be with Lenny right now. Sitting next to him in his white Jeep, happy for the day ahead of me... I wondered where he was going to take me as I chain-smoked on my bathroom floor underneath the opened sash window. This is a question I will never have the answer to now and, frankly, is the least of my worries. There are so many problems I don't know which one to focus on first. All I know is,

I feel threadbare.

I stubbed my cigarette out in the toilet water and threw it over my shoulder out of the window into the back garden. I kept my back to the view as I didn't want to see the pear tree in the centre. It reminded me of Lenny and the nightmare unfolding in my life. Yep, staying in the bathroom is safe and a non-judgmental place for now, unlike outside the front of the house. Unlike the world outside in general. Is it possible to live in a bathroom indefinitely?

I reached my arm up onto the shelf above me on the wall and blindly fiddled around until I found the metal air freshener can and knocked it down onto the floor next to me. Squirting it heavily but realised, through spluttering and a nasty taste in my mouth, the smoke smelt better. Who cares at this point if I and the bathroom look like a crack den? I followed the droplets from the sandalwood and orange spray as they fell and landed on my notepad leaving faint tiny water dots on the paper. I imagined they were forming letters, a message from above about how I could sort all this fuckery out. There was no divine word or magic message, but the pattern they made was at least prettier than ugly teardrops pelting the page.

I don't know why I'm writing about air fresheners when I am so distressed. I can't even listen to my music; I am my own wrecking ball and I've ruined my life.

By yesterday morning, the reason for my emails to Lenny bouncing and the strange antics on Monday became devastatingly clear. Writing this blog was meant to change my life for the better. Raise the phoenix within me into a life I desperately wanted, not hurl me into a public cage with lions, vultures and paparazzi.

I knew I shouldn't have listened to the VPGs and their stupid advice. Where are those bitches and their positive purple auras now? Ibiza probably. In wedged espadrilles. Making another fark-ing video.

Half of the world has read my blog. Do you understand how huge this is rock angel? The damage? Half – of – the – freaking – world has read it. This is far worse than a parent or friend reading my teen diary and I want to sack your angelic arse, but I can't. Writing to you on my notepad is the only thing I have left to hang on to, and you're the only person, puff of mist or whatever you are, I can talk to.

I wish I'd paid more attention to the blog updates instead of always being consumed with alcohol, love and fury. That one small act of agreeing to the new terms in haste changed destiny into detonation. The update wasn't a bug fix or the addition of new fonts. It turns out it was an overhaul of their entire platform and system, which entailed ALL blogs, including private ones, being made public. Unless I altered the privacy and requirements in the settings. I didn't do that. Now I am in deep, *deep* trouble.

For two days, unbeknownst to me, my Dear Rock Angel blog had been public. Under any other circumstances, it would not have been a big deal. An embarrassing glitch which would have blown away with the wind with no one noticing or caring, but with Lenny involved, it exploded. Across the globe. If the shock of this was not enough to confine me forever to the bathroom floor, the speed at which the fame vine operates is.

I didn't know until yesterday morning. As I sat to write my original blog entry for Tuesday, about my excitement of meeting Lenny on Wednesday, and the next chapter of life finally showing movement, I noticed comments popping up on my blog. For a few dumb moments, I thought they were adverts and assumed it was a new feature the platform had added to make money. The next second, the sky collapsed. Pinned to my seat, unable to catch breath, it felt like ice filled my veins, not warm blood turning me into a statue. I could barely move my hand without shaking as I saw my name in some of the comments. I began reading them and scrolling and scrolling and scrolling. New ones are being added as I read...

Will I be writing about the date with Lenny?

Strong hate towards me for being a kiss-and-tell (buckets of this).

How dare I blab Lenny's and my friends' secrets.

What does Lenny see in you, you're strange.

I'm weird, and who do I think I am?

How conveniently timed to reveal this blog when I'm launching my magazine, no one will read my magazine now. These last comments and all versions of it cut me the most.

I hated even one person thought that about me, let alone thousands. They couldn't be more wrong about me if they tried.

Some had had their perfect views of Lenny shattered by his private life drama.

Some thought it their place to cast opinions on every aspect of me and my life.

Some sweet girl only wanted to know if Bootsy had been proposed to yet. I wish I knew.

My very private blog diary of my soul has been found and read not by my mother but by half of the entire fucking planet. Had people saved it or taken screenshots of it before I took it down? I bet they have. The repercussions were spinning out of control in my mind, Lenny hating me and suing me, my magazine being a flop before it was published, my mother selling the house and I will have nowhere to live. Never having the chance to speak to Dad because he'll be mortified how the industry will know the truth about paella woman. To Bootsy never talking to me again. Although I don't believe I wrote anything bad about Boots. I can't work that one out. Why has he abandoned me too when he could have warned me sooner? And the tapes, oh my heart, I lost them for no reason. My magazine is unlikely to take off now. I hit my head hard against the back wall several times. I couldn't stop my mind from running into every dark tunnel I could find. I can't deal with any of this… the contents of my secret chamber about me, my life, and the people in it are all out for society fodder.

I'm unsure who is affected most. Everyone has a lot to lose in their own way, if only their privacy, but Lenny ranked joint first with me at the moment. Then there is *his* family, my family, friends, my future, *his* future… my God. What have I done?

Havoc has been building on the road outside my house since yesterday. The description of the hotel and Bootsy's bar, I have to assume, were enough details to give the location away. People are swarming, to-ing and fro-ing at all hours. My phone and email are going bonkers with messages, and not from the people I want to hear from or at least know. Except for Viv.

What the fuck. Bitch. Was all she said in a text.

No Lenny, no Bootsy, Martha, Dad, Mum. Not even Ronnie. I can't believe what I am living, people are circulating outside the hotel, Bootsy's bar and my house. Fans of Lenny, certainly NOT fans of mine, reporters, PR and marketing people. Wolves all hungry and using all manner of attempts to get my attention. I have had to put on my big old headphones with noise cancellation so I can't hear the doorbell ringing or all the indistinct chatter and noise. I heard it last night when I made the mistake of opening my bedroom window to tell people outside to go and do one. Do these people seriously think I'd answer their questions or the doorbell?

For a wistful second at 7 a.m. this morning, I hoped Lenny might have still come to rescue me but why would he, he'll despise me. I've wrecked his trust, his life and his career. I have become everything he thought I was not. I fear I have become everything I know I am not.

When I peeked around my bedroom curtain shortly after seven this morning to check for him, all I saw was the continuing growing crowd of people. Many, obviously reporters, suddenly yelled and clicked cameras when they saw me. Not a white Jeep in sight. I don't know if he's still in the hotel…. unlikely Monica, I remember thinking as I let the curtain fall.

I lit another cigarette.

No. 52

Wednesday 13th August

11.30 a.m.

The bathroom floor had become hard and as painful as I. Relocating, I sat in the bath on a stack of towels, hoping my change of location might stir up a solution or a miracle. All it did was let my eyes wander to the view of the pear tree outside in the garden. I can't see it without standing, but I know it's there.

11.40 a.m.

I've checked my cigarette packet. I only have two left.

Noon.

I have a packet of tobacco somewhere. I'm sure of it. It was for emergency roll-ups and Ronnie's joints. This is an emergency; I can't go out to the shop. If I can't find it, I'll have to order a packet online from the supermarket or local shop and get it delivered. I'll tell the delivery person to post them through the letterbox.

12.15 p.m.

I'd left all the curtains shut around the house when I discovered the catastrophe, it still felt risky as I ransacked the house for a pack of half-used tobacco. I made strong coffee and didn't bother with lunch. I can't eat a thing. I'm concentrating too hard on trying to ignore the commotion outside. When will they all go away? It disturbs me it might be a while as they'll all know I will have to leave the house at some point.

I found the packet of tobacco. Stuffed behind a dragon book in the cave room with a pack of rolling papers but no filter tips. Sitting on the kitchen worktop next to the hob, I tried to roll one. It resembled an origami structure, not a decent roll-up. I was always rubbish at rolling. Ronnie was the one in charge of rolling.

I pressed the fan on maximum on the oven extractor hood, pulling bits of baccy out of my mouth and checked my coffeemail account. I shouldn't check it; I'm only tormenting myself. I've only kept it open in case Lenny emails me. It's the only way he can contact me unless he asks Bootsy. I wonder if those two are talking. I wonder what everyone is doing. I wonder what I'm going to do.

Emails from the public are still flying into my inbox. Messages from newspapers, publishers and magazines asking for interviews and offering money and perks in exchange for an exclusive or extracts from the blog, join them.

I closed the laptop and vowed not to open my coffeemail account again. What once contained charm and joy is now only filled with filth and accusations. There's not a single thing in there from Lenny or his camp. I need to know if he's okay, which is counterintuitive because I know he won't be.

I texted Bootsy instead.

I didn't know the blog had gone live; I had an incident with a system update. I never meant to hurt or embarrass you and don't think I did but I miss you and want to talk to you. Outside is swarmed, I guess you know this if you're at work. Are you ok? You might not reply but I want you to know you are my soul family and we can't let this separate us. X

And then I sent another.

Also, I need to know how Lenny is, have you heard from him? X.

An hour later my phone rang. I leapt to pick it wanting it to be Bootsy, but I knew deep within it wouldn't be.

It was Martha.

Martha never rings. I'm lucky if I get a text. Her call held the same unease as it did in school when I was standing outside the headmaster's office. I went to slide the button to answer. I ran through my head how annoyed she would be and what trouble I might have caused her. I had no idea how to calculate this unknown result or what Martha was about to say. I prepared myself for a blasting and found the tiniest amount of comfort in it would be at least from a familiar voice.

"Hi," I said in a flat tone.

No. 53

Wednesday 13th August

(a day going on forever)

W ell… this is spectacular. Even for you," Martha said, "when's the next instalment I'm gripped."

"Shut up, Martha. It was an accident. It wasn't meant to be read by anyone," I said, placing the phone face down in my lap and sighing before raising it back to my ear, "say what you have to say and leave me alone. I honestly didn't mean to offend you, but I've no energy right now for you coming at me."

"I don't give a fuck what you wrote about me. It was pleasant and complimentary, mostly. Other than now every Mary and her mother want witchy predictions and magic cast into their lives to solve their every problem. For future reference, it's a side of my work I prefer to keep under my hat and out of sight... magic works better in the mystery of silence. Understand? Anyway, we can sort it out later. I'm not ringing about that. I'm coming to get you out of there."

"What? How I'm trapped? Where am I going?"

"You can stay with me at my flat above the shop until it quietens down. I know you wouldn't have done it on purpose if that helps."

I don't think it will ever quieten down, or not for an exceptionally long time. I can't get my head around what happened in the first place. Moving on from it is impossible. How do I move on from this and be OK? Martha's offer is the best thing I've heard all week, but this blog exposé will be remembered by someone or a publication for years to come.

Martha rarely pays attention to gossip and only became aware of mine from customers chatting about it in her shop, which, after the blog gained momentum at lightning speed, became the talk of Portobello Road. It didn't sit right with Martha and on its last public day, shortly before I shut it down, she visited my blog to discover the truth for herself.

This morning, ruffled by an uneasy witchy hunch Martha turned to her cards for guidance and information. Sensing I would be struggling with the consequences, she swung by my house to check in on me. Except all the mayhem outside greeted her, and she promptly turned her bike around and left.

"It's not right what they are doing and saying, regardless of whether they like you or not. I bet half of them roaming around the road don't even know why they are there.

They thought they'd join an interesting party and fan the flames."

Had she parked up earlier, she told me, and knocked on my door, it would only have made the madness worse. For her and me. People would have recognised her as Martha immediately. Her distinct style and motorcycle would have been unmistakable and, having written about her in the blog, the press and fans would have hassled her with questions too.

"Here's what we're going to do," she said. "Me, Wookie, and the rest of the group will be there in an hour on our bikes. Pack a rucksack, essentials only, not half the house. Make sure you can strap it onto your back and tight. I'll text when we are outside, Wookie and the rest of them will form a barrier tunnel against the crowd to give you a clear path. Don't worry, none of those idiots will dare mess with them. Wookie will be near your door with a helmet. Put it on and shut the visor. I'll be on the road. Get on the back of my bike and I'll zip you over here. We'll be gone before they can even think of finding their car keys."

I wasn't certain I could handle going out there in front of all those people and cameras. Not when I'm the subject of the public's entertainment, yet Martha, of all people, has gone to such lengths to help me, I can't *not*.

"Don't hesitate at any point," she added. "We need a swift manoeuvre. Wear a leather but nothing dangly. Hold on to the back handles or on to me and lean when I lean. No screaming."

Nothing dangly

Helmet on

Hold on

Lean when she leans

"Got it. I think. Thank you, Martha. You've no idea what

this means to me. I'm ruined."

"No, you're not. Don't think like that. You'll be better when it's not in your face. You can't sit there alone dealing with this."

I questioned in my mind how she knew I'd be alone, cut off from all I knew and in way over my head. Then again, it's Martha. No one understands how she knows all this stuff.

"Can you also get me some cigarettes? I'm smoking old baccy and its rank," I asked.

"I'm liking your priorities," Martha said, amused at my request. "Sure, see you in an hour. Be ready."

An hour later, I was standing in the hallway with a rucksack strapped on tightly enough it dug into my shoulders. Watching through the peephole in the front door, I watched the intimidating scene outside with the thought of riding Martha's bike playing on my nerves. What if I get it wrong and we fall off? Martha is a great rider, I'm not. I tried to ride my ex-boyfriend's scooter once but crashed it into a wall of a quiet side street where he had let me practice riding it for the first time. I didn't let go of the throttle when it started wobbling, and I rode straight into a stone wall. He charged me £500 to fix it.

I continued monitoring via the peephole until I could hear the solid roar of a convoy of motorcycle cruisers rumbling down the street. All the attention turned to their arrival and how they parked their machines literally anywhere. I located Martha hovering near the entrance to my house. I waited for her text, whilst a bunch of biker guys and women lined up opposite each other, making a short corridor for me to escape.

"Back off," all six-foot-two of Wookie yelled to the crowd as I cracked the front door open.

Realising I had no choice but to do it, I inhaled deeply, stiffened my back and fixated on Wookie. I grabbed the helmet, pulled it on, flicked the visor down and switched to concentrating on Martha. My eyes kept laser focus on the bike and I did my best to block out and ignore the shouting and clicking of buttons until I could throw my leg over on the back of the bike. I grabbed onto Martha like my life depended on it.

"Go. Go. GO!" I yelled.

She pulled the throttle back. A loud growl revved out from the bike's shiny exhaust and in a second, we were gone.

No. 54

Thursday 14th August

Martha's flat is different from what I expected. I had always imagined it to be an extension of the shop décor downstairs. Yet there was no visible altar with a smattering of spellbooks and candles. No tarot cards about the place or ceramic pots filled with mystical flora and herbs no one had ever heard of. It's spotless. Lots of white paint, leafy plants, seashells and a wooden wind chime above the window, which looks out onto Portobello Road. She said it creates balance.

"And FYI," Martha said as she made coffee from a chrome machine covering half the kitchen countertop. It was fancy enough to be in a professional coffee shop, "I don't make magical potions and lotions," she told me as a cloud of steam hissed out of a spout.

"Pity," I replied. "I'll try anything to make all this go away."

I sloped off and stood by the window in the sitting room of her two-bedroom flat, gazing down at the people promenading the street of Portobello Road. They reminded me of rows of ants constantly searching for food, their own colonies of friends or the promised source at the end of a long trail.

Martha believes all this will blow over soon and it's a matter of waiting it out. People are fickle and soon enough they will be spectating another's bonfire. I can't agree. It will be stored in the souls of every living being and devices the world over. My eyes warmed again, filling with impending tears. I didn't think they could have any more tears left in them, but I was wrong. I tapped the wooden tubes above me to make a distracting tinkling sound until Martha joined me underneath the chime and I lay my head on her shoulder.

"Thank you," I said. "Tell the other guys that too, yeah? Don't think I'll be in Smokes for a while to say it in person. None of you had to do what you did."

"No, we didn't, so what does that tell you? I know you feel deserted and exposed, and I'm sorry Lenny absconded without a thought for you," she said, propping me back upright, and I rolled my eyes as she rubbed in the obvious. "It's not your normal everyday fall out, but he will be surrounded by his pals and big shots to help him deal with it at his end. He's used to global attention. You're not, and nor do you have a squad of power folk around you advising and supporting."

"I've got you and the bikers. What more do I need," I said with slight humour.

"My point entirely," she said, returning the sarcasm. "This is my opinion only, but someone from his side or Lenny himself should have checked you are okay. That's all I'm saying about that…"

"I don't know how to make all this right. I don't know what to do… with any of it."

"It was a stupid mistake, not intentional. Right now, you don't have to do anything or abandon yourself to soothe other people who feel fractured. I don't mean to sound unsympathetic to their trauma but stick to your guns. Instead of asking how you can make it right for him or everyone else, make it right with yourself first. You'll find a way to say your apologies if you need to, but don't jump from your own ship as self-punishment. Ask yourself who of those people and situations would you have back? … your life isn't over as you fear, it's a brand new time and you get to create it on your terms."

Martha excused herself to take the coffee she'd made for her and Wookie from the kitchen downstairs. He was helping Ben in the shop as Martha had taken the day off to distance herself from customers and tarot requests, whilst using the time to keep an eye on me. She didn't trust me not to wade through the cesspool of headlines and stories on the internet, hoping to find positive news. I faltered yesterday and checked Lenny's socials and if I saw the comments 'she wrote, she'd do anything to make the jump for her success. Ride or die, she said! What a cow to do this Lenny to make her pathetic magazine popular,' once, then I've read them a thousand times.

This is the strangest experience I've had. Reading about myself everywhere in a bad and unjust light. I don't know how to handle it other than to shut myself away and wait for the hooded devil to stop heckling me to engage.

8 p.m.
Martha's sitting room

A statement released from Lenny's agent or publicist or whoever these people are. Me, Martha and Wookie read it on social media after dinner. Wookie had waited until then to tell me about it. He'd heard some kids, as he called them, talking about it earlier as they passed by when he was standing in the shop's doorway enjoying a smoke.

It wasn't an informative statement giving anything away. It simply read, 'due to some recent events, Lenny James is taking some well-earned time off and a short break from filming. He wishes to thank everyone for all the heart-felt messages and support and wants all his fans to know how much he loves you, and he will be seeing you all again soon. Please respect Lenny's and others' privacy at this time.'

"Maybe that line about the fans is code, and he means you?" Wookie piped up from the armchair he'd seated in dressed in ripped jeans with a bandana covering his head and a newly trimmed beard.

"Maybe it's code for the studio has fired him," I replied.

Martha said nothing.

No. 55

Friday 15th August

I couldn't settle down last night tousling around in bed, distracted about what Martha had said earlier. Somewhere around 2 a.m. I gave up the idea of sleep. I tried my hardest to be quiet, moving slowly and steadily as I rummaged around to find the switch for the lamp on the bedside table. My fat fingers in their clumsiness promptly knocked over a billowing plant in my bid to locate the hidden lamp switch in the dark. When I flicked it on, bits of soil were scattered over the carpet and across the tops of my bare feet, and for the first time, I realised soil is impossible to scoop up from woolly carpets. Throwing what soil I could back into the plant pot I carted the Amazon Rainforest over to the window, thrust the pot down onto the floor, and batted away its giant leaves and thick stems. *We live in London Martha, not Thailand.* As I glared at the plant, I noticed how its thick, leathery green leaves elicited a sense of peace and calm. The gentleness of its commanding presence gradually overtook me. My tense muscles all over my body gave way to release as I remained mesmerised by it. I sat down next to the plant like it was a new friend and shook the contents of my backpack out until a big brown envelope fell into my lap.

Pulling out my flight ticket, all the printed emails and notes between Lenny and me and even the paper bag I'd kept that he'd written my name on when he sent breakfast across the road to me, was bittersweet. Cycling through each piece of memorabilia evoked further regret. The chance to get to know Lenny properly and live out the wonderful inside talk no one else understood but us for a while was gone. The chance for me to live in new and better times with good friends and my dream career has gone too. All because of the click of one button. "What would you do?" I asked the plant. "You look wise, like you're special, a wisdom plant with all the answers," I whispered. "You must know something?"

It didn't. The green giant merely sat there all grandiose and important, strong and beautiful in its natural structure. I did find small satisfaction that during the hour I had to prepare before leaving home, I had thought to retrieve our letters from the MB box in my desk drawer. I'd brought them in case I wanted to read to them again, seeing as I was not going to be opening my coffeemail account anytime soon. It's a way of keeping him close to me and not left in the house unattended and neglected.

Although my real flight ticket is digital, the printed one is preferable to me and a reminder of faith. All the bits of special papers in my box made me smile and then I sobbed. The disappointment over my magazine being unlikely to work now, or for a long time as I wait for others' memories of this to fade, I cannot articulate. I'm not stupid, it's a dumb time to launch it. I miss Lenny's letters and his country music already and curled up on the floor like a comma. He turned out to be not an entitled rom-com prince but rather a man who was absolute, and it pains me to know all that is left is the possibility of what could have been. If I could keep an inch of faith, then this situation with Lenny and my search for nirvana might resolve but my tears had brought on sudden tiredness. I returned to bed with my parcel and fell asleep hugging it with the mastery of Aerosmith's ballads playing softly on my phone.

By the afternoon, cabin fever was kicking in. Martha had to work downstairs. She had a Friday the 13th sale going on, and it had unexpectedly become busier than anticipated. No surprise given all the recent hype, but Ben couldn't cope on his own. Wookie had to work at his gardening business, leaving Martha no option but to sacrifice her time off. This left me and my cabin fever flicking through daytime TV, initially thinking, I can't stay here forever and when is it safe to return home? Do I want to go back? Can I look at that street, the hotel, the bar and sit on my balcony the same as I did before, or will it all be stained and a thorn in my side? Unless... I head out to Spain immediately, tomorrow or Monday?? I could wait out my ordeal there away from London. An option which seemed great until it didn't an hour later.

To keep my mind off taxi-ing through questions I don't know the answers to, I began to contemplate those scared of Friday the 13th. I've always enjoyed the day. Thirteen is lucky for those who choose it to be and it's a number

I like. I never did understand why hoteliers, for example, wouldn't have a 13th floor or books would have a missing chapter 13. What did they think would happen? Why do so many trust superstition over believing in themselves, or is it a marketing tact? Friday the 13th began as a story from biblical times and has now been taken way out of context, a concept I can sympathise with. Fortunately, my blog didn't have a chance to become as popular as the Bible, which would have made my life doubly worse… this is the good luck I found in today's Friday the 13th, but then my mother rang.

"What did she say?" Martha asked as we chopped and sliced tomatoes, lettuce and cucumber. Wookie had brought them round from his allotment for our Greek salad and lamb kofta dinner. He'd called after finishing work. He didn't stay to eat with us as I assumed he would. He only dropped them in, washed off any gubbins from the fresh salad and put them in the fridge for her.

"Good food will help," he said to me, stepping his big boots through the flat to the front door. "I'll catch you tomorrow, Marth," he added.

I don't know what I had Wookie pegged as, but it wasn't a biker with a passion for gardening and growing fresh produce. Quite sweet really, maybe gardening and veggies are his version of balance.

My mother didn't say anything unexpected; her disappointment with me ruled her tone, followed by her embarrassment and hurt over the voicemail I'd left and my reckless blog. "It's unbearable," she told me whilst crying on the phone. No matter how angry I am at her, I don't like it when Mum cries. It brings a lump to my throat, a larger one than normal on this occasion, because I do feel bad for her. I didn't mean for her or anyone to read what I wrote about her. It was never meant to be this way.

"She did offer to come back to London, which was a surprise," I told Martha, passing her the feta cheese from the fridge and carrying on about my mother's phone call imitating her voice. "Why didn't you speak to me about all those horrible things you wrote about me in private instead of telling the world … is all she kept repeating as though I hadn't thought of that." I became bored with hearing my voice explaining it wasn't meant to be public, and it wasn't my intention to do a number on her or anyone.

"I'm sure your mum knows that deep inside, she's just upset at the moment and not listening… she can't. Hopefully, one day soon she'll be able to hear what you've been trying to tell her for years," Martha said, with a calm edge and sympathetic hand on my shoulder.

She could be right. I've tried talking with Mum before over matters such as Dad and all the other bustling fireflies trying to be heard, yet she has a knack for turning any conversation I'm trying to have about me around to being about her.

Martha crumbled the feta, and I pulled out the minty smelling koftas from under the grill and rolled them onto two plates as Martha dished up the salad with two chunky wooden spoons.

"How have you left it with her? Do you want her to come back and help?"

I shook my head, taking in a whiff from the top of the

bottle of Wookie's homemade herb dressing. It smelt weird but poured a few drops onto the salad and sat next to Martha at the round mosaic table by the kitchen window.

"The conversation was going nowhere; I told her to stay in France until this has settled and we can pick it up from there. We need distance between us. Then she switched to saying she's considering selling the house and permanently staying in the South of France."

"What do you make of that? Reckon she's serious?"

I shrugged my shoulders. Reading my mother was exhausting.

"This dinner is good," I said, stuffing half a kofta in my mouth and we changed the subject.

It was today when speaking with Mum I noticed a flash of real change. I hadn't considered this would happen with Mum. I thought my place was to find ways of tolerating her... shut up and deal with it. Yet today, I offered her and me another option. Distance. I meant temporarily, but perhaps this is how it will be between us from now on. She lives in France, and I live wherever I take my laptop.

After dinner, I did all the washing and drying up and Martha decided to head downstairs to the back room and give herself a reading. She dropped it into conversation as casually as if she was nipping to the shop for milk, but I could tell her mind had become occupied elsewhere. It had been all evening.

"I'll have a quick toot on the bong later if you want to join me?" she asked.

She must be properly bothered by her thoughts. Martha only gives herself readings when she's thinking and searching, and I can't help but wonder if Wookie's involved with it. She seemed far away earlier as she stared aimlessly in the fridge at the tomatoes. I thought Wookie and Martha were a couple, but I don't think they are. They should be a couple. The more I've got to know them this week, the more gorgeous they are together.

"Hope lady luck is on form tonight, but nah, not for me. I'm going to lie here on the sofa, watch a film that isn't Lenny's, and think about what I'm going to do with my life."

"That's easy," she said, standing in front of the mirror above the fireplace, admiring herself and tying braided fabric bracelets onto her wrist and throwing one over to me. Martha had made a few earlier when teaching Ben the art of her special braided bracelets. She swiped her shop keys from the mantle and made her way past me to leave. "Just live it."

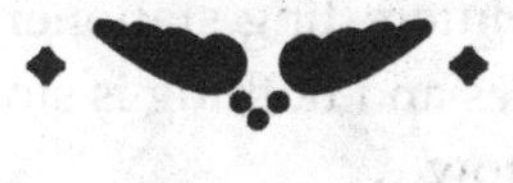

No. 56

Saturday 16th August

I sat in the shop today, only in the back room. A small yet big achievement on my way back to participating in reality. I've changed the back-room's name to the magic cove because it reminds me of stepping through a portal into a world of compelling fantasy. I was admiring Martha's spell cabinet and the rows of tarot cards, oracle cards, messages from angels and native ancients. Each deck is uniquely different, yet all of them are oddly magnetic and intriguing, like brochures of places you'd want to visit. I wasn't allowed to touch them… messes with the energy and readings, apparently.

I was down to the last page of the yellow legal notepad and needed to buy another. I didn't want to ask Martha or

Wookie. They'd done a lot already, rescuing me, letting me stay, feeding me and doing cigarette runs. I noticed how at some point this morning I felt like my normal self for a moment, like I hadn't gone away and thought for a fleeting second, sitting at Martha's table tired of being shut inside in plain jeans and a plain T-shirt, I could nip down the road myself and find a notepad. Portobello Road will have an excellent choice of interesting stationery not found in the normal boring places and nothing is stopping me from going. I can go right now…

Then the idea vanished. I vanished. Not yet strong enough to be me again and I returned to the page listening to "Hard 16" by Vixen.

Thoughts from the Magic Cove

Self-worth. It's a walk on a narrow track upon the peak of a mountain which took time and guts to climb. Have little or none, and you slip off to the left into neediness and chaotic dramas. Hold on to yourself too tightly, and it will hurl you off to the right, into isolation and rejection, and the only way through the conundrum is to keep putting one foot in front of the other and trust the mountain you chose to climb in the first place.

No. 57

Sunday 17th August

Before I scuttled back upstairs to the flat yesterday from the magic cove, I snuck into the shop whilst Martha was in the loo. She keeps a printer in the cupboard below the cash register and I swiped a stack of A4 paper and stapled it to the yellow legal notepad. It took a few hefty bangs of the stapler and a fight with the clips to make it grip. It's not perfect, but it works for now. Martha wondered about the thudding she'd heard when she returned, and I said it was a delivery truck outside as I'd opened the door to have a smoke on the top step. I could have asked her for the paper, but she would have said no in a bid to force me to go outside. The longer I leave it the harder it'll get, she says. The attention does appear to be thinning out and there are fewer people in the shop gossiping about it, which is positive. It could be a good time to consider venturing out from my Notting Hill haven, but I'm not quite there yet. Knowing I needed writing paper would have been a fine opportunity for Martha to boot me out of my comfort zone and into Portobello Road to buy some. I told Martha later that night, as we shared ice cream and watched a film about a mermaid love story, how I appreciated her letting me just *be* and sit with my writing as I figured out what to do next.

I respect Martha for understanding how my writings have become non-negotiable in my life. 'It's your version of balance,' she said. 'You, no one else, found that,' she added, spooning a dollop of cream into her mouth and yelling at the guy to 'kiss the bloody mermaid for fuck's sake.' It made me think I'm doing better than I think I am. Maybe I wasn't ready yesterday for out there, but that was yesterday and today is today.

I'm stronger than when I first came here and feel less like a dead bonfire. Martha and Wookie have been instrumental in me finding my own heat again. It's only a smoulder but it is enough to move me into annoyance and impatience and away from despair. But to return to life full-time in a powerful way? I need flames. I need to feel fire. I like fire. I have to have inner fire to live.

I rang Bootsy last night. He didn't pick up, and I tried again this morning, but he still didn't answer. I texted a paragraph to him. He can't keep throwing his toys out of his pram forever, and it's now becoming a bigger question... What's more important to him, a stupid blog I wrote or us? Going separate ways or keeping a sibling kinship?

None of this would have had the impact it has had if Bootsy hadn't been adamant about playing cupid with

Lenny and me. I'm not blaming him; Bootsy didn't hit the button or write my words, but I told him it wouldn't end well for me with the hat. No doubt Lenny is planning damage limitation manoeuvres with his fancy dancy people not thinking about me and my broken heart at all, whilst I wait for mañana all over again.

I wrote in my text to him.

You've made your point, and I'm sorry this has all happened but happened it has. We have to find a way forward. I want to know how you are or are you injured in a ditch. Are you back at work or avoiding that, too? I happen to care about you and right now you are being unfair when I am repeatedly trying to sort out this mess with you. And I can't because I'm working blind. I don't know which part of what I wrote caused our fallout or how I can help. I'm at Martha's. I couldn't stay at the house; it was too crazy, but I'm coming home soon. I don't appreciate being ignored, which goes for Lenny too, if you speak to him. I'm not texting or calling again, despite my life being two lights darker if I never hear or see either of you again.

He didn't reply.

Fuck you, Bootsy. Fuck you, Lenny. Fuck all the people.

Martha tapped on my door around 7 p.m. all pretty and floaty, asking if I wanted to go to Smokes with her tonight. She was dressed markedly different from her standard rocker biker style, and I liked it. Jeans with suede chaps teamed with a white floaty blouse with embroidered flowers on it and lots of turquoise and silver jewellery with feathers hanging from hair braids. It suited her. I thought about my days-old dirty jeans and scruffy T-shirt and suddenly, I was no longer hiding and healing, I had become a dingy woman with a strange smell.

"Come on. You can ride on the back of me, now that you're a pro," she said, but I screwed my face up to the idea. "You need to start getting out, and you'll be in a safe space at Smokes. They won't give a rat what's happened. Most of them won't even know."

"I know they won't, but not tonight. I'm washing my hair," I joked.

"No offence but you need to," she said with a laugh. "See you when I get home."

I'd worn the same boring clothes for days, no makeup, no jewellery or big hair. It's all gone. I disappeared in a flash. I'm disappointed I'd let myself become a bedraggled outcast, when my style, attitude, passion, my dream seeds were always my, erm, err, what is the word I'm searching for. Were… were… were… MY FIRE.

"Martha," I called out as she was closing my bedroom door. She popped her head back around bearing a hopeful expression that I'd changed my mind. "On the way over to Smokes, can you ride by my house and see if the circus has left?"

"Sure thing," she said.

…and washing my hair is exactly what I did.

No. 58

Monday 18th August

Mid-morning, I finally found Martha and Wookie in the kitchen drinking mugs of coffee sitting on wrought-iron chairs at the mosaic table by the window. The shop is closed on Mondays, and I'd been waiting for Martha to return from her morning errands to speak to her.

A few paper carrier bags were nestled on the worktop with bottled water, food and bread poking out of the tops. Sprigs of green herbs lay next to the bags, which I guessed must be from Wookie. Whilst they were both gandering at a sign being taken down on a shopfront across the road, I stuffed a £20 note in one of the brown paper bags and rattled about with the beast of a coffee machine. I've been shown numerous times how to use it. It doesn't help, I always get one part of it wrong. This thing doesn't work, I told them, banging the metal implement which holds the coffee onto the worktop. Wookie came over, moved a metal lever, pressed a button, sat back down and told me I'd never make a barista. Whatever happened to classic filter coffee, I muttered as Martha shook her head at me. Wookie did his fresh produce meetings whilst Martha shopped earlier this morning, and now they've decided to hang around here for the rest of the day, preparing for their week ahead.

"What are your plans for today?" Martha asked.

"Glad you mentioned this," I said, sweeping the top half of my hair into a top knot and letting the rest hang wild like a Viking. "As instructed by Madame Martha, I'm not checking my coffeemail… I'll explode if I read any more garbage about me from fans and requests from lowlifes for interviews. However, I need to know if the incoming mail is slowing down and if anything important is there before I close the account. Would you mind doing the honours, Martha?"

She jolted her head back. Taken aback by my move to close it when, for the past week, I'd made it clear, cutting off the only communication avenue to Lenny was a no go. Martha said she would have shut it down immediately due to the barrage of enquiries and trolls. Lenny knows where you are if he wants to find you, she'd say. It's easy to agree with her, harder to do in real life. If Lenny chose to contact me, I knew it wouldn't be via our old coffeemail yet I had to give *what-if* a chance. This week my opinion is different, my coffeemail account has become torture music in the background and I need to turn it off.

"Smart thing to do," Wookie said. "We rode by your place last night. Not much about, it's fizzling out but I recommend we check again during the day. You thinking of going back?"

"I have to… and it's my house. It's not right. I've been driven out of it and imposed myself on you two."

They both insisted I wasn't imposing I fist bumped both their shoulders but I knew it was time to leave.

"I'll check your cofffemail on one condition," she said, "you go out there first. Today," pointing toward the kitchen window with her coffee mug. "Wookie can go with you. You need to go out on a test run first before you tackle being in a huge house on your own. And also, because you need a new notepad, so you won't steal my paper again."

"How did you know about that? And if you tell me psychic superpowers, you can't be human."

"I'm exceptionally talented but… security cameras, love. I know what delivery trucks sound like and those weren't what I heard yesterday. S," she said. Wookie was sniggering into his beard.

"Shut up," I said, smacking Wookie's upper arm.

"Go, both of you and I'll sort your account."

I handed Martha my laptop and login details, patted my chest and gave her the V-sign as I officially left the building with Wookie. I'd dressed deliberately in plain clothes, a long sleeve white top to hide my tattoos, no makeup and a pair of sunglasses. A normal outfit which fitted in with everyone else, I felt naked. And utterly ridiculous.

Every day in summer, Portobello Road is busy as people of all ages enjoy its artistic flair and tourists coo over stalls and trinkets. The place comes alive from early morning when coffee shops open their doors and deliveries arrive with goods for the day. It's a unique part of London and if I didn't live in South Kensington with a burn for travel, I'd live in Notting Hill. In one of those white houses with lilac wisteria on the front and I'd have my own writing studio or magazine office.

I had intended to zip down the sloping hill, dart around all the people and shops, purchase the notebook and be back in Martha's quirky kitchen as quickly as I left. A short while after Wookie and I set off on our tentative journey, my need to rush de-accelerated and my guard gradually dropped. I realised no one noticed me, shouted things, clicked a camera or seemed bothered by my presence. My disguise left little to suggest it was me. I fitted into the mainstream and blended in. At any other time, I would have had a problem with this, but for today, it was perfect. It allowed me to slow down and forget the storm, to listen to Wookie's tales of his allotments, gardening work and love of growing, as we investigated each shop and stall that sold blank journals.

"What about this one, Monica?" He shouted, holding a thick leather journal up in the air from a stall on the opposite side of the road to me. The journal and my name did elicit a few head turns, but I pushed my way into a small crowd of people, pretending to look at tacky vapes. I ignored Wookie completely.

"Don't call out my name waving a bloody journal about," I said to him, laughing as we carried on meandering still empty-handed a few minutes later.

"Don't leave me hanging either," he retorted.

We must have searched through all the journals in Notting Hill and I couldn't find the right one. Wookie didn't understand this at all and kept repeating, 'Just pick one, they all do the same thing.' He doesn't understand, they don't. I need a connection to it, a meaning. Despite our disagreement over journals, he was happy I was out and being left alone by people and that he didn't need to beat anyone up for hassling me.

On the verge of dropping the task of finding my ideal writing partner, it dawned on me, I already knew. I knew what type of paper I did feel connected to… my original. The yellow legal notepad. It's where all this began. There are many beautiful journals, but mostly their pages are too decorative and small for me. After a detour to a standard stationery shop, I purchased two yellow legal notepads. We'd made it all the way to the end of Portobello Road and bought a wrap each from the Street Food Market at Ladbroke Grove. Sitting on a bench to eat, the air was thick with inviting street food smells, Wookie wanted to make a note of the stall's name to speak to the owner about who supplied their veg, salad and fruit.

"Paper," I said, handing him a sheet from my notepad.

Whilst we ate, Wookie told me if I could make it through this last week to this point here and now. Eating in the middle of a hectic location, I can do anything. Handle all situations. Run your own show he said… I can do anything but bring Lenny back and resurrect my magazine I returned. He disagreed, saying the only problem he could see with the magazine is the timing. It's too soon to publish it, he continued and advised simply to delay the launch.

"Use the time to your advantage," he said nonchalantly, mid-bite.

"It's as good as dead in the water, like Lenny and me," I said.

"Listen," he said, throwing his screwed-up wrapper in

the bin as if it was a basketball, "I know Marth thinks this Lenny guy should have stepped up more in this mess, and there's truth in that. I don't know the fella, but he sounds alright to me, and Marth can be harsh at times."

"She's right! He thinks I sold him out, and he left me alone to deal with all this. If Lenny believes that's what I would do, then he doesn't know me at all. Not even a tiny bit. I would never do that to him."

"You can honestly say you know with 100 percent certainty that is what he thinks?"

I couldn't answer him. Not a word would leave my mouth, no matter how many times I stuttered.

"I thought not. Regardless of what he *actually* thinks, give the man a minute. Let him do what he needs to do at his end first."

On our walk back up Portobello Road I refused to roll up the sleeves of my top despite the sweltering heat. I preferred to sweat than people recognise me from my tattoos. Wookie said I had become paranoid, and maybe he's right, but he hadn't had to live with the last week as I'd had to, and Wookie wasn't me. Then he knocked the wind out of me by complimenting my controversial blog, saying he enjoyed reading it. Not the private tales of others, but what I'd written about my own life, my opinions, learnings and dreams. It made him take another look at himself and I loved that he told me this. It raised me up. My words *really do* have a good impact. It didn't matter a jot. It was only one person I'd inspired. I was purposeful. At that moment, he asked if he could give me some advice.

He said, "None of this what's going on in your life is about the update mishap. It's not about Lenny, or your magazine, your dad, mum, friends, money."

It's not?????

"It's about you. You wanted to find nirvana… and you have."

I had to pause walking and stare at him dumbfounded.

"Have you been on the bong, Wookie, as I can assure you this is not what I had in mind."

"You misunderstand what nirvana is. It isn't people, places and things. Nirvana is pure love, the Pura Vida. The connection you hold within, found in your… secret chambers, I think you called it. That same inner truth you made wrong for fear it was inappropriate, and you hid it away to stop others from finding out how wrong that essence of you was… as you'd made yourself believe it to be. Except it never was wrong. You understand? Nirvana is you, Monica, the kooky and the not-so-kooky.

Friends, fam, boyfriends, career, it's all the same. And if you accept your inner truths are not twisted or inappropriate, and instead live with wide-open wings, you will find success, love and all you seek will no longer be kept from you. Including from the Lenny James' of this universe."

No. 59

Tuesday 19th August

It was the wrong side of 7 a.m. when I heard a foot hit the bedroom door, followed by Martha yelling for me to get up. Hazily, I shuffled barefoot through her apartment in pyjama bottoms and a T-shirt, squinting at the offensive early light. Martha, far too perky for this hour, sat fully dressed with makeup done at the mosaic table in the kitchen. My laptop lay open in front of her as she muttered how unbelievable the emails were people had sent me.

"Thanks for dragging me in here to tell me. I wasn't aware of that," I said.

Martha, ignoring me, continued and according to her, not all of them were bad. I'd missed some of the more complimentary ones supporting me and telling me how I'd inspired these individuals to dream, to feel possible and to change.

"Tactics. To get me to respond. I hate all those fuckers with a passion, but what's the bugle call about?" I said, tackling the coffee machine with a prayer I keep my patience with it.

Martha, not moving her eyes from the screen, explained she didn't have a long as Ben didn't work on Tuesdays, and she needed to open up shortly. Since yesterday she had scanned over and checked through the wrath of messages, deleting the majority of them into the trash bin. She'd kept the suspiciously positive ones along with those from the hat to leave their fates up to me.

"Before you close the account, there is one interesting email you should consider," she added, turning to acknowledge me in the eye for the first time this morning.

I quit rattling the coffee machine, my fingers instantly turning into fat clumsy stumps and I almost dropped the mug on the floor in my hurry over to the table. Sitting opposite her, my mood had flipped, the annoyance over the rude awakening gone, as I found myself leaning toward her with bated breath, asking if it was from him.

"Who?" she asked.

"The Pope. Who do you think?"

My stomach tightened, and my chest fluttered thinking the *what-if* moment had been worth waiting for after all…yet it soon sank like a setting sun over the sea. The message wasn't from Lenny or the Pope but from the London Newspaper. The same newspaper I sometimes read in Bootsy's bar; the same one I wrote to all that time ago pitching a column they ignored.

"I don't want to hear about a stupid paper, and I am not talking to anyone. I don't care what they're offering."

"You might want to read what this one has to say and if you'd be quiet for a minute and get down from your horse. I'll tell you."

With deflated interest, I listened as to why the editor-in-chief himself had contacted me. Eye-rolling pleasantries and an apology for contacting me this way opened their communication. Since they couldn't find any agent who represented me, they resigned to reaching out using the coffeemail contact and hoped I would receive it.

"Get to the point Martha,"

The editor went on to say, they appreciated the live version of my blog had not been intended to be read, yet in its short life, it had caused an influx of unexpected interest from their readers to hear more from me. Email and calls are received daily by the newspaper. The readers' interests do not surround any of the people mentioned in my blog, but my own quest. The lessons I learned and those I discover, my approach to myself, to life, dream seeds and finding nirvana as a young woman living in London. London's most popular newspaper wishes to offer me a position as a columnist with my own Monica Blue column. Would I please contact them regarding this matter?

"It goes on to pay, conditions, yadda yadda but people are fascinated and inspired by you. Same as the emails I mentioned, but you didn't believe," Martha said.

I thought about what Wookie had said yesterday. With the information Martha has unveiled this morning, I'm questioning if my rock angel is knocking on my door with a hunch.

"This is worth thinking about. They've handed it to you on a plate because–"

"I work alone," I said, interrupting her.

"I don't mean writing for them, although it's a good

and secure option to consider. They've just handed you gold. They told you hands down the best marketing research and information you could ever need."

"Keep talking," I said, slowly narrowing my cautious eyes.

"They've confirmed you – you – Monica Blue"–stabbing a pointed finger at me repeatedly– "has an audience. They want more from you, they want to read your work, and they love what you are doing, who you are and your perspectives. Not Lenny's or anyone else's. Yours. Newspapers don't hire paid columnists easily, which tells me this is bigger than they are letting on." She leaned back smugly into the back of the chair. "You could either write the column for them… or do it yourself online and keep full control. Just don't drink on the job."

I snarled a sarcastic lip at her for the last remark as she rose out of the seat, telling me she'd had to go downstairs. An early morning reading before the shop opened was due in shortly and she needed to tune herself in.

"Leave it with me, I'll think about it," I said. Intrigued, I snatched the laptop and turned it around to face me.

Martha smiled to herself as she grabbed her bag from the kitchen worktop, moved the lever of the coffee machine, and pressed the button.

"It'll work now," she said.

But I was lost in the email and the ideas she suggested, and I could only muster a muttered and staggered, 'Yeah, bye,' to her with a weak waft of my hand.

Tuesday Evening

Fire within roared once more. There is nothing like the burn of real passion. I pondered life and career choices for most of the day, unchanged from my pyjamas. A columnist, in a London Newspaper, and not any column, my own. A long-standing wish granted. The dream of many a writer. If I had been offered this six months ago, I'd have taken it immediately. It would have been a hell-yes making all else fade out into nothing. Then there's Martha's suggestion to take the golden ticket from the newspaper and run like the wind with it. Yet do I have the muscle to make it a success without the backing of a named publication and pro editing team?

And what about my magazine? The whole enchilada I have fought for. It's on the brink of materialisation and being a tangible readable publication. I can't disregard it because an easier option rolled in.

I can't ditch my magazine.

I can't.

I can't drop the baby.

Or can I?

Wouldn't backtracking mean I don't believe in my dream at all and everything I stand for? Wouldn't ditching it make me a faithless fraud unable to put my money where my mouth is? I don't want to be that person.

Newspaper. Online. Magazine. One of these three places is the home for my words. My words, straight outta nirvana, I am discovering, do matter. Do make a difference to people, but where is the right place for me and my tête-à-têtes about life? Until this morning, I would have fought anyone to the death who said it was not my magazine. I have been convinced for so long my own magazine built from the ground up is what I wanted. My purpose. My dreamseed. Now I'm not as sure. Back at Martha's kitchen table, thinking into the distance, I watched the shop across the road have a new sign fitted on the front where the old one had been. Deliveries of large boxes made by a man in a white van were taken inside before he drove off hanging his cigarette out of the rolled-down window beeping his horn when I remembered *why* I wanted to have my magazine… not solely the glory of having one.

If my *why* has always been to let my freak flag fly, for my words and expression to matter, to cause meaningful change and disruption to society, to give others the courage to be original too, then does the platform I use in which I do this matter? This is the dreamseed, this is what it means to be a writer. It occurred to me in my continued silence watching the workmen wipe final marks off the shop's sign, the platform is secondary to the purpose. It's the words that matter and like homing pigeons, words and stories find their own way home to where they belong.

Writing for the newspaper, my own indie column or my own magazine, are all realities I can choose to step into. Each has its own benefits, advantages and drawbacks and I have tried to deliberate and apply a process of elimination all day to my conundrum. I've weighed all the facts with logic and linear thinking. If I take nothing else from what I've learned from writing the blog, it's never to violate the mystical wink of a rock angel. An inner knowing, a hunch, a sixth sense, a funny feeling, call it whatever the fuck you want, but once you notice it, you had better pay attention and I know exactly what I am going to do.

No. 60

Wednesday 20th August

I awoke this morning still lingering in a dream where Lenny and I exist. It fooled me for a sweet moment. I was cosy and serene, held in a bear hug of happiness, but the vision became hazy and left when Def Leppard's Hysteria song barged into my mind, reminding me of the mess. Reminding me Lenny isn't here, he's not on the other side of my email, he's not coming back to me and sending me messages. Although I'm undecided if I indeed dodged a bullet and the brightest biggest orange carrot I've encountered to date. Part of me can't blame the man for thinking I sold him out and for severing our connection. It doesn't matter what has happened, because the point is, regardless of how I dress this up, Lenny James will always be the one who got away, and I oddly feel at peace in admitting this. Those feelings I have for him, which I made wrong and avoided, are true. I need to let this be good, not bad. This acceptance does not ice my heart but warms it. There's power in owning the truth and I get to keep that, whether I see Lenny again or not. No one can take that away from me, not even him.

A few coffees later in Martha's shop…

"I've taken about fifty pictures. What's wrong with them?" Martha exclaimed, dismayed at my demand for the perfect picture for my new profile image.

"I don't know. They're all odd," I replied, scrolling through all the images, zooming in to examine them in detail.

"That's how you look, it's not my handy work" she said. "Hmm," she said, checking them again and sounding dissatisfied at her artistry over my shoulder. "Ben, get over here, you're younger than me. What's wrong with these pictures?" Martha asked.

Ben hooked the last of the tops he was hanging out on one of the rails and wandered over to the cash desk. I sat on top of the desk still in the same ripped jeans I'd been in for days and a new plain black vest courtesy of the shop. I'd also blagged my way to using Martha's makeup and hairspray and talked her into letting me borrow a few items from her shop in the name of art; symbolic rings, metal bracelets, black wristbands, a bunch of alchemy chains, I made sure one pendant had an Ankh on out of respect for my ancient Egyptian sisters, and a pillar candle to place in front of me. I'd left my house with barely a toothbrush and didn't possess one item from my normal attire, not even an earring. Realising Martha never switches off from thinking about business, I bargained for her time and props by buying a pair of black lace fingerless gloves and a cigarette holder from her using my tape money. All I needed was a picture of me with big 90s hair, full makeup including my signature eye-to-temple side pattern, a thickly lined cat eye and jewellery. The lit pillar candle would sit in front of me as I smoked a cigarette in the holder wearing my new lace gloves.

"It's the angle. You hold the phone at the wrong angle," Ben said. "Here I'll do it." He took my phone and asked me to recreate the pose and within five minutes it was done. We all beamed down at the chosen image, its added filter, also chosen by the newly appointed photographer, Ben, enhanced it further.

"It's a great picture, Monica," Ben said. "I'm sorry I took your job too,"

"Thanks, and no you're not," I said, pushing him on his chest in a playful manner, "Good you did though, otherwise who would be my photographer?"

Martha let Ben go home. She'd decided to close up three hours early as our mission was complete, and the shop was dead. I began placing all the borrowed items back in their rightful places, draping chains over their holders and fighting with the ring tray to fit the rings into their tiny slots. As Martha cashed up early for the day, her mood turned distant, I asked her what the deal was with her and Wookie and if they were a couple. Telling her they made a cute match. They care about each other, look after one another and spend a lot of time in each other's company.

"We're friends that's all."

"Yeah?" I responded with raised eyebrows. "Friends don't stare at friend's tomatoes like you were in the fridge the other day."

She soft punched the side of my arm knocking the ring tray from my grip onto the floor and stared softly at the notes she was counting in her hand.

"Maybe not but Wookie doesn't see me in that way. We've been friends for too long. It's all good."

I heartily disagreed and as I gathered the rings from the floor, I couldn't keep my opinion withheld from her. When I'm convinced about a matter, I can't hold back. Martha and Wookie are written in the stars and one of them or both of them need to catch up to the idea.

I dismissed Booty's sincere belief and excitement for Lenny and me in the beginning, but witnessing the situation between Martha and Wookie makes me understand his drive to bring us together. I wish I'd taken his intuition more seriously in the same way I wish Martha would take mine now. She needs to wake up, smell the damn coffee and say something to Wookie. I can tell Martha is in love with him. I thought back to that day when she said to me with a heavy heart how the card's messages were for me, not her… I see it now. She was hoping for the predicted *love storming in* to be about Wookie riding into her arms with declarations of his heart for her. Perhaps the message is still for Martha, because whilst she was correct, love did sweep into my life quickly, it also left just as quickly and, in my book that doesn't count. I recalled my talk with Wookie on the way home and I think he might need to take his own advice too. What if Martha and Wookie have loved each other for years and neither one of them has dared to move the needle? All the time they have missed and will continue to be a waste. And for what?

"Can you say in complete honesty, you know 100 percent that is how Wookie feels?" I asked, smug for remembering his words and I slid a perfectly organised ring tray to her across the counter for the second time.

"That sounds like something he'd say. Anyway, forget Wookie, we're sorting you out before you leave tomorrow. Don't you have work to do upstairs?" she said.

"You'll miss me when I'm not here," I retorted, sliding my phone in my back pocket poised to leave as Martha flicked all the lights off and activated the alarm.

"I'll cope misses," she said, the alarm beeping its intimidating countdown beeps in the background, bringing on panic about leaving in time before sirens blare. "Besides, I'll have your new column to keep me amused," she said as we passed under the dangling birdcage. I opened the door, and we stepped outside, banging into someone checking the shop's name on the sign above, not watching where they were walking.

"Bootsy," I shouted out too loud and too shocked, letting go of the door handle.

"I have the right place then," he said in a friendlier tone than when I last heard his voice.

Then the alarm sounded off. A blue light flashed annoyingly above the T on Martha's shop sign, piercing all ears in Notting Hill because I hadn't shut the door in time. This is why I hate alarms.

All the people were staring at us, wincing and covering their ears with their hands. I tried to stand in front of Bootsy to block the view of faces staring at me, it triggered me into remembering the horrors of last week. Martha rolled her eyes, complaining it's never a dull moment when I'm around and marched off to reset the system inside the shop.

"Clocking off early, are we?" Bootsy said half smiling.

A minute later, the beeping returned, and Martha darted out, locking up and handing me the key to the flat's side door, telling me and Bootsy we could go up as she had somewhere she needed to be.

"Wookie's," I asked with a nudging elbow.

"Mind your own," she yelled back as she walked up the road, "nice to meet you. Finally," she added, tipping an outstretched hand toward Bootsy.

"You too," he replied, holding his arm up, but she'd vanished into the busyness as only mysterious Martha can do.

No. 61

Thursday 21st August

I decided yesterday to return home today. I'm not back in South Kensington yet, I'm writing this entry as my last one at Martha's before I leave. I couldn't leave without writing one for the road. A few days ago, I didn't think I would be able to go home again or if I wanted to. The place I once loved stabbed me in the back. Some might say I'd swung the machete too far around and pierced my back with the point of my own blade, without any help from another or dark force. Life doesn't do a number on you unless you do a number on yourself, which is why I am choosing to turn down the newspaper's offer and shelve the magazine. I'm running with the indie column sealed with a prayer for good wind beneath my wings.

My magazine hadn't been smooth. It was hard work, yes, but more than that, it was a struggle. Banging a square peg into a round hole, forcing it to come together thinking I was being focused and talented and becoming the Anna Wintour of my generation. I learned that hard work and struggling are two different things. If I am honest and admit the truth in my secret chambers, it was turning into a heavy stone around my neck and a knot in my stomach. It became more noticeable and stronger each time I sought to work on it. Since yesterday, I've been in disappointment pondering if the fire my magazine once held had shown its true identity and was, in the end, a smaller guiding fire and not the main event. It was a protest against the world I had been living in. A creation from the head, not the heart and those two spaces are easily misconstrued because, whilst the difference is vast, the discernment to know the difference is slight and often missed. To find that discernment is to find oneself. Writing a new indie column feels like me. It's pure love from my heart and love mends things. I didn't expect this turnaround and before the disaster, I would have made this choice wrong by telling myself it was being unfaithful to the magazine dream. I would have scoffed at the suggestion of it and stuffed it away. I am not making the same mistake as I have done my whole life. This time I choose my love. This time I choose the secret chambers. This time I choose nirvana… it somehow knows better than I do.

And that's why I'm giving the people and myself what they want. Reinventing the controversial blog as a brand new one, redesigned, repackaged and buttoned with an unmistakable MB edge. In contrast to the magazine and using the skills I have learned these last few weeks; the new blog was easy and smooth to create. Within a day and a half, everything fell into place, it was as though Mary Poppins had arrived in town. I secured the first two paid adverts to run on it to start generating income… Martha's shop and now Wookie's new shop. I learned last night the store across the road being re-fitted with the sign is Wookie's debut organic fruit, veg and allotment advice shop. The opportunity to have the place had apparently crossed his path once before, but he'd turned it down, leaving a nip of regret lurking in his mind. Having been inspired recently to revisit the option, he'd called up the owner of the building and, eventually, they reached an agreement. It opens next month.

My personal blog to my rock angel, and anything bat shit crazy in my life, will stay here on the yellow page as I can't give it up. The public blog will be written with the intention for the world to read it. Heavily edited, it won't discuss people, circumstances, mention names or cause a Hollywood uproar. The Dear Rock Angel blog is in response to demand and will feature lessons I've learnt and will learn, my unique views on life, style, interests and oddities. It's life according to me. Who knows, I may end up with a classic vintage sexy newspaper all of my own one day. I am writing the opening piece when I get home later today after Bootsy drops me off.

Which reminds me… my wingman is back.

We talked for an hour at Martha's kitchen table. Bootsy did not appreciate me disclosing his private life. Fearing I had caused his bromance with Lenny to suffer, my blog had also informed some of his family and work circles he was gay when they didn't know. It wasn't the gay thing he particularly cared about; it was a few words Lenny had said to me when he turned up at my house that night that I had documented…

'Bootsy is away on a romantic night.'

Because he was away on a romantic night, but not with Marco. Bootsy the sly dog had met a new guy not too long ago, a British DJ who spends the winters in London and the summers touring Europe. He met this chap randomly in the biscuit aisle at the supermarket and both were hit by cupid's unexpected love arrows, which explains the peppy mood he'd suddenly acquired recently.

Bootsy had to face an ugly truth and admit the life he was building with Marco was not the one he wanted after all. The accidental release of the blog railroaded Bootsy onto tricky land, requiring quick thinking. He knew he didn't want to be a fixture in minimalist corporate-driven living. He had known for some time, he told me. Bootsy wanted free living in cargo shorts and to own a beach bar, with surfers, tourists and hideous pop music, but finding the right time to tell Marco had escaped him. Marco had the unfortunate experience of reading his fate for the first time online in the blog. However, the blog forced Bootsy into being what he should have been – honest. Bootsy and Marco didn't deserve to have their skeletons blown out of the water by me. No one did, but Marco also deserved the truth Bootsy had struggled with how to tell him.

"Oddly, after it all came out, and I had no choice but to solve what I didn't want to deal with, it was sorted out. Quickly, within a couple of days. I didn't enjoy any of it, but in a way, I need to thank you," Bootsy said to me, "You gave me no choice but to change. I guess the universe only gives a person so long to do what must be done, or it will do it for you." He said, with tired eyes. Marco, understandably devastated and angry, moved out of their apartment to one further across the city nearer to his office.

"I'm taking a sabbatical from the bar and touring around Europe with Aaron and his decks for the rest of the summer, see where life goes after that."

I am outrageously happy for him. I thought he was mad because I'd lifted the lid on Marco's impending proposal and his life in general. Not because he'd met the love of his life and was trying to navigate a big, unexpected change he'd never considered would happen. He wanted to find a way to leave quietly out the back door but received the opposite, realising a quiet, non-hurtful way to tell Marco would have had him wait a very long time because it didn't exist.

"I am sorry about how it all happened but relieved to know you're a happy pirate," I told him with a huge honest grin. Then I thought about romance for a moment too long and my smile dropped. I paused the conversation and swirled coffee round in the mug I held close to my chest. I couldn't avoid the elephant in the room. I spoke into the mug containing a mini whirlpool of coffee rather than maintaining eye contact with Bootsy trying not to break.

"Can I ask," I said, lifting only my eyeballs upward to meet his, "have you heard from Lenny? Do you know where he is? If he's doing ok?"

"All I know is, he went back to New York as soon as your blog news became known to him, which didn't take long. He texted me to say he was leaving, hoped I was alright considering, and he'd be in touch. That's all I know, Monica. I wish I had better news for you, but I don't. Please don't ask me to text him for you or give you his number, because as much as I love you, I can't do that. I can't break his trust."

"New York? He went back to New York… that's so far away." I trailed off knowing I had royally messed up; I missed him badly and didn't know what to do.

Bootsy ended up staying for beers and dinner with

Martha, Wookie and me. I don't know where Martha had been this afternoon, but it wasn't to see Wookie. He had been at one of his allotments making wooden boxes from old pallets for display units at his new shop. He had meant to ride past my house and down the street to check for activity but had gotten lost in time. Fortunately, Bootsy has been back at work the past couple of days and monitoring the area.

"I get asked in the bar about it all, to which I pretend I don't know what they're talking about. It's fizzling out as these things do after the initial hype… other than people keep taking pictures of your balcony," he said, turning towards me as Martha and Wookie sniggered with increased volume.

"Are you being serious? Why do people want pictures of my balcony?"

"No rhyme or reason to the public's fascination of the month. It's become more popular than photos being taken of the hotel where Lenny stayed… who needs Romeo and Juliet's balcony in Verona when you have Monica Blue's balcony in South Kensington."

Martha and Wookie were roaring with laughter and whilst there was humour in what Bootsy said, I wasn't sure how I felt about the balcony thing. It's my balcony. It's where I hang out with my tape deck and listen to music, it's where I write and talk to the moon. It's my space. And it gave me the smallest of the small insights into how Lenny's life must be all the time.

"Anyone up for a game of cards and another beer before we call my cab home?" I said, hopping up and grabbing a bottle out of the fridge, anything to stop myself wallowing.

No. 62

Friday 22nd August

When I arrived back last night, I could have been revisiting high school or a former place of work, not home. It had almost become part of my past, and it pulled out all the feels from the depth of my psyche. It was later in the evening when the cab rolled up outside my white home to drop me off. Dusk had fallen, and it appeared most had left South Kensington's suddenly most interesting street. To be certain, I'd sent Bootsy ahead to open the front door whilst I held back in the cab, so I could walk straight in. Eliminating the stress of having any questions or cameras pounced on me from out of nowhere whilst I fumbled with door keys.

It was a smooth arrival. Not a flash flashed, or a word

hit my ears nor left my mouth. The stillness of an empty muted mess left after an out-of-control party.

Once inside, I dumped my backpack on the bottom step of the staircase and told Bootsy to take the cab back to his place as I would be fine. He offered to stay, but I preferred to be alone, to walk the boards again and retake it all in, after my life had all but been obliterated.

I noted all the curtains remained closed, the stack of towels in the bath was exactly as I had left them, and bits of baccy still littered the kitchen floor. I pushed the button on the extractor hood to turn off the fan. I must have forgotten to switch it off in my rush to leave. It had been left whirring all this time. At ten p.m., I stood leaning against the worktop next to the extractor hood and coffee maker in a thickened silence, which oddly seemed louder and more pressing than when the fan had been cranking. Everything had stayed the same, except everything had changed.

This morning at eight o'clock I stood in the same spot, hugging my laptop, tentative about the day ahead and I couldn't help but stare hopelessly at where mine and Lenny's den existed for one night only.

Enough, I told myself.

"Enough already," I said out loud monotone, and as quickly as night turned into day, I decided no longer to dwell on what happened, the risks I may face going forward or the very real truth I am unlikely to ever hear from or meet Lenny again.

I can't change anything by dwelling, wondering or wallowing, it turns one into the Viv's of this world. I refuse to curl up and die and, as I once wrote, *only I can leap for the future, and leap I must.*

Bootsy thinks everything about turning my blog into an indie column is a bad idea. I disagree. My energy is far from defeat, despair or dumbass, it's rocketing at the thought of writing the first blog and leaving for Spain. I unhugged the laptop and placed it on the island. I flicked the fan on for company, pressed play on an old Anastasia album on my phone and after opening the laptop's lid, a renewed feeling of power streamed from the ends of my fingertips.

I'm back, bitches, and I began to type.

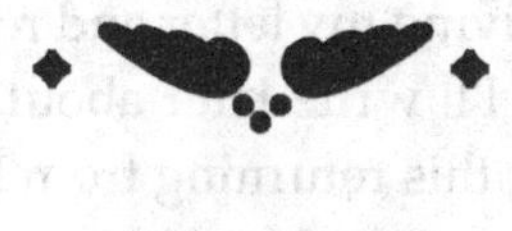

No. 63

Saturday 23rd August

Ignoring beeping car horns, I barely missed the traffic as I rushed over the road and pushed my face against the bar's row of windows. The bar wasn't overly busy, although the lunchtime crowd proved enough to dissuade me from popping in to see Bootsy as I'd planned to. As I used to and as I miss doing. I rattled a knuckled fist on the window instead, the people inside sitting below the window on the cushioned seats turned their heads like owls to locate the interruption. Bootsy, the muppet, didn't hear a thing. I knocked louder until he did and mirrored a screwed-up face back at those seated by the window.

Eventually, satisfied with a hand wave from Bootsy and comforted by seeing old friends… my stool, my space at the bar, John the Knight, the chair where Lenny sat and rows and rows of glass alcohol bottles watching Bootsy place olives in fancy glasses for fancy people, I left for Martha's. I wanted her to read the first blog before I hit publish. Her comments wouldn't alter what I'd written, but it was a mark of respect I guess, rather than permission. I also wanted to let her know Dad – my dad – called *me* this morning, after receiving my letter and reading about all the recent commotion. I'll write later about Dad as I'm sitting on the tube writing this returning from Notting Hill.

I'd agreed to help Wookie with moving and arranging baskets and crates ready for his produce and products. It doubled as a timely opportunity to show Martha my blog, but she wasn't in her shop when I got there. Ben said she was across the road at Wookie's shop. Portobello Road is the epitome of constant change and unfolding edginess, who knew vegetables could be rock n roll, I thought as I pushed Wookie's new shop door open. Wandering in, I quickly absorbed the sight of a rustic biker's veg store for the first time in my life. On thinking about it, it was the first time I'd been in a proper veg store, period.

"Guys, hey guys… it's looking good!" I said, peering around the empty space until I found an open door into a back kitchen unit. "Guys?" Martha and Wookie clearly were not interested in my arrival or aware I happened to be standing there. They never heard me open the door or me calling their names. Their passionate kisses and rovering arms had taken them to another place. They gently embraced each other all over like they had waited their entire lives to touch each other's faces and not an inch of their skins wanted to be apart again. I tiptoed back awkwardly and tore off a piece of paper from Wookie's many lists on top of a bunch of crates.

About bloody time. I'll help with your boxes later. Check your emails for the preview of the new Dear Rock Angel blog … advertises perks. MB

And placed the note on top of his pile of papers and weighted it down with a rogue potato I found rolling about the floor.

No. 64

Continued...

THE DAD CALL

Dad's phone call came this morning before I left for Martha's. I thought it deserved its own space and not merely mentioned in between the other words of Saturday. I'd finished the final draft of the new column and was planning which clothes to pack for Spain and how to fit them all in my holdall. I remember thinking it was impossible and sighing at the array of shorts, t-shirts, dresses, trousers, headwear and unsuitable shoes spread across my bed. I wished the 1st of September would hurry up. *I want to leave summer and leave London.* That's when he called. Out of thin air. It wasn't an expected call; I'd half forgotten about him; it made me drop the holdall as though it was suddenly burning my hands.

It wasn't a long call between us. All the things I thought I would say or yell at him, I didn't. None of them came to my mind, let alone became words capable of leaving my mouth. I didn't hear his voice and poof; all was forgotten and chat away as though it was only last week I saw him. His call didn't arrive with a magical funfair either, it was just, well, kinda normal. It didn't faze me. Moreover, it fitted nicely into Saturday like Notting Hill.

"Monica, it's erm. It's Dad. I got your lovely letter this morning. How… how are you?" he said. His voice still gave warmth the same as it did when I'd hung, the same as it always had.

"Is it? I wasn't sure it, or, I would be after all this time," I replied with a protective coolness. I didn't know how far up the friendly scale to be.

"I've waited years for this; every phone call or letter I received… I hoped it would be you."

"Today's your lucky day then," I answered. Feeling a sense of relief at hearing Dad's uncertainty and nerves lacing his last sentence. Dad is one of those people who knows exactly what to say at all times and doesn't second guess his confidence. It was comforting, therefore, he was feeling the pinch here as much as me.

"Tell me, how are things? How's London? Seems strange not to know," he asked.

"You sort of lost that prerogative."

Silence backed up the line as though he was returning to a dusty cobwebbed room, once filled with light and joy.

"I deserved that. Monica… if you want to throw anger and insults at me, go for it. You won't say anything I haven't since said to myself."

I couldn't help but believe his honesty and I began to physically ache, as I heard his voice crack. Only once but it cracked. I bet he was sitting in his office with papers plastered everywhere, a million computer screens open with weird recording graphs on them that only he understands. He'd be rubbing his brown eyes from underneath his round glasses, like an emotionally mad professor.

"Remorse sounds good on you… I don't want to throw abuse; I've done all that. I've raged and beaten pillows. I've cried rivers in silence because it hurt that much." I replied. I stuttered as I tried to find the rest of my sentence. "It was all so far-fetched and confusing. Only recently have I realised the only thing left from all the warfare is… I still miss you. But perhaps now, I've grown enough to deal with unconventional situations."

He paused once more, clearing his throat before telling me how proud he was of me and always had been. How he loved me, and we needed to talk this out properly. He had gotten wind of the blog and Lenny, I mean who hadn't at this point, and asked if there was anything he could do. Did I need help or media guidance and yadda yadda. I told him ten days ago yes, but no, not now. I'd sorted it the best I could and explained a new indie column was about to drop. I can't deny it was validating-ly good when he said he looked forward to reading it, but I didn't know how to respond to his lovey-dovey words.

"I realise the last one was not meant to be read," Dad said, "but it was good, Monica. Really good. You have talent. A flare. I am not surprised people want to hear more from you. Ignore the haters, or try to learn too, and don't engage with them. Call me for anything"

He tumbled into asking if we could arrange another call to talk more or a video call if it's not too much or he could fly in, or this or that. Whatever I wanted.

"I'm flying out to Barcelona on 1st September; how about we start with coffee…?"

No. 65

Sunday 24th August

I had forgotten about the interest in my balcony. Earlier this morning, I'd resumed my throne on the lounger and had stood up for an alternative view to proofread the debut column for the eighth time or was it the ninth. I held my laptop in one hand, and with half an upturned mouth found a sense of fulfilment as I finished reading it. *I'm happy with it. Happy. And ready.* About to hit the publish button, out of the corner of my eye I saw a group of people on the pavement below pointing a phone up and snapping a sneaky picture of me. They soon scarpered after I accidentally-on-purpose angled my coffee cup, held in my other hand, and let the hot coffee pour out on them from a height.

"Oops," I said, peering over, speaking extra loudly as I had music blaring in my headphones. I saw their mouths move back at me as they walked off and wiped away coffee splashes from their faces. I didn't hear what they said, and I didn't want to know.

One hour later...

I returned to a laid position on the sun lounger and hid behind sunglasses and headphones. Pretending the busy inquisitive streets below didn't exist, I attempted to write this daily private entry on my yellow legal notepad, but writer's block had swooped in like a bird. I couldn't find the words, let alone inscribe them onto the page. I had become too distracted with thoughts racing over how the new version of my blog, which I'd now published, would be received. Half of me didn't care, and I love this grainer side of me. Except, the new indie column is incredibly special. It's important to me and I cared a whole lot about every part of it. Not only for my ego, satisfaction and success but because the words I had spun right of my centre were the vistas and personal revolutions others sought. I couldn't be sure they were.

I decided to lay under a cloudless sky soaking in the morning city heat and log this entry later.

Later still...

Today, the magazine I had envisaged for years did launch, but a no frills edgy indie column to a rock angel did. It bore a simple colour and structure and two decently designed and sizable adverts for Martha's and Wookie's Portobello Road shops sitting along the right-hand side of the column's text. They were my first paying advertisers. A business deal in daylight, although I have a sense those two will be with me wherever I am, either as digital beings or fully formed humans.

Now it's real and alive, my writing and I are once again out there. I can't deny I feel anything other than nervous as a first year. I'm convinced my stomach is eating itself. Is the column being read as I think about it? I don't know. There are no comments as yet and I'm trying not to check those for the rest of the day or check visiting traffic numbers. A watched kettle never boils and all that jazz. Instead, I will pray tonight to *my* rock angel, for the success of the column that she inspired, because what else has anyone got but their nirvana and an angel to hang their hat on?

Welcome to Dear Rock Angel; Autobiographical Blogs about Life According to Me.

This is what I wrote.

Dear Rock Angel.

Sometimes life can become a bit fucktangular.

At such a time, it can seem the only viable option is to hide away in the bathroom and hope to fall through a crack in the floor tiles, where you've been sitting for hours or maybe days unable to move because fear has frozen you still. Waiting and wishing for an alternate universe or the ability to turn back time. Anything really to make the distrust, disruption and distress go away.

Except it doesn't go away. Not until you realise, as I eventually did, that it isn't life or circumstances you fear. It's love, of all kinds, that is feared. Which really means we fear ourselves, because a fear of love is a fear of our own love. Why would I fear myself? That's the real question to ask on the bathroom floor. Not stupid empty ones like, why did I do this, say that, think those thoughts, not read properly and press the wrong bloody button. If you are reading this, I assume you have arrived here due to the backstory of its creation.

You may think it is risky for me to start a new column, it is, but I have returned to the page for positive reasons not to make another faux pas.

I have spent my life advocating for depth and originality, fiercely fighting against superficial living. Yet in my recent pain, I discovered I only dared to care for certain deeper and more serious aspects of my life from a surface level. I would not make the choices I truly wanted for fear of that choice being a wrong or inappropriate decision made by my wonky heart. This sounds ridiculous coming from a person who is not – and never will be – politically correct. Sometimes the battle you fight for is the very lesson you also need to learn yourself.

In the blink of a drunken eye, every inch of me was exposed to the world. My soul naked. Motherfuckers all over the planet reading about my life and secrets I'd privately confessed in a blog to an angel, and it terrified me. The mass of negativity I received in reaction to the exposure, confirmed my wrongful and skewed self... We are all self-fulfilling prophecies after all. The thing is, a phoenix cannot be stoned. It will always rise if one is brave enough to let it.

After one darkened hour too many, I decided I'd be damned if any part of me would be superficial. I'm no surface lover searching for a tepid life. No. I want a fierce life with non-flakey people and wild, raw passionate love. My heart is not wonky. My love is not wrong, regardless of wherever whatever and whoever I choose to give it to.

Therefore, to all those who tried to stone me, to all those I hurt. To all those who were surprised and to all those who felt betrayed or placed at a distance from me. To all those, I caused problems and chaos for. To all those I was close to and didn't speak to when I should have, and to those who appeared in my life wearing a hat and made me believe in tinsel, I offer no apologies. To any of you.

None.

I meant everything I wrote. The good, the bad and the quirky. I own every word, thought and feeling because it was all true. But, to all those who stunned me with support, kindness and love for the blog and my journey you changed the trajectory. Made me look twice and listen to your interests and demands. I have never been one to disrespect my spirit and hence I shelved the magazine and created this indie column specifically for all of you instead. A new entry will be added every Sunday evening, because, of all the

twilights of the week, Sundays are the strangest, don't you think?
Let your inner rock angel live,

Monica Blue

P.S. If you came here for gossip and scandal may I suggest you piss off.

No. 66

Monday 25th August

Last night was fidgety. Falling asleep but never enough to stay there for any decent amount of time. In the early hours, I must have dozed off among the disorderly sheets and cushions, only to wake shortly after with a start.

A flurry of messages, notifications and calls all jumping my phone. I thought I was reliving the same stressful experience as when my original blog mistakenly went public, and I had made the worst mistake ever, again by writing the indie column. I was triggered all over, convinced people hated it and were cancelling me, until I calmed my arse down and saw the truth.

Read the truth.

And the sun shone again as I realised my fears were wrong. Traffic is running in droves to the blog and site. Comments are rolling in, and are mainly good, supportive and positive; numerous readers citing their situations or questions for advice, which I answer in a general column post as I'm no agony aunt. Some comments on the blog are, of course, dark and courtesy of trolls and haters. They disapprove of me yet take time to follow me, comment and mention how right they were about me. I ignore their darkness, but quietly thank them for the exposure their negativity gives the column, as the more publicity and attention it gets, the more people who do enjoy my writings and gain something from it, can find it.

My indie column is loved. I chose correctly and I feel dazzled inside. I didn't know this level of happiness existed and it makes me wonder how many more levels of dazzle and happy there are to experience. We think we know it all until we discover we don't and that's exciting.

Bootsy is still unsure about the entire thing. He did, though, send a thumbs up and a 'yay' for the opening piece this morning and told me to go over to the bar later to see him. I hope to turn his opinion around in due time, but if I don't, it won't stop me. Martha and Wookie are my biggest fans, but I already knew that, and they are revelling in the extra customers the adverts are bringing in for them. Viv and Ronnie, once big and bright friends in my life, became smaller flames some time ago, before reducing to embers and now they have gone out completely. Turning to bits of ash that fell through the fire grate. I've not heard from either of them and, to be honest, it's what I prefer.

Dad sent a congratulatory text message about the post I wrote and an emoji of a coffee cup. It is still a novelty seeing his name appear on my phone screen, which makes me both nervous and excited simultaneously. Once we meet in Spain, our relationship possibilities will be clearer. I am clueless about what to talk about with him, but I can hope, not too far from now, I will know what it is like to have a dad in my life again. Mum sent a message of continued disbelief, and I replied with continued distance. A message which was all but a shrug of my shoulders.

And Lenny, my dear hat. You'll be in my heart each day. I'll think of you always, and I will be regretful for years to come that we didn't get a chance to experience what could have been.

No. 67

Tuesday 26th August

The front doorbell buzzed late in the morning, and I was dubious about opening it, not having answered the door to anyone since I'd returned home. I checked out the peephole to find Martha dragging two large-sized cardboard boxes one by one up the steps. I opened the door and saw a black cab parked on the street behind her as the cockney driver yelled through his open window.

"You alright there, love?"

"You're timing to ask me is ironic," Martha shouted back, rolling her eyes as she placed both boxes at my feet. "Wait there," she instructed the guy.

"Morning," I said inquisitively, staring down at the boxes.

"I needed to drop these off to London's newest favourite

writer," she said grinning, "but can't stop as the meter's running," signalling to the cabbie.

"You, frugal biker Martha, are paying to ride in a cab? When you haven't even been drinking?"

"Unbelievable, I know, but I couldn't fit those in the bike's side panyas, could I?" she replied, indicating the boxes. "Besides, I'm not paying. The sender of those is," she tapped a box with her booted foot as she stood in a super-woman pose catching her breath.

I shot her a completely confused expression and began to shuffle the boxes into the hall. "What's in them, and why have you bought them? I don't understand."

"You will," she winked, turning to leave. Halfway down the steps, she retraced to meet me at the door again, "I'm proud of you. Make sure you come for dinner before you leave for Spain, OK? If you're lucky, I might give you a card reading as a free bon voyage gift."

I stopped corner walking the boxes into the hallway to meet her violet eyes, which care more than she lets on.

"Thank you. Yes, to dinner. No to the card reading. You caused me mayhem last time."

"I did no such thing. I pulled the foretelling insights from right out of your universe, not mine. It all turned out to be true... no?"

"Goodbye, I'll call you later."

With that, she slipped off into the back of the cab, pulled the door closed from a half-hunched stance over the seat and waved out of the window. I gave her a two-fin-gered salute and closed the front door. Baffled by the con-tents of the boxes, I went to retrieve a pair of scissors from the kitchen to cut all the tape off. Whatever the contents are, I thought, they had to be kosher, or Martha wouldn't have brought them or been involved with their delivery.

A force had built in my stomach turning it into a human lift. One second the stream of energy would whizz up to my chest, and the next second it plummeted to my pelvis, then back up to my chest and then down again. Up and down, up and down, growing stronger each time. A large part of me hoped the gift was from Lenny and I thought my tightened body might fracture as I anxiously pulled back the flaps of the box, only to find the mysterious contents covered in cream tissue paper. A letter sat on top addressed to Monica.

It didn't look like Lenny's handwriting, but I opened that envelope quicker than a sharpened knife and sat on the floor with my back to the front door to read it. I'm trying to let him fade out of my mind like he does at the end of his movies, like he did to me in real life, without giving me a chance to explain, but I don't wish to forget him. This experience will haunt me forever.

The letter was not from Lenny.

The inner lift set off back down from my chest, instead of plummeting down, it stopped. Hovered midway and I read the letter's message.

Monica,

Martha here. I write on behalf of your dad, Warren. I spoke with him for around half an hour the other morning. It wasn't an early morning tarot reading as such, your dad isn't into mumbo jumbo as he called it, but he said he needed help to break a spell. My spell, that I put on your tapes. Nice guy, by the way.

He discovered you'd sold the tapes when he read your blog. My work remains true to my claim. It appears the guys at

SK Music have been unable to sell the tapes. Either they were the wrong albums, or the wrong bands people wanted. Payment card machines would stop working if someone did choose one, or the buyer didn't have the money, and many customers were browsers only. The universe cooked up all sorts of ways to prevent their sales. Then your blog broke and word got around, causing a rumour the tapes are cursed (these city civies understand nothing). Anyway, no one in three hundred miles is interested in them. Your dad rang the store to buy them back, but his credit card wouldn't work over the phone either, which is when he rang me to 'sort out the ridiculous spell.'

That's where I was going the other day when Bootsy called round, reversing spells in music stores and assuring the owner nothing is cursed, I'm not weird and there are no demons in his shop. Then only I could arrange their delivery back to their rightful owner...

Ta-da. Your babies have returned safe and sound.

P.S. Your dad paid. For everything. The tapes and my time, which is expensive in these circumstances. You need to repay him (sorry).

PPS. He was mad you'd sold them, just a heads-up.

PPPS. Yet did say you are a Blue. He would likely have done the same thing in your shoes; he also told me to tell you he loves you and can't wait to see you in Barcelona.

Blessed be,
Martha

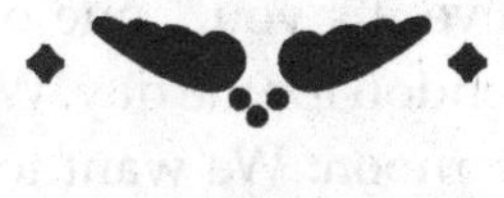

No. 68

Wednesday 27th August

I posed for a selfie in Bootsy's bar. POSED. For a SELFIE. With two unknown people, God I'm distasteful. I'd realised around 5 p.m. I was starving with no food in the house and any cares about being heckled no longer concerned me. I marched across to Bootsy to see if he could sneak a dish from the hotel restaurant for me. Bootsy can wangle meals from their main menu occasionally, but he couldn't leave the bar as it was getting busy, and he had no help. I resorted to a vodka and orange, with a bar sandwich and a packet of peanuts. Not what I had in mind, but as I mowed through the free food, I noticed two women out of the corner of my eye muttering to each other, checking me out from across the other end of the bar. As I stared back at the two women around my age, they embarked on a fluttery approach towards me. My stomach tensed as I took a gulp of my drink and rose to a stand from my bar stool. Sliding the glass back on the bar, I kept my guard hard.

"Evening, ladies. Can I help you?" I said defensively, shoving the last piece of sandwich in my mouth.

"We can't believe it's you," one of the women said. "We only came to London for the day. We bought ourselves new dairies this afternoon. We want to sort our lives out too," she continued, waving a small carrier bag in the air as her friend did the same. "Then we thought, as we are in London, we would come and visit the street where you lived and the bar. We didn't expect to see you though… can you sign them," she said with hopeful yet lost eyes, "our, er… dairies?"

A smile etched its way onto my face and became increasingly wider. Softly laughing to myself in my head as I allowed my guard to lower and fly away, and I happily signed their new journals. How could I not help these two young women? Not too long ago, I was them. Parts of me still are, so for me to be *that* inspiring person to someone else, like those that I look up to are to me, feels beyond anything I can describe at this moment, and I took her pen and wrote…

I hope you find nirvana too.
~ Monica Blue

They thanked me for my message, which they repeatedly read. I could tell how much it meant to them, they were excited with their impending journeys, and I silently wished them peaceful ones. I had purpose, I thought, as we wrapped up our selfie moment and they left the bar. I re-seated myself, still dazed by what had happened, and noticed Bootsy watching on.

"You'll be getting duck lips and a cocktail dress next," he chuckled to me as I ripped open my packet of peanuts and threw some at him. When his attention was elsewhere, I emptied two sachets of salt into his cup of coffee he'd left on the bar.

A full moon was out patrolling the London sky by the time I I was able to sit out on the balcony. It was perfect for listening to a mixed tape I'd made for myself because spending evenings out on the balcony with the moon and my music would soon become part of my past. In a few days, I'll be leaving for Spain. I wanted to reflect on this summer with vodka, my red tape deck playing loud rock music. Whilst certain things are still lost and sadly unlikely to be found again, I can turn my face to the possibilities of a bright future. Tomorrow I will finish packing, reply to column inquiries and note ideas for next week's post. But tonight, tonight is for me.

I lay down squishing the back of my head into the sun lounger, gazing at the moon forming brighter and brighter in the darkening sky. I was soaking in my appreciation of this space when I saw something fly past the side of my eye and land on the ground next to me. At first, I thought it was a bat, but I don't think we get bats in South Ken, which is disappointing, as I'd love a pet bat. When I looked down to my side, placing my drink on the floor to locate what had flown past me, I saw the last thing I expected to see. Not a bat. A Stetson hat.

I gasped forward, knocking my drink over as I swung my legs over the lounger to stand. I picked up the hat and immediately ran my fingers softly around its outline and over the brim. I wanted it to be his more than anything and not a cruel passer-by trying to provoke me. I couldn't be sure it was Lenny's, but it sure looked like his. I held it up to my nose, and it smelled like him too, making me close my eyes and think of him deeper. There wasn't any note attached to it, but it had to be him. It must be. My heart raced me to the balcony, and I peered over the ledge, but he wasn't there and there was no white Jeep. No one was standing there other than a few people going somewhere I didn't care about. I had a hunch. He's here. He's back, I know he is. I propelled myself as fast as I could down and round the stairs to the hallway, still holding the hat and puffing for extra air. I swung the front door open and drew in a long audible breath. My eyes landed on suave alpha elegance which would render even the most emotionally dead among us alive. Lenny, bold and dapper, dressed in a cream and beige pinstripe suit and stark white shirt with a few buttons undone. His skin freshly sun-kissed by the American weather. As he had the first time I saw him, Lenny engulfed me with an uncontrollable fire. It grows stronger each time I see him, hear him, think of him, and read his name. It always will. It will always follow me.

"So," he said, casually leaning against the doorframe with a raised eyebrow and the grin of a mischievous boy, "tinsel. Huh?"

No. 69

Seeing him standing there with his hands in his pockets being all beautiful and authoritative sparked both the dark and light within. Did I feel small, tall, embarrassed or special? I couldn't tell. I hugged his hat, trying to find a smile but struggled. Had fate brought us to meet again for a second chance - fuck - how romantic would that be? If I let myself, I could run away with the idea of it, but dreamy love stories are usually reserved for the silver screen, and this isn't a movie. This is my life. My life he left as quickly as he had arrived in it. I didn't know if this was a hello or a goodbye and it hurt too much to consider either because my heart was doing fine before him, and now it's not fine.

"Possibly... I mean, so I read," I replied eventually, my hands infinitely relieved for the distraction of his hat to fiddle with.

He smiled warmly at me with a small attempt at a

sympathetic laugh and shuffled himself upright from the door frame with ease.

"Can I come in?" he asked, sounding more serious. I hesitated; his voice had paused me in my world for a few seconds until I automatically stepped aside to let him in. He clicked the door closed behind him, and we stood in silence taking in the sight and closeness of each other. I wish I'd curled and back-combed my hair, applied extra liner and worn half an arm of bangles.

"I heard you were back in New York, after the slight… fuck up," I said breaking the magic or was it tension between us.

"Slight?" he replied, widening his eyes. A sense of disbelief swept across his face, "I'd hate to see your major ones," he added, sort of laughing and sort of not. I dropped my shoulders with a sigh, attempting to find the funny, but failing.

"I get it," I snapped. "It shouldn't have happened, but it did and trust me, out there," I pointed to the front door with his hat whilst gesticulating it in the air, "have made me pay. I've been living in the devil's inferno but… oh yeah wait. That's right. You wouldn't know as you took off. Left me to deal with it all on my own."

"I know, and I regret my actions like you wouldn't believe, I –"

"Surely you knew I published the blog by mistake. And if you didn't, you could have asked me. It wasn't fair of you, Lenny… you're used to mass attention and fame. I'm not. You have an entourage to protect you. I don't." I said, stiffening up all mad about it and stewing in my memories of the ordeal. I wanted him to know the truth. Yes, I deserved some of the public bashing for my signature recklessness, but I wanted him to know the pain I can never forget. Not only from the world reading my private life and the humiliating backlash from it, but the heartache of realising I missed him. A lot… and hurting because he didn't even care enough to check if I was okay.

I told him I tried to get hold of him to see how he was and to try to rectify the disaster. I said how untouchable and invisible he was and that I didn't know what to do or how to respond for the best. "I had to resort to hiding in the bathroom for nearly two days until Martha rescued me," I informed him, which he smiled slightly at. I wanted to know if the studio had fired him, what his agent had said, how his dad and Rosie were. But above all else - above all of this giant mess - I told him I would have stood by him in the aftermath. Given a united front even in the glare of it all, because I stand sturdy with those I care about. "That's the difference between us, though, isn't it?" I rampaged. "I would have done that, if the circumstances were reversed. You didn't." I don't think I stopped for five minutes straight nor left space for him to reply because suddenly there appeared to be a great amount, perhaps too much to say. I slumped down on the bottom step, placing his hat next to me and stared at the hallway's cold tiled floor, disappointed with how his return was going.

Lenny stepped forward and gingerly picked up his hat from the steps and for a moment I thought he was turning around to leave. Instead, he sat down next to me and reached his arm across to move my strands of loose hair covering my face to behind my ear. Electric eels spun about in my stomach in fast circles, and I wondered if his stomach was doing the same thing, but he was too composed and sure to be nervous.

"Making the blog public might have been a mistake. What I want to know is, as it appears, I cause you turmoil and always have you conflicted. Am I a mistake too?"

I shook my head, still staring at the floor. "Sometimes I don't know how to just *be*. I never expected you to move me towards the sun and give me feelings I've never had before, and I don't know how to *be* with that."

He twirled the hat around, nodding his head and dropping his chin as though he knew exactly what I meant.

"I can't sit here and pretend I was okay with what happened." he said, "I wasn't. The press has been unreal. Was I angry at you? Yes… but I don't believe you did it on purpose." He nudged closer to me, leaving only an inch between our bodies. I could sense his eyes fixated on me, and then he flicked them back to his hat and then back to me. "But I was a jerk to do that to you and I'm sorry from the bottom of my heart. For leaving and for how the fans and press treated you… It wasn't right, and you didn't deserve it. Bootsy filled me in. At the time, everything was moving at such a rapid pace, people all around me were saying this and that and, I was hurt, you know? Uncertain. Confused. Confused by you, by what had happened. By what you had written about me. If I could do a retake, I'd do it differently."

"It's not a film you know," I said trying to lighten the situation, "thanks for saying you were a jerk," I replied, slowly turning to him. He took the side of my face in his hand and moved it until our eyes locked. His hand remained on my cheek. "I'm sorry too, for all the trouble and chaos I caused you," I told him.

He rubbed his thumb across my cheek and took my heart with those cornflower blue eyes.

"That night I saw you on the balcony for the first time, a force put a spell on me or something," he continued. "I wanted to know who you were and everything about you.

I've never known anyone to be like you. I can't forget about you; I tried but I don't want to. Some might say you're a liability. I say you cause welcome disruption. I see a person with a rare authenticity living in a world where it is difficult to keep that. Someone who reminds others to walk to their own beat. Someone special who wants to be loved and supported, because no one ever bothered to take the time to do that before."

I couldn't find a word to reply with, he could see right through me, and I couldn't turn away from him. I touched his fingers and the side of his hand, the connection propelled a burning ache to want to run my hand through his blond wavy hair, touch him, touch all of him and not let go until June. Trying not to let emotions run out is tricky when the man who I've done my best to keep at arm's length for every reason in the universe, is the reason for me finally discovering what love might be.

He told me I'd appeared in his life from out of nowhere, expanded his world beyond sense, and then, in the same way, I managed to implode it overnight. I couldn't say anything but sorry again to him, it was true. My wake had caused a lot of wreckage… "You weren't the only one who didn't know what to do," he paused, filling his chest. "We were both dealing with a situation neither one of us knew how to. You're beautifully dangerous and I needed space and privacy. Time to think. I couldn't stay here waiting for the circus to come to town. I had to leave; you must understand that?" I wasn't sure I did, but I refrained from interrupting and thought about how his words, beautifully dangerous, reminded me of the song by Slash and Fergie. I didn't think it was appropriate to be thinking about music so dismissed the tune from my mind and continued listening.

He explained he'd left in the middle of the night as soon as he'd heard about the blog and read it all. It was the night before our date at 7 a.m. the following morning. That morning as he was leaving, Lenny had asked his driver to stop by my door, and he got all the way to the bell before turning around, getting back in the car and telling his driver to go. Unsure of what to say to me, what to think and what was true.

"There are casualties for sure. It's cost me a few friends, fans and a couple of smaller work deals. I'm not fired, you'll still see my handsome face on the screen - or not - given you don't watch my films," he giggled as I playfully knocked his knee with mine. "There's a damage limitation plan in place, which you'd expect... being in the spotlight, my life has to work differently. It has perks, obviously, but it's also frustrating, intimidating and crazy at times. It's not a lifestyle for everyone," he said, waiting patiently, as though I was meant to give him a reaction. When I didn't, he carried on. "Dad and Rosie are disappointed, mainly over the drugs, which is worse than falling out with me, but we're working on it. Oddly, they said they know me better now and I'm learning more about myself. All good when I think about it. Rosie's gonna work with horses too, I'm made up for her," he grinned, looking outwards and distance.

We still hadn't moved from the bottom step, as I listened to him intently. In inquisitive silence, I waited until he'd finished all that he wanted to say.

"Why are you here?" I asked, no longer locked in a feeling with him and I let my hand fall from his. "I'm pleased it's turning out ok for you, relieved. But I don't want someone who thinks I'm only beautifully dangerous or merely a fascination that makes their life more exciting.

I'm looking for the dream that loves me back. If you can't do that then please leave."

He turned sideways away from me, raising his arm and I thought he was walking out for good, instead, he hung his hat up on the end of the bannister.

"I'm not going anywhere. Monica, I've come here from New York just for you… all the hoo-ha, filming schedules, your writing schedules, travel plans, the long distance between us is, it's not important. It's nothing that can't be solved. When I read your new column, I got the first flight I could get here because it's killing me not having you and your hocus pocus in my life. I did fuck up, we both did, but I don't want to lose you or hide you… I've fallen for you. Simple as that." He stopped talking, placing his hands over mine, moving me closer to him and I swear we were powering the house. "I want to be with you, we can find ways. Our way. What do you say to doing unconventional life together?"

My plan to stand my ground in the name of righteousness and flying solo disappeared. I could hold on tight to my values, I'm not scared to face a future without him and he knows that too but I could also miss out on the love of a lifetime.

I could choose differently. I could wield the dagger a different way.

I started to smile, which grew stupidly big. Feeling like goo I gazed into his eyes romancing me, they looked a far cry from the wild coke eyes not too long ago.

"Let's keep moving towards the sun," I replied.

Our heads pulled towards each other, he leaned over me, and I tilted my head up as his mouth reached for mine and I let my lips meet his. They faintly brushed together, and my pelvis tingled as I muttered through our entangled mouths ─

"Yes, by the way. Yes, to everything," and I enveloped the middle of his back losing myself entirely. I let him lead as he kissed me as I have never been kissed before, let him hold me as I'd never been held before, and I thought I might self-combust from a slow rush as I entered a new unknown era of my life.

I have no idea how we or any of this will work out. No one, not even more normal people, can be certain about matters of the heart, but I'm willing to find out. Lenny told me I need to understand a few rules and fame etiquette, for protection, safety and privacy.

"Like, not publishing private material and annoying folk?" I replied.

"Exactly like that," he mocked.

"I don't do well with rules."

"I know you don't, and I don't care," he replied, returning his mouth to my neck, my chest and finally my lips again.

The song Halfway to Heaven by Europe began strumming in my head as he lifted me from the steps. Holding me firmly in his arms he carried us to our official first date. Coffee – in person – sat in my kitchen.

"You ever been to New York at Christmas time?" He asked, flicking the button on the coffee machine to turn it on and grabbing two mugs out of the cupboard, as I doodled on one of the envelopes from today's post.

Blessed by a Rock Angel...

If you would like a free copy of the track list featuring all the songs and artists featured in Dear Rock Angel visit my YouTube Channel or access it here:

https://annaliesemorgan.com/books

Connect with me here!

Newsletter:
https://annaliesemorgan.com/newsletter

Track list from Dear Rock List:
https://annaliesemorgan.com/books

Website: https://annaliesemorgan.com

Instagram: @annaliese.morgan

Facebook: facebook.com/annaliesehmorgan

X: x.com/miss_ahmorgan

Email: hello@annaliesemorgan.com

About the Author

Annaliese Morgan is an English author for young and new adults. Originally from Yorkshire but based in London, she lives with her two sons, a Basset hound called Pineapple and too many books. Her writing career began in the late nineties and has produced non-fiction and fiction work. Annaliese primarily writes fantasy and contemporary stories and has been featured on BBC Radio, Stage 32, Woman Magazine, Woman's Own Magazine, Stylist and many others. Annaliese and her two boys (The M's) are also avid travellers and a creative family doing life their way.

Find out more at www.annaliesemorgan.com